Gumbo Justice

Gumbo Justice

Holli Castillo

Oak Tree Press   Taylorville, IL

Oak Tree Press

Oak Tree Press books may be purchased for educational, business or sales promotional purposes. Contact Publisher for quantity discounts

First Edition, June 2009

Cover by MickADesign.com

ISBN 978-1-892343-51-2
SKU 1-892343-51-7

LCCN: 2009927824

This book is dedicated to my husband, Julio "Big Who" Castillo, and my two best friends, Sophia Louise and Hailey Cecelia.

ACKNOWLEDGMENTS

There are many people I have to thank for helping me turn a single what-if into a published novel. First, my thanks to my publisher, Billie Johnson at Oak Tree Publishing, who gave me this opportunity and who has always been most accommodating in answering my questions. Second, my family — my husband Julio, who is the inspiration for the character of Big Who, my children, who tolerated the hours I spent on the computer, my mother, who watched my children so I could write, my sister, who endured the endless torture of my request for comments on rewrites, and my aunt, Theresa Acosta, a nurse who answered a multitude of questions on ways to kill people. I also have to thank several friends for reading my work and offering feedback- Susan Talbot, Sherry Lozowski, Jane Beebe, Gwyn Brown, and my best friend, Lisa Fogarty, who not only read the novel in its various forms, but drove all over New Orleans with me, including through the dangerous St. Thomas Housing Development, to make sure I had the street names and geography correct. Last, but not least, I would also like to thank my boss, Jim Looney, who always supports his staff and never tells me when he thinks I'm crazy.

FOREWORD

Although I tried to keep everything in this novel as accurate as possible, I have taken artistic license with some things for the sake of simplicity. For instance, while the New Orleans Police Department is divided into eight districts, the makeup of the districts is a lot more complicated than what was necessary, or interesting, for me to detail in a novel. I also combined the two Uptown districts to create a single district for Ryan's crime scene duty rather than unnecessarily complicate the storyline. So my apologies to the NOPD for playing around with the districts and organization of the police department. My intent was not to be inaccurate, but to write only as much as would entertain a reader.

Criminal law changes nearly every legislative session in Louisiana, and both the Louisiana Supreme Court and United States Supreme Court constantly hear death penalty cases. It is possible the death penalty for rape of a child under twelve mentioned here may be invalidated by the time this book is being read.

Finally, this story is set in pre-Katrina New Orleans and many things have obviously changed since that time. For instance, the D.A.'s Office building in this novel flooded during the storm and has yet to be repaired. The courthouse is open again, but there is talk of moving it to a new location. The streets and neighborhoods remain basically the same, however, Jazz Fest is still a huge success, and if you want a good shrimp po-boy, you'll have no trouble finding one.

Monday

3:30 A.M.

Does it hurt yet?

The shrill peal of the phone penetrated Ryan's dream, banishing the chilling voice and macabre image from her foggy mind. She glanced around the room in a panic until she finally caught sight of the clock on the dresser. The green neon numbers wavered until she blinked. Three-thirty a.m. Why couldn't murderers and rapists wait until the daylight hours to commit their crimes? She exhaled slowly. At least the nightmare was over. For now, anyway.

Ryan picked up the phone and groaned. "Yeah." Her head was heavy, her mouth furry.

"Thirty in the St. Thomas. Shep will pick you up in five." That was the extent of the conversation, but she immediately knew that it was her brother, NOPD Detective Sean Murphy, calling to report a homicide in one of the city's ten housing developments. Detective Anthony Chapetti — Shep — would be there in five minutes to drive her to the crime scene.

She untangled her clammy legs from the rumpled sheet, and groaned again as she sat up. Even with the air conditioner blowing full blast, her hairline was damp. And it was only the end of April.

Clad in a thin tank top and white cotton underwear, she rolled out of bed and stood in front of the window unit with her arms raised above her head, exposing her armpits directly to the cold blast of air for a minute. She didn't want to think about how hot it would be by July.

Reluctantly, she stumbled away from the air conditioner, averting her eyes from the mirror as she flipped on the light switch. If she looked at all like she felt, the mirror would only hurt her feelings.

Making a cursory attempt to brush through the network of auburn tangles, she admitted defeat when the bristles made contact with a tender lump on the back of her head. A vague recollection surfaced of falling off of a bar stool last night, her head landing in something wet she hoped was beer. It had seemed hilarious then, when she was full of tequila, but now that she was painfully sober, not so much.

Sighing, she rummaged on the floor and grabbed a pair of well-worn running shorts that she had borrowed from one of her four brothers years ago, and debated whether she really needed a bra. After all attention would be focused on the dead body, and nobody would be paying too much attention to her.

But then again, her father, Sixth District Police Captain Kelly Murphy, would definitely notice and have quite a lot to say about it later. While the captain didn't ordinarily put in an appearance at crime scenes, he had so far shown up at every one during Ryan's week of crime scene duty.

She resigned herself to wearing the bra, and then grabbed a black half-shirt from the dresser, knowing her father disapproved of the tight shirt, in part because it revealed her belly-ring. A pair of faded tennis shoes was the final touch. The other assistant district attorneys could wear expensive suits and fancy shoes to the filthy crime scenes if they wanted, but not Ryan.

She thought back to her first night, last month, when she was called out to another crime scene in the St. Thomas. Dressed like a proper assistant, she had ruined a pair of $300 Ferragamo pumps, stepping in a pile of what she hoped was dog mess, but thought might possibly be of human origins. Never again. With what the D.A. paid his prosecutors, Ryan couldn't afford to lose another pair of shoes.

A horn honked. Ryan flipped the light on her porch twice to let Shep know she was on the way, and then hastily brushed her teeth. The horn honked again. Not bothering with makeup, she sprayed a shot of perfume on her neck and rolled deodorant into her armpits until it disappeared into her skin. While people might call her a bitch, Ryan wasn't going to let anyone say she stunk.

She finally ran out of the front door and was immediately assaulted by the pervasive heat. The air was thick with the smell of narcissus, although the nearest ones grew two houses away. Usually, the sticky sweetness of the small, white flowers was comforting, reminding Ryan of playing in her own backyard as a child. Right now the scent was too redolent, more reminiscent of a box of deodorant tampons, and made her stomach heave slightly. She tried to swallow the nausea as she slowed her step. The man waiting for her inside the Crown Vic was tapping his fingers impatiently on the steering wheel when she slid into the passenger seat.

"About time," he said, raising an eyebrow before gunning the car backwards out of the covered driveway. His gaze was intense, with coal lashes framing eyes the grayish-blue of the Gulf of Mexico. "I guess you had another late night."

Ryan reached over and clicked the A/C switch to high, determined not to let Shep's perfect looks make her feel self-conscious. His dark hair stopped just at his shoulders, and even now, in the middle of the night, looked as if it had just been washed and blow dried. Although department regulations required all personnel to be clean-shaven, Ryan had never seen him without stubble, nearly camouflaging his high, chiseled cheekbones. The dark shadow added a hardness to his otherwise almost-pretty facial features.

He made a U-turn in the middle of the street, ignored the stop sign on the corner and drove halfway across St. Charles Avenue, only pausing to let the streetcar pass. The conductor jangled the bell and gave a wave in passing.

Ryan aimed the side air vent at her face, and then took a chance and glanced at herself in the passenger window. She had been wise to avoid the mirror at home. Her almond-shaped eyes were sunken-in without makeup, the purple crescents underneath them emphasizing her fatigue. The normal tan of her face was reduced to an unhealthy gray hue, the result of too much Cuervo Gold and not enough sleep.

"I spent the day at Jazz Fest, and most of the night at the Hole," she finally said, mentally cursing herself for feeling the urge to explain herself. If she had been in court, she would have ignored Shep's comments. Of course, if she had been in court, she wouldn't have looked like a cross between a swamp witch and Alice Cooper. "I forgot I was on death patrol tonight."

It wasn't so much she had forgotten, but more that she hadn't cared that it was her duty week that had kept her out so late. The Hole was a bar across Tulane Avenue from the D.A.'s Office, owned and run by Ryan's oldest brother, Dominick, consequently making it a safe haven for her when she wanted to drink away the problems of her day. And she wasn't about to miss the Jazz Fest for crime scene duty. The New Orleans Jazz and Heritage Festival came around only once a year. Crime scene duty came around every month. Just like her period.

"And if it was up to me, I wouldn't be going at all," she added, covering her mouth as the sentence ended in a yawn.

Shep activated his police light and ran the red, accelerating as he headed down the deserted St. Charles Avenue. "I still don't understand why your boss thinks his attorneys are needed at crime scenes."

Ryan shrugged. "He does this every election year. The voters seem to like it."

Something dark scurried in front of the car and Shep veered sharply from the center of the lane in an apparent attempt to avoid it. There was a bump, and an armadillo waddled on stubby legs to the right side of the road.

Ryan watched through the side mirror as the armadillo made it out of the street in one piece, knowing it would probably die anyway. The appearance of swamp creatures such as armadillos, nutria rats and even an occasional alligator in the city was one of the many paradoxes that New Orleanians accepted without question.

Shep ignored the animal and pointed at Ryan. "And you, of all people, don't mind being used as a prop for the D.A.'s commercials?"

"If it gets me a promotion, Peter can use me as a footstool in his commercial. And, anyway, I looked really good on TV." The commercial had featured six prosecutors in the background at a fake crime scene, with the D.A. standing in front of the camera emphatically expressing his concern about the crime rate. Ryan had thought she had stood out from the other prosecutors, if for no other reason than for the size of her boobs. Watching herself in the commercial on television for the first time had been an almost religious experience.

Shep turned the A/C down a notch. "It's still a waste of everyone's time. Most of the attorneys are totally useless outside the courtroom."

Ryan didn't mention that many of the attorneys were just as useless inside the courtroom as well. This was the second time Shep had voiced his feelings about the necessity of the assistants at the crime scene to Ryan, and while she wasn't convinced it did anything other than bolster her boss's campaign, she wasn't going to let Shep minimize her job.

She turned the air back to high. "Well, maybe if ya'll actually caught a criminal now and then, the crime rate wouldn't be so high and Peter wouldn't feel the need to defend himself every time he's up for re-election."

The car accelerated through the intersection as a yellow light changed to red. She waited for Shep's obligatory defense of his department, but he changed the subject, an amused look on his face.

"Nice belly-ring. Makes you look like a stripper."

Ryan weighed her words as the Crown Vic flew too quickly down the single lane of St. Charles Avenue, past the antebellum mansions and the lush magnolia and crepe myrtle trees that jealously guarded them.

"Knowing how much you like strippers, I'm sure that's supposed to be a compliment, but don't get any ideas. I'm not really your type." As if Shep had a type. If a woman had legs that opened on command, she was pretty much his type.

"Have you been reading the bathroom walls at court again?" he asked. A deep dimple in each cheek was revealed by his slow-spreading smile. The smile was off-kilter, and made him resemble the cartoon alligator a local French Quarter artist painted on T-shirts to sell to tourists. The alligator, named Gilbert, pronounced in the French dialect, Gil-bear, had a mouthful of even, white teeth, and light lines that crinkled around his eyes. The T-shirts depicted Gilbert charming the shotgun away from a Cajun in a pirogue. Something Shep would probably have no trouble doing himself.

"Yeah, and from what the girls are writing about you, you have nothing to brag about." She glanced at his hard, athletic body in a way she hoped seemed disinterested, thinking Anthony Chapetti probably had quite a bit to brag about. His body was lean and cut beneath his black SID T-shirt. Her eyes wandered down, inadvertently ending at the bulge in his jeans. The thought trailed away as she realized Shep was watching her watching him, and she finally looked away, slightly embarrassed.

Gilbert's smile widened. "If I take you out for raw oysters at Acme, will you quit throwing yourself at me?"

She resisted the urge to smack him. He was obviously trying to get a rise from her, and she refused to give him one. Instead, she dismissed him with a wave of her hand. "If you put as much energy into catching criminals as you do into trying to get laid, you might actually get an arrest credit now and then."

Gilbert's smile gave way to Shep's, and Ryan was satisfied that she had won the round. Shep had been best friends with her brother Sean since grade school, and Ryan had always had the same typically hostile relationship with Shep that she shared with her own brothers and had still not quite outgrown.

He rounded the corner onto Felicity on two wheels, and continued speeding in silence toward the Mississippi River. Within a block, the lavish, imposing mansions gave way to shabby, impoverished shacks, revealing another New Orleans paradox, the filthy rich living spitting distance to the poverty-stricken destitute. The continued trek down Felicity brought them to Magazine Street, and the closer they got, the bleaker the neighborhood became. Just beyond Magazine Street, the St. Thomas Housing Development loomed ahead, like a brick and cement monster waiting for its prey.

The silence was awkward, and when Shep finally slowed to make a right onto St. Thomas, one of the few streets that ran all of the way through the project, Ryan let out a barely audible sigh of relief. Shep's eyes darted to her before he pulled to a stop between two marked units, their red and blue lights strobing frantically. The area was teeming with uniformed officers, one of who indicated to the second building from St. Thomas Street.

This side of the development was bordered by Tchoupitoulas Street, but a massive brick wall kept it hidden like a bastard child from the main thoroughfare. The buildings here had been condemned years ago, and were supposedly going to be torn down at some point in the future. Some of the council members talked of tearing down the entire development and relocating all of the occupants, because several prominent companies were looking to invest in the area. While it would have been beneficial to the city to revitalize the crime-infested neighborhood, so far, the talk was just that — talk. The council didn't seem to be in a hurry to pay for the mass relocation.

The St. Thomas was one of the larger housing developments in New Orleans but, until recently, not one of the more dangerous. Then again, none of them was exactly Disneyworld. Ryan took a deep breath as she walked away from the Crown Vic a step behind Shep, trying to calm the wave of apprehension rolling through her stomach.

"What do you have?" Shep asked a short, Hispanic patrolman.

"Black male, approximately twenty years old, single gunshot wound to the head."

Ryan quickened her step to keep pace with Shep as they followed the officer to building 21, a three-story brick unit, with boarded windows and a set of cracked cement steps that were partially sunken into the soft Louisiana ground.

"Watch your step," Shep said, reaching for Ryan's hand to help her over the foot-and-a-half gap between the steps and the building. She ignored him and stepped over without his assistance. He shook his head and continued into the apartment.

"Have fun, kids. Your vic was also naked, bound and beaten." The patrolman seemed relieved to be leaving the area, whistling as he walked away.

The area was beginning to attract a crowd, despite the late hour and lack of lighting. Ryan stopped behind Shep in the dismal, unlit foyer, which smelled of urine and some other smell she thought was familiar but couldn't quite make out. Her father stood near the open door of the first apartment, holding a flashlight. He looked as if he wanted to say something, but remained silent when he walked up, towering over her.

The captain stood six-foot-four, 275 pounds, and Ryan, for all her twenty-eight years, barely five-feet tall and somewhere in the neighborhood of the 110 pounds she would admit to, looked like a child next to him. Her father's lips were a thin line of disapproval as he looked her up and down.

Ryan surveyed the apartment, which was lit only by a handful of battery operated halogens. Even without proper lighting, it was apparent that the conditions here had been unlivable for some time. The ceiling panels in the combination living room/kitchen were missing, exposing raw wooden beams, and the sheetrock on the walls was fraught with holes and graffiti. Ryan caught a whiff of a familiar odor, and checked her tennis shoes quickly to make sure she didn't have a repeat of last month. At least the stink wasn't from her shoes this time. She carefully watched her step, trying to avoid the needles, syringes, and numerous glass and metal tubes that littered the floor.

"Find anything?" she asked, directing the question at her father.

"Just him." The captain pointed to the body, and then wiped beads of sweat from his forehead. "And what in God's name are you wearing?"

"Clothes," Ryan answered, as she picked up one of the halogens and flashed the light on the body.

"If you say so," the captain said, a note of doubt in his voice. He turned as a uniformed officer walked into the room from the hallway.

"Nothing in the bedroom or bathroom," the young officer said. "Well, nothing but drug paraphernalia. Oh, and rats. We're going to have to start shooting them if the coroner doesn't come for the body soon." A scuffling sound came from a shadowy corner of the room. The officer pointed in the direction of the noise. "See what I mean? Puddy and Daubert are checking out the other units, but I seriously doubt this guy is waiting around for us to catch him."

Ryan finally walked over and aimed the flashlight on the body — a naked black man, with close-cropped hair and a scabbed-over scar on his chest. His hands were bound together in front of him with white rope, and his face was severely bruised, half of his lip split, hanging nearly to his chin. But the tiny hole in his forehead was the fatal wound. When he died, his bowels and bladder had relaxed. A small puddle of urine had spread out underneath him, and the proximate odor of feces was unmistakable.

"Is this L'Roid Smith?" Ryan asked, even though she already knew the answer. She knelt by the body for a closer look, careful not to touch anything. She almost hadn't recognized him. She definitely hadn't recognized the flat, vacant look in his eyes. Ryan had never seen the man without a cocky expression or an ominous warning look on his face. But then, she had never seen him dead before. He certainly wasn't giving her the evil eye now.

"You know this clown?" the captain asked, his gray brows furrowed in a deep frown.

Ryan nodded. "Leader of the Soldiers, street name G-Pimp. He was set for trial this week for the murder of three Warriors." The St. Thomas Soldiers and the Ninth Ward Warriors were the two most dangerous gangs in the city. "He was out on a 701."

The state had 120 days to try a case after the defense filed a 701 motion, and had failed to meet the deadline in Smith's case. Not that missing the cut-off date was unusual. More than one murderer had found his way back to the streets via a speedy-trial release, often just to end up back in prison when the jury convicted him. While the pre-trial release relieved the defendant of his bond obligation, Article 701 had no effect on the actual charges. Although L'Roid Smith wouldn't have to worry about either one of those now.

Ryan stood back up. "I tried to prosecute him for a murder last year, but my witnesses disappeared. I had to dismiss the case after we picked the jury, and after Smith got in my face in the hallway and told me he would never serve a day for the murder. Really pissed me off. The D.A. wasn't too thrilled either."

The captain scowled at Smith's body. "I can't believe some stupid judge let this punk out of jail on a 701."

Ryan smiled. "Looks like the stupid judge did us all a favor. Smith wouldn't have served a day on this case either. What are the chances the witnesses would have testified? If they're even still alive. Some people don't give murder a second thought." The casualness of homicide among certain elements of the New Orleans community was something Ryan thought about a lot during the course of murder trials, and now she stared at Smith's lifeless form as if it somehow held the answer. "Not that anyone will lose sleep over this one. Except maybe Bo Lambert." Her smile inadvertently widened.

Bo Lambert was Ryan's main competition in the office, both of them vying for the same promotion to the elite Strike Force. Ryan thought about calling Bo to deliver the news of L'Roid Smith's death personally, but decided she would let him wait until he got to the office the next morning to find out he was losing a major homicide trial credit.

"Nice," Shep said, rubbing the shadow on his chin. "This ought to be easy to solve. Lots of cooperative witnesses on gang cases."

The apartment was too hot, and the stench from the quickly rotting body and its released fluids was overwhelming. Ryan wondered why she bothered with deodorant and perfume when she was going to smell like dead body and human waste by the time she left. She turned toward the door to leave when she noticed a dark tube-like shadow slightly protruding from underneath Smith's body.

She started to kneel down, thinking the object might be a crack pipe either Smith or his killer had been smoking, when the tube turned to face her, wriggling antennae and hissing. Ryan jumped and let out a slight shriek, her heart pounding furiously.

"Just a cockroach," she said, feeling a shiver run down her spine. The two-inch roach took a step in her direction. She jumped again, and Shep quickly brought his boot down on the offensive insect. Ryan felt another chill when the body of the roach made a crunching sound under Shep's boot.

The roach was no longer crawling, now just a crushed brown shell of oozing, snotty-looking guts with still-moving antennae.

"Could you step on it again?" Ryan asked, stepping behind Shep. "As long as the antennae move, they can come back to life."

Shep stepped on the roach one final time, grinding it hopelessly into what used to be cheap carpet, but was now mostly green fibers and strands forever embedded in dirty cement.

"Just like a female," she heard a deep voice behind her. "Digging all up in the dead body but scared of a little roach." She turned to see Detective Monte Carlson standing in the doorway, a grin playing on his lips.

If Ryan hadn't known him, she might have mistaken him for a gang member. Monte Carlson was a light-skinned black man, with a bald head and unlikely green eyes. He had a bandanna around his bald head at the moment, and wore a sleeveless white T-shirt. A Cobra tattoo coiled around his well-formed right biceps, and a tarantula clutched his left, offsetting the miscellaneous other artwork running up and down his arms. He had multiple piercings in his ears, and wore a small gold hoop in his eyebrow. There was a rumor his penis was pierced as well, which Ryan didn't know from personal experience but had come damn near to finding out last Friday night.

Today, he also had a solid black teardrop drawn on his face under his right eye, a common prison tattoo signifying that the inmate had killed somebody. The outline of a teardrop meant the inmate had shot someone, a filled-in teardrop meant the victim died, although no one with the mark would ever admit that to a prosecutor. Ryan knew that Monte's teardrop, unlike his other tattoos, was not real, but part of his undercover look.

"Little? That roach could help the coroner move the body." She tried to control the heat rising in her face. Monte had given her a ride home from the Hole Friday night, and she had been pretty drunk. She had a vague recollection of climbing on his lap in his police unit. Not that he had complained. "And what brings you to a homicide anyway? I see you're wearing your wife-beater, so you must be working undercover somewhere." She pointed to his shirt, knowing Monte's personal mode of dress didn't usually include a Stanley Kowalski white tank top.

Monte was a detective in narcotics, also under her father's command, and primarily conducted buy-bust operations. He drove through the high crime neighborhoods in an unmarked police unit equipped with a hidden video camera, until somebody flagged him down and sold him crack cocaine. Once he was safely out of the area, the take-down team would arrest the dealer, and the drugs, prerecorded money and video would all be used as evidence. The job was dangerous, and Ryan was sure it was part of Monte's allure. That, and the whole forbidden fruit thing.

Monte nodded at Smith's body. "Your homicide might be connected to a drug bust we did a few hours ago. We arrested a Soldier who gave up some information that a hit might be going down in the St. Thomas, but wouldn't say who. G-Pimp here could be the answer." Monte shook his head. "Then again, the night's not over yet. We could find more than one dead banger tonight. I just wanted to check it out. Your buddy Lambert was doing this one, huh?"

Ryan made a face. "And he'll probably want the perp to get the death penalty just for messing up his stats."

The captain's voice cut into the conversation. "Ryan, are you finished here?"

Ryan watched her father wipe his forehead again, and then search his shirt pocket for a cigarette. She wondered if he had picked up on some vibe from Monte. She knew a relationship with Monte would be unacceptable to the captain, and was thus out of the question for her. Of course, what she had been after Friday didn't exactly fall into the category of relationship. And they hadn't done anything, really, although she doubted her father would see it that way.

"I want to talk to crime lab before I leave." She glanced over at the body again, struck by its nakedness. "Do you think he was sexually assaulted?"

The captain pointed at Ryan before anyone had a chance to answer. "I'll be waiting for you in the car." He stalked to the door, pausing as Sean walked in.

"Crime lab and coroner are both rolling up now," Sean told the captain. "And you've got some press out there waiting for a statement."

"Make my whole goddamn night complete, why don't you," the captain's voice was a growl over his shoulder as he stomped out.

Ryan waited until her father was out of the doorway of the apartment to aim a question at Monte. "Just out of curiosity, is that normal for a dead body, or is it true what they say about black men?" She raised her eyebrows at L'Roid Smith's penis, which was grotesquely large and swollen. Monte might have only been to first base, but she would make sure he remembered.

"It's all true, baby." Monte grinned and gave her a wink.

"Outside, now!" The captain's voice was more like an enraged bear than a mere growl this time. Ryan wondered if he had heard the exchange with Monte, knowing she would catch hell in the car on the way home if he had.

Two crime lab officers walked in before Ryan could get out of the apartment.

"What a cesspool," one of them said immediately. "We can't do anything here until daylight." Henry Cooper stood with a slouch, his shoulders slightly rounded and his hands in his pockets. His sloppy posture did nothing to detract from his belly, which was straining the laws of physics by the T-shirt tautly stretched over it. The shirt had a picture of a smiling crawfish wearing a bikini and the words, "I love sucking heads and eating tails, New Orleans Jazz Festival."

"Are you going to try to lift prints?" Ryan asked. She knew Cooper as a competent but somewhat lazy criminalist. He was good at his job, when he bothered to do it, and Ryan had enjoyed more than one run-in with him in the past, trying to get him to show up for court when he was supposed to.

Cooper looked at her dubiously, his deep-set gray eyes clouding over, and waited a second before he spoke. "I don't see the point. There must be a million prints in here. This place is the equivalent of a crack house. And not too many surfaces in here are going to be suitable for latent prints." He made a pretense of looking around the room.

"What about the doorknob?" Ryan pressed. "It's worth a shot, isn't it? I mean, you're here anyway. You might as well do something."

Cooper looked annoyed. "I'll do the doorknob if you want. But being here gives me the heebie jeebies."

"Yo dawg, you not scared of the projects, are you?" Monte asked, slapping Cooper on the back.

"The projects don't scare me." Cooper's frown transformed into a sly grin. "The people in them, that's another matter."

"Oh, so you just scared of us black folks. Well, you can always go wait in Eulah Mae Simpson's apartment," Monte said, and the others snickered. The demographics for each of the city's housing projects had been released several years ago, and the St. Thomas had noted a single white female, seventy-year-old Eulah Mae Simpson. She had lived in the St. Thomas development since its inception in the early 1940's, when the project was predominantly white, and continued living there today, among the some thirty-four hundred black people.

Cooper took his hands out his pockets. The slouch remained. "I just don't see the point in wasting time trying to lift prints that won't be good anyway."

"Do them right and maybe they will be," Ryan said. "And on the very slight chance that a suspect is developed, a fingerprint just might come in handy. I don't know why, but for some reason juries like it when we have the defendant's prints at the scene. So even if you get a million prints off that doorknob, if just one of them matches my defendant, I have a much better chance of winning my case. Can you see that at all? Or maybe I should ask your captain for his opinion."

Ryan could feel the officers' eyes on her as she walked away, and she knew they thought she was being a bitch. Why couldn't everyone just do what they were supposed to do? Then she wouldn't have to be so mean. And why hadn't Sean or Shep ordered Cooper to lift the prints? Obviously because they didn't think printing the apartment was worth the bother either. Once somebody was arrested, the police officers didn't care about the difficulty Ryan would have convincing the jury. Losing the case would be her fault, not theirs.

She turned back once and caught Monte's eye. He winked at her again, making her feel a little bit better. She smiled back, and kept her hands balled in fists at her sides to avoid the temptation to chew her thumbnail.

Halfway to the captain's car she had an uneasy feeling that someone was watching her. She stopped and whirled around, half-expecting a confrontation with

Henry Cooper, half-expecting Monte to stop her. Nobody was there. She looked at the abandoned apartment buildings surrounding her, wondering if someone could be inside one of them. Then she felt goose bumps rise on her arms and laughed at herself. Cooper just had her spooked. Plenty of bums lived in the empty buildings, and they were probably just watching the action. She started walking again, glancing back once more, still seeing no one.

Two press cars were parked near the captain's Crown Vic. Ryan threw a big smile and wave to Chance Halley, a blonde-hair, blue-eyed babe of a reporter from WDSU, the feeling of unknown eyes watching her temporarily forgotten. Chance was young and good looking, even by TV reporter standards, and Ryan thought his lack of air time was a tragedy. Chance waved back, and made a motion with his hand to his ear like a phone, as if he was going to call her. The captain made a rude noise. Ryan smiled, knowing Chance Halley had no idea who she was, but figured he would try to find out. Reporters were whores for inside information.

She got into her father's car, sat back and waited for the lecture du jour. She didn't know which one this would be, about her clothes, about the way she talked to the guys, about being a prosecutor. She always managed to do something that didn't quite measure up to the Murphy standards. And the captain was never shy about letting her know it.

Not that her father didn't love her — Ryan knew he did. As a matter of fact, of the five Murphy children, she was his favorite, being the youngest and the only girl, even if she wasn't his biological child. But she knew her father would never make that the topic of conversation.

She wondered if she should tell the captain about her feeling of being watched, but then vetoed the idea. He would undoubtedly tell her she wouldn't have to worry about people watching her if she would wear more clothes. She put the thought out of her mind once again as her father backed onto Felicity.

The captain made a right on Tchoupitoulas, and then drove along the great wall that separated the street from the housing development, finally taking another right on Jackson. He could have driven the direct route straight through the project on St. Thomas to get to Jackson, but Ryan knew that he wouldn't with her in the car, as if he was protecting her by not letting her see any more of the project's ugliness. The streets outside of the St. Thomas were empty at this time of the morning, even the drug dealers in their beds.

She waited for her father to say something, hoping he would ease into the issue of the day so she would have a few seconds to build a defense. Instead, he silently cranked the air up to high, and headed in the direction of Ryan's apartment, taking a left on Magazine Street.

The bead lady, a homeless woman famous for the dozens of Mardi Gras beads she wore around her neck, had parked her shopping cart at the corner. She was staring at herself in the plate glass window of an antique shop, adjusting a feather on her hat. Ryan almost wished she could trade places with the old woman, at least for the duration of the ride home. Her father's silence was somehow more unnerving than his usual ranting.

Ryan decided to get the jump on him. "You know daddy, that crime lab tech Henry Cooper is a lazy slob."

A beer truck ran over the curb, cutting in front of the captain's Crown Vic.

"Asshole," the captain muttered and leaned on the horn. He turned his attention back to Ryan. "I really don't want to talk about Henry Cooper." He paused. The silence pounded in her ears until he spoke again. "Lawyers got no business at the scenes of crimes. If the D.A. wants to take a chance with those other idiots that work for him, that's on him. I'm not taking a chance with you. You're not doing it anymore."

Anger flooded Ryan's pores.

"I am an adult. You can't tell me what to do. And it's not up to you whether I go to the crime scenes or not. In case you've forgotten, that's part of my job."

"I can change that with one call to your boss."

Ryan tried to calm the heat coursing through her veins. Uncontrolled rage was never a productive weapon against her father. She would need to switch tactics.

Envisioning a Hallmark commercial that always reduced her to tears, she sniffed. A second later, the waterworks began. "Daddy, if you tell Peter I shouldn't be at the crime scenes, he'll think I put you up to it. I'll look like some fat kid trying to get out of gym class. I guess I can kiss Strike Force goodbye — probably trials too. I'll be too embarrassed to stay at the D.A.'s Office when I get moved to a desk. I'll be miserable, but I suppose I'll manage to find a new job somewhere."

She allowed a single tear to roll down her face. "I just always thought you wanted me to be happy. I thought you loved me." She ended by placing her hand on her forehead and slouching down into the seat.

Her father had a pained expression on his face. "You can stop being a drama queen, Sara Bernhardt. Your act might work in the courtroom, but not with me." Then he softened his tone, and Ryan knew that, despite his words, he was caving in. "I just worry about you, baby."

"But you have no reason to worry about me."

The captain let go of the steering wheel and threw his hands up in the air. "Look at how you dress to come to a crime scene, for Christ's sake. The only thing missing was a pole for you to dance on." He was getting worked up, but he was also changing the subject.

Ryan gave him a look out of the corner of her eye, trying to contain a smirk. "You and Shep been hitting Big Who's? You both seem to have the low-down on strippers these days."

Big Who's was a strip club, nasty even by Bourbon Street standards. The owner had set the "W" on the sign to blink, alternating the name Big Who's with Big ho's. The NOPD had frequent dealings with Big Who when his girls failed to wear the obligatory pasties and G-strings as they danced in the club's windows.

The captain turned red, but remained silent.

"Don't tell me I'm right." Ryan knew she was pushing too far, but couldn't resist. "Somehow I just can't picture you shoving a dollar bill down some stripper's thong."

"The way you talk to me! I have never been to a strip club in my life, young lady. Well, not voluntarily. I mean, I've gone undercover a few times —"

"I bet you have," Ryan interrupted, and then smiled the smile of the victorious. Topic deflected. Her father was no longer thinking about her crime scene duty. She used the lull in conversation as an opportunity to change the subject. "So, do you think you're going to come up with any suspects for Smith's murder?"

The captain shrugged, and Ryan knew he wasn't going to discuss the case with her. Not that his reluctance would stop her from prodding. One of the things she enjoyed about her job as a prosecutor was being in the loop.

"Do you think Shep is right that Smith's murder is going to be impossible to solve?"

The captain glanced over at her cautiously. "Let me worry about that. And what's with your sudden interest in Chapetti? You've mentioned him twice already."

"Why would I be interested in Shep?" she asked, avoiding the question. "I'm not exactly his type."

"Well, I'm glad you realize that, at least." The captain seemed a little too relieved.

Ryan decided to not let him off that easily. "Now that we're clear on Shep, what about Monte Carlson? Are you going to warn me about him next? Because you know," she lowered her voice and looked around the car as if someone might be listening, "I've heard he's black."

"Monte Carlson? Jesus Christ, Ryan, I was worried enough you might be interested in Anthony Chapetti. Are you trying to drive me to an early grave?" The captain put his left hand over his heart.

"And you would have a problem with that?" She feigned surprise. "Me going out with a black man?"

Her father pointed at her. "Never mind the fact that he's black. Jesus Christ, Ryan, Carlson's not even Catholic." He turned onto Napolean, where the houses were sizable, but not quite the mansions of St. Charles Avenue.

They were still several blocks away from Ryan's house when she said, "Well, Daddy, Shep is Catholic." That would most definitely give the captain something else to think about other than complaining to the D.A. about her presence at the crime scenes.

"We are not talking about Chapetti again." From her father's tone, Ryan knew better than to push this time. "He's a good cop, but with all women who call him at the station I'm surprised he ever gets any work done. And don't get me started on the poor girls who have shown up at the station for him. I didn't think my little girl would be happy being some gigolo's plaything."

"Nobody uses the word gigolo," she said as her father pulled into her covered driveway. She knew her father was exaggerating, as he always did when he was trying to convince her of something. Her father's propensity for embellishment, however, didn't stop Ryan from wondering exactly what Shep did to all those women to make them pursue him so aggressively.

When they were out of the car, the captain finally said, "I won't call your boss about this crime scene bullshit. Yet. But so help me God, if you so much as get a broken nail at one of these scenes, my size 15s are going to be embedded in somebody's ass." He pointed to his boots.

Ryan smiled with relief. No matter how she got there, she always managed to get what she wanted.

They walked in silence toward the front steps of the shotgun double she rented. The house was raised three feet from the ground, set on cement blocks like many of the houses in town to protect them from the frequent floods. All of the rooms were in a single row, lined up directly behind each other, and locals said a shotgun slug fired through the front door would travel through each room and exit the back door, hence the name. The house was a double, but the adjacent apartment was used as storage by the owners, so Ryan had no immediate neighbors.

The captain detoured from the Camellia-lined cement path to the page wire fence that surrounded the back yard. His eyes scanned the length of the yard before joining Ryan on the porch. He then walked into the house ahead of her, checking the house for intruders, stopping in the kitchen. "I'm glad to see you finally took the key out of the back door."

Ryan was glad that her father had something positive to say for a change. She wasn't about to tell him she had no idea where the key was, and couldn't remember the last time she had seen it.

He had lectured her when she first moved in about not leaving the key in the double bolt, because an intruder could break the small panel of glass in the door and reach the key inside. Ryan had pointed out that if someone was willing to break the glass to get to the key, he could just as easily break a window to get in. Her father had told her that her attitude invited trouble.

She followed the captain back to the front door. He started to say something, but Ryan suddenly noticed the deep lines etched in his face, and his words were lost. Every now and then, she caught a glimpse of her father, and saw him, not as her overprotective parent, or even as the stern, commanding police captain, but as a tired, worried old man.

Ryan impulsively threw her arms around him and buried her face in his chest, comforted by the familiar scent of stale cigarette smoke, pungent sweat, and just a tad Old Spice. "I love you, Daddy. I'm sorry I make you worry so much."

He planted a kiss on top of her head. "I know, princess." He reached into his back pocket and came up with his wallet.

Ryan squeezed him as hard as she could, barely able to get her arms completely around his mid-section. "I don't need any money," she said, embarrassed that her father assumed her affection was born of an ulterior motive. "Thank you for not going to the D.A. about the crime scenes. I promise I'll be careful." She finally let go of him. When she looked at his face again, the tired, worried old man was gone, and her father was back.

"I love you too, baby," he said, and walked out, remaining on the porch until Ryan locked the front door and set the alarm.

Ryan looked at the clock and realized in just a few hours she would have get ready for work. As exhausted as she was, Ryan jumped in the shower and scrubbed herself with the hottest water she could stand, trying to get the St. Thomas stink off of her body. She hoped that when she fell back to sleep, the voice and image from her earlier nightmare wouldn't return.

JACOB

His mother had named him Jacob. For some reason, the new parents had thought they could erase the first eight years of his miserable life by changing his name. But they couldn't, and, after more than twenty years, he was still Jacob, no matter what the new family had decided to call him.

He grabbed a plastic CD jewel case off the entertainment center, and used a razor blade to chop the off-white, crystal-like chunks on top of it. The pieces could easily have been confused for rocks of crack cocaine, but were actually chunks of crystal methamphetamine, readily available to purchase at clubs and college campuses. Of course, part of the thrill was in stealing the crystal from evidence. One hundred percent free, and impossible to trace back to him.

The crystal turned into a coarse powder, which Jacob divided into lines with the razor. He took a hundred out of his wallet, rolled the bill and snorted the powder through it. He felt the sting in his nasal passages, and then the burn. The drug left an acrid, phlegmy taste in the back of his throat, a minor inconvenience for the bright, Technicolor rush he began to experience almost immediately. Now he was ready.

He returned the CD case to the entertainment center, ignoring the brown vials neatly lined up next to the other cases. The vials contained extremely rare, highly-concentrated liquid heroin, also taken from evidence. Jacob hadn't decided yet who would be the lucky recipient, but realized that such a deadly drug could surely serve a worthwhile purpose at some point in the future.

He strode to the window, turned off the lights in the apartment, and opened the curtains. Using binoculars, he peered through the tiny hole he had cut in the window shade, glad that he had spent the extra money for higher power magnification lenses. He was a good distance from the crime scene, but he could see her almost as clearly as if she was standing right in front of him.

Hatred burned deep in the pit of his stomach. Jacob had assumed that a woman as self-centered as Ryan Murphy would have at least sensed when somebody detested her as much as he did. Fortunately, he had been wrong.

He stood motionless at the window, watching her until she left, wondering how he would be able to stand waiting to carry out his plan.

8:55 A.M.

Ryan vaulted out of her Jeep, turning back hastily to make sure the "Official NOPD Business" sign with the NOPD logo was in place in the windshield. She then flew up the front steps of the Orleans Parish Criminal Courthouse, past the dozens of reporters milling about on the steps outside. Ryan was not quite late, but would have been had she not parked illegally in a police zone on Tulane Avenue.

A reporter called her name and tried to catch up to her, but Ryan raced ahead. As much as she enjoyed the spotlight, she didn't want to agitate the judge by being late. Although if the reporter had been Chance Halley, she had to admit she might have risked it.

"Ryan, wait up." Mike Boudreaux, her junior assistant, ran up the stairs behind her. Mike had been an offensive lineman for the New Orleans Saints prior to going to law school. Six foot five, he had weighed in at 365 while playing, but, as he frequently stated, had slimmed down to a "lean" 310 pounds since his football days. With his square jaw and large blonde head, he still looked more like a ball player than a lawyer. "I'm all set to go on the molestation case, if he doesn't plead," Mike said, his green eyes revealing his excitement at the possibility of going to trial.

Ryan glanced behind her, double checking to make certain Chance was not among the reporters, and was disappointed that he wasn't. "He'll plead. Janet never goes to trial," Ryan said, referring to the public defender in the section. "Did you hear about L'Roid Smith?"

Mike stuck out his chest. "I wish I knew who killed him. I'd like to shake his hand."

"I guess Bo has the week off now." Ryan tried not to smile. For the most part, individual statistics determined who received promotions, the number of each prosecutor's jury trials one of the more important factors. The Smith trial would have tied Bo with Ryan for the total number of jury trials she had prosecuted. Now, Ryan was ahead by one.

"So, how was the murder last night?" Mike bounced on his toes as they waited behind a short line of people entering the courthouse. "I can't wait until I get assigned to a duty." He showed his D.A. badge at the top of the steps, and the uniformed deputy, already recognizing them, signaled for them to go around the metal detectors.

"You'll be assigned any day now. Although I don't know why you want to be." She waved down the hall at two police officers she knew.

"So was the murder scene cool?" Mike gave a nod in the officers' direction.

Ryan covered her mouth as she yawned. "I almost got bit by a cockroach. And you have no idea how difficult it is to get the smell of dead body out of your hair."

"Cockroaches don't bite," Mike said, as if he hadn't heard the rest.

"Those big German roaches in the projects do. And they hiss like cats."

They continued up the second flight of stairs, a circular, double set of marble steps. Ryan would have preferred to take the elevator, but, as usual, it was out of order. Only the individual courtrooms had air conditioning, and moisture was already beginning to form on the back of her neck.

Mike pushed the Section B door and held it open. "I still think going to the crime scenes would be cool, even if a cockroach does bite me. I can't wait until they put me on the schedule."

Mike was so idealistic. That would undoubtedly wear off in time. The two prosecutors walked on the plush carpet down the center aisle, taking a quick inventory of the people already waiting in the heavy wooden benches on either side.

Everything in the courtroom was first class. In fact, as Ryan often pointed out to jurors, the court scenes in the movie *JFK* had been shot in this very room. The velvet window treatments, solid oak furniture and crystal chandeliers were replaced every two years at the expense of the tax payers. The musty smell, however, was always prevalent. Ten thousand dollars could keep the courtroom looking pretty, but apparently no amount of money could stop it from smelling like feet.

As they approached the state's table, Mike gave her an admiring glance. "You look really nice today."

She gave him a quick smile, feeling a little uncomfortable.

The day Mike had been assigned as her junior, Ryan had taken him out to celebrate. Mike had gotten drunk, and admitted he liked her. She had thought it was cute, until he had said he was having second thoughts about marrying his fiancée, and Ryan had felt it necessary to snap him back to reality. She had told him that it wouldn't be appropriate for them to become involved as long as she was his immediate superior. The entire situation had been a bit awkward, and sometimes Ryan got the feeling Mike still had a crush on her.

Not that she wouldn't have considered dating him under different circumstances. His body alone would have held her interest for an indeterminate amount of time. But not while he had to answer to her in court, and not while he was engaged to another woman.

Mike seemed to sense Ryan's discomfort, and quickly changed the subject. "So, do you really think the judge will sentence Johnnie Lee to death? And if we don't go on the molestation, what are we going to start working on?"

The previous week, a jury had found Johnnie Lee guilty of raping his ten-year-old daughter, LaJohnnie, in a two-day trial that had ended in an impressive twelve-minute verdict. It had been an emotional trial, as was usually the case with child victims, and Ryan was glad that the jury had come back so quickly. After the verdict, the two prosecutors had begun preparing testimony and evidence for the penalty phase.

On capital cases, Louisiana law required a separate mini-trial for the penalty determination, where the state was required to prove aggravating factors or circumstances in order for the jury to choose death. The state usually put on evidence of the defendant's prior criminal record, as well as any relevant aggravating circumstances of the crime. The defendant had the opportunity to put on mitigating evidence, which usually included his mama, begging the jury for his life. But Johnnie Lee's mama never showed up, and the jury came back with the death penalty after deliberating for three days. The only thing left now was for the judge to actually impose the sentence.

"The death penalty for rape was upheld by the Supreme Court a long time ago," Ryan pointed out. "The judge has no legal reason not to impose it. And all those reporters out there are just waiting to let the public know if Judge Jackson wussies out." Ryan had made anonymous calls to the press herself, to let them know the possibility existed that the judge could try to reduce the penalty, an unlikely, but not impossible, scenario. "And anyway, after hearing LaJohnnie's testimony about all the horrible things that man did to her, I can't imagine a judge in this building who would have a problem imposing death."

Getting the death penalty on this case should not only have made history, but Ryan figured the jury's verdict should also have secured her shot at the promotion. Since the law had been upheld, no prosecutor in Louisiana had ever convinced a jury to vote for death on a rape case. Until now. All she needed was for the judge to impose the verdict, and she was certain that the Strike Force position would be hers.

"The next big trial in here is Gendusa," Ryan went on, answering Mike's earlier question, aware that he already knew the answer. The Gendusa case was a five-victim murder, alleged Mafia hits of state witnesses. Mafia or not, the state had a strong case. Marcelo Gendusa was on tape, courtesy of a recording made by his girlfriend, admitting to the murders.

Unfortunately for Ryan, two special prosecutors had been assigned to it. She would have loved to try the case, being that mob cases were rarely handled in state court. But since no money was recovered to forfeit, the Feds didn't want the case and had taken a pass, allowing the D.A.'s office to prosecute the state charges. Ryan was still indignant that she wasn't allowed to at least sit second chair.

"But we're not even doing that one. So we don't have anything big set for a while." He seemed as disappointed as Ryan.

"State, call your first case." Judge Jackson had appeared on the bench while Ryan and Mike were talking, looking peeved, as always. The judge was nearing retirement, and everyone knew that he hated it. Not that Ryan blamed him. Despite his age and graying hair, he was still sharp, with the athletic build from his days in the military. He also had the distinction of being the first black judge to sit on the bench at Orleans Parish Criminal Court.

Ryan smiled, although she knew social pleasantries had little effect on the judge's disposition. "We're ready to pick a jury on Jones, and for sentencing on Johnnie Lee."

"Hmph," the judge said to no one in particular. "Public Defender, get up here."

Janet Johnson, a large, bosomy black woman with giant red lips and seemingly hundreds of long, colorful braids exploding out of her head, sauntered up to the bench. "He's going to plead," Janet said with a slow drawl. "Ya'll can go on and sentence Johnnie Lee and I'll be drawing up Mr. Jones' paperwork."

"Donna?" the judge asked the gray-haired clerk.

As usual, Donna knew what the judge wanted without him actually asking anything. "Johnnie Lee's attorney is on the way."

The judge looked irritated. "Hmmph. Five minute recess then." He pounded his gavel and went back into chambers.

A second later, Donna made a sound in her throat like a lion growling. "Take a look at what the cat dragged in."

Ryan looked up as Shep swaggered into the courtroom, smiling at all of the females in the audience. He stopped momentarily to shake hands with Nero, the court bailiff, and then continued to the front of the court. At the clerk's table, he nudged Ryan slightly with his hip and grabbed Donna's hand.

"How's my favorite clerk?" he asked, giving Donna a smile.

The sixty-year-old clerk smiled back. "I bet you say that to all of the clerks."

He then put his arm around Ryan's shoulder and looked her up and down. "I liked you much better in that tight little shirt last night." He turned to Donna. "Did you know your prosecutor has a belly ring?"

Donna raised her eyebrows and peered over her glasses. Ryan could see the other woman calculating the gossip potential. "Had an interesting night, did you?"

"We were at a crime scene," Ryan said, her face starting to flush. She ducked from under Shep's arm and quickly walked over to the state's table.

"If that's what the kids are calling it these days," Shep said with another smile and a wink at Donna, and then followed Ryan.

"What do you want?" Ryan asked. "You don't have anything in here today." Shep sat in the chair next to her, so close his leg was touching hers. A masculine, woodsy smell emanated from him. Ryan tried not to notice it.

"You have a motion hearing coming up on a crack possession. Clint Perkins."

Ryan shifted slightly away. It was difficult to pay attention to what Shep was saying when he smelled so good. "So?"

"Sanchez saw him throw down a bag of rocks. We were on proactive patrol because of the hospital rapes."

Ryan frowned. "And what?" Sanchez wasn't with the department any longer, but Shep should have been able to handle the hearing without the other officer. As soon as the judge ruled the evidence was admissible, the defendant would likely plead to two years and Sanchez's current whereabouts would become irrelevant.

"I didn't actually see the throw-down," Shep said. "Sanchez told me Perkins dropped the bag of crack. Maybe you ought to write this up for a deal. He'd probably plead to attempted possession if he got probation."

"You know I don't give deals to crack heads," Ryan said. "And why does Sanchez's report say that you both saw Perkins throw down the rocks?'

Shep shrugged. "You'd have to ask him."

"That's really cute, since you know I can't." She tapped her fingers on the top of the table, no longer enamored with the way Shep smelled.

He smiled and put his arm around her shoulder. "Look, babe, if giving a deal bothers you that much, just tell me what to say. You want me to say I saw the throw-down, I saw the throw- down. Problem solved."

"Have you been smoking crack today yourself?" Ryan asked, trying to keep her voice down as she pushed his arm away. "Of course I don't want you to commit perjury. Are you insane?" He knew better. Ryan wondered what he wasn't telling her. She looked at him suspiciously. "Are you sure there's not some other reason you want this guy to get a deal?"

Shep put his hands up. "Why would I care what happens to him? I'm just trying to help you out. You don't have much of a case without Sanchez. I can either say what you need me to say so your evidence doesn't get suppressed, or you can give the guy a deal. I thought I was being nice by letting you know now, instead of waiting until you put me on the stand. Give him a deal or don't give him a deal, it's nothing to me."

Ryan was skeptical, but Shep obviously wasn't going to say anything else. "I guess I don't have much of a choice." She scrawled a note to herself on a legal pad. Shep stood up and walked to the door, turning back once to wink at her again. She felt her face turn red, realizing how it would look to anyone who was watching. Luckily, Johnnie Lee's attorney Louis James walked in at that exact moment, drawing everyone's attention.

Donna knocked on the judge's door and a second later he took the bench. "Ready for sentencing, Mr. James?"

Johnnie Lee was led to the podium in the center of the room, shackled at his hands and feet. Louis James stood next to him. "Louis James for the defendant, Johnnie Lee. We're ready for sentencing, your Honor."

The judge nodded. "This case comes before me for sentencing, the jury having recommended the death penalty. During the guilt phase, the jury found beyond a reasonable doubt that Johnnie Lee committed the rape of a person under the age of twelve, specifically, his ten-year-old daughter, LaJohnnie Lee.

"During the penalty phase, the jury found eleven aggravating factors and one mitigating factor, thus arriving at their decision to impose death. Finding that the jury's recommendation is proper, it is the sentence of this court that the defendant, Johnnie Lee, is sentenced to death by lethal injection."

Ryan stopped listening. Several reporters who were sitting in the back of the courtroom hurried out of the door, while Johnnie Lee was led away, stone-faced. A press conference would be held the following afternoon, and although the D.A. wouldn't let her say much, she would get to answer a few questions on TV.

There was no way Bo could top this.

Shep couldn't help but smile as he walked down the hallway. Ryan was pissed. She hated to give deals, and Shep had no doubt she realized something was up. Ryan was too smart not to see through him.

He couldn't tell her the truth, that Perkins was an unregistered confidential informant, something against department policy. He might have shared this information with a different prosecutor, but Ryan wouldn't have cared about how useful Perkins was to Shep. She would have still wanted to nail him, despite the fact that it could have gotten Shep reprimanded, not to mention cost him a valuable CI.

He had known that if he offered to lie on the stand to make Ryan happy, she would adamantly refuse. She didn't have a clue about the real world. To her, everything was black and white.

He smiled at the minute clerk out of habit, but was still thinking of Ryan's pained look when he suggested she give Perkins a deal. Shep had been close with Sean for years, and had always thought of Ryan as a spoiled brat — the favorite who could wrap her parents around her little finger to get herself out of trouble, something she was definitely no stranger to. And while she was certainly not hard on the eyes, Shep could never get past her big mouth.

Then, several months ago, something had happened to make him see Ryan in a different light. Shep had testified for her on a case where a retarded homeless man, "working for food" on the corner of Claiborne and Carrollton, was savagely beaten by a group of college students. By the time the drunken frat boys were finished with him, the man was $2.50 richer, but required an extremely painful emergency room procedure to extract the loose change from his rectum.

At trial, Ryan had steamrolled over the defense attorney and the defense witnesses in her usual aggressive way, keeping just civil enough not to alienate the jury. She was good, knowing just when to stop.

And then during her closing argument, tears had streamed down her cheeks as she relived the agony and shame of the victim for the jury, making him seem like a human being to people who ordinarily would have considered him nothing more than a pesky nuisance. Shep had realized for the first time that Ryan genuinely cared about more than just winning cases, and it had caught him off guard.

"Shep!" A high-pitched voice barged through his recollection like a storm trooper. He finally noticed the tall, well-built blonde — not natural, he knew from personal experience — straining to get his attention. She was leaning over her desk, her ample rear sticking out, no panty lines visible through her tight skirt.

"Wanda, how's it going?" He kept his tone casual.

"Fine, now that you're here." Wanda's red lips formed a pout. "Where have you been hiding? I haven't seen you around much lately."

And there's a reason for that, he thought, but just gave her his number three smile. He and Wanda had a casual, off and on relationship for the past two years. They would date for brief periods of time, if having constant sex was equated with dating, and then they would drift apart. He had decided the last time they had gotten back together would be the final time. Wanda was still having trouble accepting the breakup.

"I'm a little busy these days. We've got all of these unsolved homicides, and the captain's been on my ass."

"The captain is a very lucky man," Wanda said, running her hand up Shep's leg to an inappropriately high spot on his inner thigh. "I would trade places with him in a heart beat. And you know what they say about all work and no play."

"Yeah, it keeps my job security." Shep moved his leg out of her reach, keeping his number three smile in place. His number one or number two smiles would have given her too much hope, and he had no intention of giving her his real smile. She hadn't even gotten that when they were sleeping together.

Wanda gave him a knowing look, her tone no longer playful. "When you're finished with whoever you're doing this week, you'll come back. You always do."

He shrugged without comment, remembering the last time they were together. After one of their sex marathons, he had tried to have a discussion with her, not about anything deep like Plato's Dialogues, but about a murder in the tight-knit New Orleans East Vietnamese community. Shep was frustrated with the reticent witnesses, who refused to give him any information because the shooter was also Vietnamese. Wanda's contribution to the discussion had been to tell Shep about how a Korean woman always cheated at the Bingo game Wanda went to every Thursday evening. That's when it dawned on him that they had nothing in common, and decided that he had to end the relationship.

Shep was disturbed that it had taken him two years to figure it out. Looking back, he had been confronted with the sad truth that he had never dated a woman with whom he could actually have an intelligent conversation. He guessed that's what he got for thinking with Shep Jr. his whole life.

"What number is my case on the docket?" he asked.

Wanda wordlessly handed him the docket, turning her back to him and her attention to a defense attorney, in an obvious attempt to make Shep jealous that was completely wasted on him.

TUESDAY

2:00 A.M.

Ryan was just getting into bed at two a.m., exhausted and with the beginning of a headache. She had gone out after work to celebrate her big win. The judge had cancelled court for the next day, something he rarely did, and Ryan didn't see the harm in kicking back and enjoying herself for a couple of hours.

Shooting tequila had seemed like a good idea then, but the pulsating in her temples now had her questioning her earlier decision. Even if she could sleep late the next day, she still had to go into the office in the afternoon for the press conference, and she did want to look her best on television. Maybe the party should have been postponed until the weekend.

The phone rang. The caller ID registered Unknown.

She frowned as she picked up the receiver. "Yeah."

"I'm giving you another gift."

Ryan's heart sped up. The caller spoke through a voice distortion device that gave his voice a demonic quality. Ryan had received a similar message on her answering machine the night before, and had dismissed the call as a prank. All of the prosecutors received such calls from time to time, but the distortion device made the voice sound so eerie and ominous, she found it difficult to keep her hands from shaking.

"Oh really?" she asked, trying to sound unaffected, eyeing her gun on the nightstand as she waited for the obscene part of the call explaining what the "gift" would be.

But the caller hung up without saying anything else.

Ryan climbed into bed and put her gun on the pillow next to her, drawing the blanket around her body, chilly despite the heat. A second later, the phone rang again.

She thought about letting the machine answer, but didn't want to give the prank caller the satisfaction of thinking he had scared her. She saw Sean's cell phone number on the caller I.D..

"Yeah," she answered, her heart rate returning to normal.

"Another 30. I'm on the way."

One day down, six to go. Then she would be free for a month before she had to worry about being called out in the middle of the night again. Unless she made Strike Force. The Strike Force attorneys were not on the crime scene duty schedule, yet another reason for striving for the position. She put on a T-shirt and shorts, and pulled her hair back with a clip.

A horn honked. As she grabbed her shoes, the phone rang again. She ran outside, refusing to glance at the phone on her way out.

Sean drove in silence for nearly five minutes, his mind obviously elsewhere. He hadn't told Ryan where they were heading, but she had an idea from the route they were taking. She didn't want to mention the prank caller, knowing Sean would blow it out of proportion.

"Why are you so quiet?" Ryan asked, unable to stand keeping silent herself for so long. "Some woman breaking your heart?"

Sean shrugged, a flush creeping into his face. Sean's problems always seemed to revolve around unrequited love.

"What's the deal with the pretty boy from Channel Nine?" he finally asked. Ryan assumed he was only trying to take the focus off of himself, but the subject was too tantalizing for her to pass up.

"There's no deal." She pulled down the sun visor and looked at herself in the mirror. She still had circles under her eyes, but at least her hair was clean and beer-free tonight. "Why?"

"After you left last night, he came sniffing around. He was up our asses, asking questions about the homicides. And then he mentioned you."

Ryan couldn't subdue her smile. "I can't help it if men find me irresistible."

Sean cocked a cynical eyebrow. "He asked who the hooker with the captain was."

Ryan laughed, not offended. "Really? What happened to him?"

"He got away with a warning this time." Sean parked the Crown Vic in almost the same spot Shep had stopped yesterday. "If he bugs me tonight, he might not be so lucky."

"Deja vu," Ryan said as she and Sean walked to building 21.

The captain was standing by the broken steps, smoking a cigarette. He reached for Ryan's hand to help her over the gap between the steps and the building.

The captain's flushed face was beaded with sweat. "Victim is Jeremy Jeremiah. Forty-five-year-old black male, looks like he was beaten to death." He tossed his cigarette to the ground as he walked in front of Ryan into the apartment directly across the hall from the one where Smith had been found.

The captain pointed to the body on the floor. "He's a nobody. No substantial record, just a few DWIs and a domestic on his rap. No drug arrests, and at his age, new gang connections are a little unlikely."

Ryan stared at the body. "Well, well, Mr. Jeremiah, so nice to see you again."

The captain's head jerked in Ryan's direction. "You know him?"

Ryan nodded. "I had Jeremy Jeremiah in Magistrate a few years ago." She remembered the day vividly. "He was arrested for beating his pregnant wife with a baseball bat. At the preliminary hearing she backpedaled. She said she got beat up in a bar fight, and that she put charges on Jeremiah because he yelled at her when she came home drunk. I had never seen a pregnant woman beaten before. And instead of being thankful that she was safe from him, she lied to get him off. And then cursed me out in the courtroom for trying to press charges anyway."

"Got you all riled up, didn't it?" Shep asked, crouching by the body.

"Somewhat. And I fixed her little red wagon. I had her arrested for filing a false police report."

Shep whistled. "Why would you put a pregnant victim in jail?"

"I was mad," she admitted. Arresting the victim in court had been quite a big deal. Even the D.A. had commended her for the action, although Ryan realized in retrospect she could have gotten fired if Peter hadn't approved. "And I thought after spending a couple of days in OPP for lying for him, she'd realize he wasn't worth the trouble. She was probably safer in jail anyway."

"What happened to the case?" the captain asked.

"Peter eventually refused the charges on the wife, so she was released. She still refused to prosecute, so Jeremiah's case was also dismissed. No victim, no case."

"He still has his wallet," Shep said, his gloved hand holding up a battered wallet. "No cash, but he still has two credit cards and his driver's license. Probably not a robbery."

"Coincidence that he's across the hall from Long Dong Smith?" Ryan nibbled the new hangnail on her thumb. "Why beat somebody to death in a building that was the scene of another homicide just the night before? I mean, they had to break through the crime scene tape to get in here." She looked over at her father, who was now standing in the doorway, staring intently at two patrolmen outside. "And what happened to your cop on the dot? Isn't that the whole point of COMSTAT?"

COMSTAT was an abbreviation for Computer Statistics, a crime tracking program implemented several years ago. New Orleans was divided geographically into eight police districts, each district commanded by a captain with a full staff of officers and support workers. The captains had to report the status of every investigation to the police superintendent at a weekly meeting. A giant map of the district was hung on the wall, with red dots placed on the crime scene locations. Putting extra patrols in those areas was referred to as "cop on the dot." Captain Murphy frequently compared the map of his district to a pimple-covered ass.

The captain suddenly darted over to the two nervous-looking patrolmen, like a large, overweight lion pouncing.

"Not a good time to bring that up." Sean walked closer to Ryan and lowered his voice cautiously, a habit picked up from their mother. "Abbott and Costello over there were supposed to sit parked all night, when Abbott wanted to go for a doughnut at the Krispy Kreme. So there you go." He indicated to the two patrolmen who were now getting reamed by the captain. The two officers were saved from further embarrassment when Monte Carlson walked up from his police unit.

The captain abruptly stopped yelling and turned his attention to Monte. "Carlson, what brings you to a homicide scene for the second night in a row?"

Monte nodded at Ryan briefly before he looked back at the captain. "Cap, we just picked up a kid across the project in a heroin bust. Donnell Jones' little brother, Devon. He claims he has information about your homicide last night."

Donnell Jones was a frequent flyer in the criminal justice system, well-known to both the NOPD and the D.A.'s Office. Apparently, his younger brother was following in his foot steps.

"Why didn't you call one of these guys to come pick him up?" the captain asked, and Ryan had an idea he was thinking about his conversation with her the night before. "Some reason you had to tell me in person?"

Monte looked around and lowered his voice. "He'll only give the info in exchange for a walk. He heard that an Assistant D.A. was out here, and said he'll only talk to her."

"How would he have heard that?" the captain asked with a frown.

Monte flashed a smile at Ryan. "Ain't every night we get a white woman D.A. in the projects."

Ryan smiled back. "Seems like it to me."

The captain wiped beads of sweat off his forehead with the back of his hand. "Carlson, do you think the kid is involved in dealing?"

Monte shrugged. "We did surveillance for a week. We only saw Donnell dealing, but there was a shitload of heroin in that apartment. Devon would have to be blind, deaf and dead not to know what was going on."

"You want to talk to him?" the captain asked Ryan.

"As long as you're not going to arrest him. I don't want to be in the position where I have to ask my boss not to accept charges somewhere down the road."

The captain nodded to Monte. "We'll meet you at the station."

Monte shook his head. "Kid doesn't want everyone to know he's pimping to the cops. He said he'll talk here, and only to the prosecutor. No interrogation and no taped statement, or you can charge him with the dope deal."

Ryan wasn't surprised the boy didn't trust the police. Gizelle Jones, the mother of Devon and Donnell, had been convicted of prostitution three years ago, after being arrested in a massive police sting. She was serving ten years as a multiple offender. A year later, Devon's father had been shot to death by police after robbing a gas station on Canal Street.

The captain made a noise in his throat bordering on a growl. "So I guess now even the goddamn criminals get to tell me how to do my job?" He threw his hands in the air. "He's got one minute."

Monte roughly jerked a small handcuffed boy of about twelve from the back seat of the car. Long dreadlocks hung from his head, and his shirt featured a picture of a rap group flipping the bird, the words "Fuck dem Niggaz," spelled out in bullets underneath them. His pants were pulled so low half of his red boxer shorts were revealed. "Any bullshit and you going to Juvie, got that, podner? Ain't nobody playing with you." Monte shoved Devon toward the captain. "He's a punk. Unless he gives you gold, I'd put his ass in the system."

The captain grabbed Devon and pushed him against the building, searching the boy thoroughly before turning back to Monte. "Put him back in the car and leave him cuffed. And you," he pointed to Shep, "make yourself useful and go talk to Sisko and Malette. If I have to so much as look at those two imbeciles again, I'm going to give myself a stroke."

Monte thrust Devon into the backseat of the car, giving him a warning look before opening the front door for Ryan.

Shep reluctantly approached Sisko and Malette. He wanted to hear what Devon had to say, and had absolutely no interest in questioning two cops he knew were going to be on the defensive. He would try to make this as quick and painless as possible.

Shep stopped in front of Sisko and Malette, who were both eyeing him with distrust. "You're sure you didn't see anybody walking around here or driving off when you got back?"

Sisko shook his head. "Nobody was here. No cars driving off, nothing."

Shep pointed to the building Jeremiah was in. "Unless that guy beat himself to death, I'd have to say you're wrong."

"I'm sure somebody saw or heard something," Malette said with a shrug. "But drug dealers are the only ones likely to be out around here, and they're not exactly forthcoming with information."

"Well, if the two of you hadn't needed a doughnut fix maybe we wouldn't have that problem right now." Shep hadn't intended on provoking the men, but Malette's attitude pissed him off.

"I needed some coffee," Malette said, an edge to his voice. "We didn't go for doughnuts, for the record. We been sitting in the same spot since eleven, watching a whole lot of nothing. I was about to fall asleep, so we went for coffee."

"Yeah, you stick to that story, Malette. Unless you guys have anything else, you can go back on patrol." Shep nodded toward the street. "If you think you can manage it." He turned to walk away, but Sisko grabbed his arm.

"So Chapetti, off the record, what's the story with the captain's daughter, little Miss Tits?"

"What do you mean?" Shep asked with a frown.

"You know, what's her story? I heard she's into cops," Sisko said, making an obscene gesture with his tongue.

Malette made a big point of adjusting his crotch. "I wouldn't mind getting a little piece of that."

Shep shook his head in disbelief. "Didn't I just tell you to get back on the street?" He nodded in Ryan's direction. "And I doubt either one of you could handle even the smallest piece of 'that.'"

"Looks like Chapetti's got a hard-on for the captain's daughter," Malette said, nudging Sisko with his elbow before turning back to Shep. "And here I thought you'd be getting enough pussy from your court reporter."

Shep grabbed Malette by the front of his blue uniform shirt. "Do you know where the street is, you doughnut-eating mother fucker? Because I can show you, if you need me to."

"Fuck you, Chapetti," Malette said, pushing Shep two steps backwards. "And get your hands off me."

Shep moved forward to buck up against the other officer, but Sisko grabbed Malette by the arm and pulled him toward their police car, looking in the captain's direction the entire time.

Shep thought about chasing after Malette to finish the discussion, but decided it wouldn't be worth making a scene, and walked back over to the captain instead.

"Those jerk-offs have anything?" the captain asked.

"They went for coffee," Shep answered. "They didn't see anything. Sort of like the witnesses out here." Shep stopped his explanation as Ryan got out of Sean's car, a smug look on her face. "Maybe the juvenile delinquent gave Ryan something useful."

"What are the chances?" the captain asked, heading in Ryan's direction.

Ryan was excited to have information nobody else knew, and wanted to prolong the drama as long as she could.

The captain was not in the mood to wait. "So what does the junior drug dealer know?"

"Well," Ryan said slowly, trying to drag the story out, "Devon said about a half-hour before the patrolmen showed up last night, he saw three men going into the empty apartment."

"Can he describe them?" Sean asked, his eyes big blue dots on his freckled face.

"The first two he recognized as L'Roid Smith and Jeremy Jeremiah."

"What about the third one?" Sean asked.

She paused before she answered. "The third guy was a white man."

"White?" Shep asked. "The only white men that ever come out here are cops."

"Well, that's the really interesting part," Ryan paused, longer this time, for effect. "He said the white guy is a cop."

"Jesus Christ, Ryan, why didn't you say that to begin with?" the captain asked. "How does the delinquent know the guy is a cop?"

"He said he's seen him investigating some of the crimes uptown."

"Did Devon happen to say what he was doing out here at that time of night himself?" Shep asked. "Was he out here dealing?"

Ryan shook her head. "He said he had 'found' a bike earlier in the day and hid it in the next building back. He had come to pick it up when he heard a car. Nobody comes to this side of the development except to sell drugs or commit murder, so he hid. He saw a white man getting out of a black Taurus. The man met Smith and Jeremiah outside building 21. They went inside and then Devon heard a pop. A few seconds later Jeremiah left, carrying clothes and shoes. The white man made a call from the payphone and then drove off." She pointed to the payphone near the street.

"Well, that checks out," Sean said. "The calls came from that payphone. The phone's already been printed. Maybe we'll get something."

Ryan shook her head. "You won't get the killer's prints. He wore finger rubbers."

"He wore what?" the captain asked.

"Those little rubber finger protectors," she explained.

"And Devon can't identify him?" Shep asked. "It seems if he could see well enough to see fingertip protectors, he probably got a good view of the guy's face."

"He only admitted he recognized Jeremiah and Smith because he knows they're both already dead. And he said he didn't think he could ID the cop."

Her father narrowed his eyes at her. "Did he at least give you a description?"

"He said the cop was overweight, not too tall, and acted nervous, like Archie Bunker on crack."

"That should be easy to narrow down," Shep said. "Short and fat. He just described half the force."

"Good thing they get Nick at Nite in the projects, or you might not even have that," Ryan added. "And Devon's not talking again." She began ticking points off on her fingers. "He won't give an official statement, he won't testify, and if you want anything else, you might as well just bring him to jail right now." She handed the captain a piece of paper she had torn from the back of a note pad in Sean's car. "But he did give me this." It was a picture Devon had drawn of a somewhat elaborate devil face. "The white guy had this inked on his upper right arm."

"We might be able to trace it," the captain said, doubt in his voice. "I better call the superintendent before this story gets out." He handed the drawing to Sean before walking away.

"There's a tat place on Carrollton. If I remember correctly the guy is a biker who specializes in devils," Shep said. "Maybe he'll know something."

"Jimbo," Ryan offered. "He'll probably help you out if you mention me."

"Jimbo?" Sean began rubbing his temples. "You're on a first name basis with a biker that does tattoos?"

"I get around a little," Ryan answered, trying to gauge if her father was paying attention. Luckily, he was already engrossed in a conversation on his cell phone.

"You have a tattoo?" Shep asked, looking her over as if searching for it.

"No," she answered quickly, glancing at her father again.

"Is the kid getting a walk?" Monte asked.

Ryan nodded. Monte and Sean walked back to Monte's car.

"If we believe the kid, the cop wanted to make sure we found Smith's body," Shep said. "And tonight's body was called in from the same payphone."

"You think there's a connection?" Ryan asked, pleased to be in on the investigation.

"I don't believe too much in coincidences." Shep rubbed his chin. "Looks like somebody wanted us to find Jeremiah, too. How long would it have been before we found these bodies if somebody hadn't made the calls?"

"It probably wouldn't have been that long, with this heat and all." She made a face and waved her hand in front of her nose. "I can smell dead body from here already, and it's only been a couple of hours. I just hope Jimbo knows something about the tattoo."

"Unless Devon will look through some pictures and make an ID, we don't have much else to go on. Just keep it to yourself that both bodies were called in by the same payphone, okay? We don't need people talking about a serial killer yet."

"Do you think this might be a serial killer?" Ryan wasn't sure whether she was more scared or excited by the prospect.

Shep shrugged. "I didn't say that. But knowing how much you like being on television, I just want to warn you not to mention it to any reporters."

Ryan made a face to Shep's back as he walked away to building 21. She waited alone, bored now that she was no longer the center of attention, annoyed that the reporters who were pulling up on the street didn't seem to have any interest in her. Shep could have saved his breath warning her about keeping her mouth shut. Nobody wanted to talk to her anyway. After a few minutes, the captain walked back up, flashing an angry look at the news vans.

"I've got to meet with the superintendent right now. Get Sean to give you a ride home." He pointed in the direction of the press. "And for God's sake, don't talk to any of them." The captain then walked quickly to his car, red-faced and sweating.

Ryan wondered if her father could possibly be in trouble. While she knew the superintendent couldn't possibly blame the captain for this murder, she also realized that the big boss would want to hold somebody accountable, and the district captain was usually at the top of that list. But then again, the captain always said shit rolled downhill, which put Sisko and Malette in an unenviable position.

She started to walk over to Sean when Shep waved her over to his Crown Vic. Sean was apparently too tied up with the crime lab, and the on-duty tech, Suzie Chin, to give Ryan a ride home.

Shep drove slowly through the development down St. Thomas Street, not bothering to take the long way like the captain had. The streets throughout the project were in deplorable condition, full of even more potholes than the rest of the city streets, and Shep's deliberate pace allowed Ryan a glimpse into a subculture she never would have gotten to see otherwise.

People were still mingling outside the breezeways of the development, under the sparse streetlights, and on the steps leading into the buildings. Ryan wondered what they were all doing up at this hour. The crime scene was too far away for the activity to have disturbed anyone here, so she assumed they were just up for the sake of being up. Several teenage males were standing in an open door of one of the units, talking and laughing. The adults nearby ignored them, engrossed in their own conversation. She wondered why those kids weren't in bed sleeping, getting ready for the school week.

"So, when did you get a tattoo?" Shep's voice brought her out of her trance.

"One night when I thought it would be fun to mix shots of Tequila with Jagermeister. What's the big deal anyway?" She was only half-focused on Shep, still wondering about what kind of chance those boys had when nobody even cared where they were in the middle of the night. Maybe there was a reason for the L'Roid Smiths of the world.

Shep had a slight frown. "Tattoos just seem so, I don't know, what's the word I'm looking for?"

"Dangerous?" Ryan suggested, forgetting about the St. Thomas teens. If their own mamas didn't care, who was she to worry about them? She turned to face Shep, putting her back to the project residents.

His frown relaxed. "I was thinking trailer park."

"Bite me, Chapetti. You don't happen to have a cigarette, do you?"

He turned onto Jackson Avenue and picked up speed, leaving the development behind them. Just like the night before, the streets were empty and quiet.

Shep shook his head. "Smoking is so bad for you. For somebody so smart, you sure do a lot of bonehead things."

Ryan made a face at him. "How lucky for me that you got to drive me home. I got a public service announcement and the chance to be called stupid all in one night. You must be taking lessons from daddy."

He crossed Magazine Street, obviously intending to take the quicker St. Charles route. "You might find this difficult to believe, but sometimes your dad makes sense. He definitely has a point about the way you dress, especially to come out to a crime scene."

"If you're trying to earn some brownie points with my dad, hotshot, you might want to note that he's not around to hear you." She indicated to the back seat of the car. "Kissing booty only works if the booty is actually close enough to feel the smack. And how did we get from the tattoo on my ass to my daddy's antiquated ideas about how young ladies should dress to look at dead people?"

"The tattoo is on your ass?" He paused, seeming distracted. A second later he shook his head. "Well, anyway, I don't think you realize the impression people get when you dress like you do."

"There is nothing wrong with my outfit. And what people are you referring to? The stiff on the floor?" She was getting annoyed. While the T-shirt and sweat shorts wouldn't earn her any fashion awards, the clothing was far from revealing.

"I'm thinking about the patrolmen." He turned left onto St. Charles. "Do you have any idea how some of the guys talk about you?"

Ryan pretended to be excited. "Really? Which ones?"

Shep gave her a deprecatory look. "Sisko and Malette. I think I have their phone numbers, if you're interested."

She smiled. "I'll pass. But everyone's entitled to an opinion, even about me. Last month I overheard Henry Cooper saying I was so mean he bet my vagina had teeth. Of course, he's so crude he called it a snatch instead of a vagina, but it was still pretty funny."

"I can't begin to tell you how wrong it is that you don't seem to be the least bit offended by that comment. And how do you think your dad would feel if he had heard Cooper?"

Ryan could feel her nostrils flaring. "It's none of daddy's business. Or yours, for that matter. Why do you care so much about what daddy thinks anyway?" She poked him in the arm. She was surprised when he stopped the car in the middle of St. Charles Avenue and grabbed her finger.

"If you were my daughter, and I overheard somebody that worked for me making those kind of remarks, especially in front of my other men, I'd have his job and his ass." A car pulled up behind them on the single lane street.

"Well, good thing you're not my daddy then, huh?" The car behind them honked. Ryan jerked her hand from Shep's grasp.

"You know, you really are a spoiled brat." He ignored the honking and stared at her, an expression on his face Ryan couldn't interpret.

"Would you please just drive?" she asked, pointing to the street, uncomfortable with his level of attention.

The car behind them seemed to get the message and the honking stopped. Shep finally shifted his focus back on the street ahead and drove forward again. "I don't think you even realize how lucky you are to have a family that cares so much about you, in spite of all your crap."

"That's really none of your concern," Ryan replied. "Why don't you worry about your own family, and let me worry about mine."

He drove the rest of the way in silence.

In front of her house, Ryan started to get out of the car. "Thanks for the ride, Mr. Personality."

Shep grabbed her arm and waited until she looked back at him to speak. "Not everybody respects the fact that your father is a police captain. I just don't want anything bad to happen to you."

She pulled away and ran up the front steps of her apartment, slamming the door behind her. She watched out of the window as he sat in his car for several minutes, and then finally drove away.

JACOB

Jacob watched from his vantage point in the St. Thomas apartment. He was concerned when he first arrived. A patrol unit was parked right outside the complex. If the police stayed all night, he would be unable to proceed. And then he finally relaxed as the car drove off.

He dialed a number. When the man on the other end answered, Jacob simply said, "It's time. Go." He knew within minutes the plan would be in action, and unsuspecting Jeremy Jeremiah would be victim number two.

Jeremiah, like most people, had no idea just how precarious life was. He likely wouldn't realize it until the second before he died. Jacob wondered if Ryan would be the same, unsuspecting until the moment of death.

Jacob had spent a long time on his plan, and thought it would be a shame if Ryan only realized the immanency of her own death for a second. As much as he had suffered because of her, it wouldn't be fair. And after all, he had given her ample opportunity to prove she didn't deserve to die.

Jacob focused the binoculars on the crime scene, watching Ryan in anticipation. The maximum magnification brought her so close, he could see each perfect white tooth of her barracuda-like smile. A slow, painful death would most definitely suit her.

Enjoy yourself now, bitch. You won't be smiling for long.

5:00 P.M.

Ryan hid in the hallway near the restrooms while the press rolled into the seminar room. When it looked as if most of the reporters and cameras were jammed into the room, Ryan walked out of the shadows and sat in the waiting area. She needed a few seconds to focus.

The day had been a whirlwind. She had been in meetings for the first part of the day, discussing the press conference with the D.A. and his First Assistant. Then she had to speak at length with a rape victim who wanted to dismiss the case against her attacker. Ryan thought she had succeeded in talking the woman down from the ledge, but couldn't know for sure until the woman actually testified at trial in three weeks.

Throughout her day, Shep's words from the previous night kept intruding on her thoughts. Why should he even care about what the other cops thought? And then she had started to wonder if he might be right, if she should be more concerned with how the officers viewed her. After all, if she believed Devon Jones, a bad cop lived pretty close to home.

She had eventually decided to dismiss Shep's concerns. Whoever killed Smith had nothing to do with her. She was in no more danger from officers like Sisko and Malette than she was from Shep.

She directed her attention to the press conference, rehearsing in her head how she would answer any questions that were thrown at her. She knew she wouldn't get much air time, being as the D.A. enjoyed the limelight even more than she did, but Ryan had several prepared responses, just in case.

She was distracted from her task by Bo Lambert stepping out of the elevator. She tried to think of a way to duck back into the hallway without having to talk to Bo, but couldn't figure out how to accomplish it without being obvious.

Bo smiled as he approached, pushing the glasses up on his nose. "Congratulations on the death penalty. I'm really happy for you." He seemed sincere, but Ryan refused to let her guard down.

"Thanks," she said, giving him a fake smile.

Competing with Bo wasn't the only thing that bothered Ryan. Something about his appearance also annoyed her. His suits were expensive and tailored, his brown hair always meticulously cut and styled. He looked like all of the other prosecutors who came from money. Except for the large, black framed glasses that were always sliding down his nose. With all of his money and attention to detail, Ryan wondered why Bo would wear such ill-fitting glasses, or better yet, why he didn't just wear contact lenses instead. She suspected the glasses weren't even prescription, thinking Bo may have worn them to make himself look smarter.

"I heard you were at L'Roid Smith's crime scene," Bo said. "You're so lucky you got the uptown district."

Ryan listened for any hint of malice in his tone, but unexpectedly heard none.

"I haven't had any murders," he continued, disappointment filling his voice. He looked around and then lowered his tone. "I heard that Kellie hasn't bothered to show up for any of the crimes in her district."

Ryan wasn't surprised. Kellie Leblanc was the type who would decide to simply ignore the D.A.'s orders. And then she'd try to sleep with him to get out of trouble for not doing her job. Ryan refused to comment, knowing anything she said would likely make it right back to Kellie. "I guess that's between her and Peter."

Bo nodded. "She also said if she had a police escort like you have every night, she'd be more inclined to show up at the crime scenes."

"I'm sure she's banging some patrolman in the Third District who would give her a ride." The words popped out almost involuntarily.

Bo just laughed. "Without a doubt. But if she gets caught ignoring the D.A., she could be out of the running for Strike Force."

Ryan wondered if that was Bo's way of dropping a hint that she ought to tattle on Kellie.

"As long as her skirts are easy access and her favorite word is yes, Rick will consider her anyway." Rick Martin was the Chief of Trials, and was the person primarily responsible for doling out promotions. Ryan hadn't planned on discussing the Strike Force spot with Bo, but she couldn't stop herself from criticizing Kellie.

Bo shook his head in disgust. "You and I work our asses off. Kellie hardly ever goes to trial because she gives everybody deals. I don't think she would even be able to handle a Strike Force case."

Ryan nodded in agreement, but was still wary, wondering why Bo was being so nice to her.

He looked over her head and pushed his glasses up again. "Here comes your press conference."

Ryan stood up as the D.A. walked up and shook hands with Bo, and then put his arm around Ryan's shoulder.

"Showtime," he announced, a big smile plastered on his face, and Ryan followed him into the seminar room.

The captain watched the small TV set in his office at the station, waiting for Ryan to speak at the press conference. He was proud of his daughter, no question about that. He just sometimes wished he didn't have to worry about her so much. The five o'clock news cut live to the conference. The captain recognized the local reporters, as well as a guy from CNN and another one from Fox News. Ryan was making the big time.

Peter Berkley spoke at length about the significance of his office getting Louisiana's first death penalty on a rape case, interrupted frequently by the press. The conference was almost boring, until an unexpected question came from the back of the room.

"I have a question for Ms. Murphy. Can you confirm that you have a link to both of the homicides in the St. Thomas this week?"

The camera closed in on Ryan, looking toward the back of the room, a vaguely interested look on her face. "I'm sorry, but I don't think I got your name."

"Chance Halley, WDSU TV."

The captain frowned at Chance Halley through the TV set.

Ryan smiled brightly. "Mr. Halley, the focus of this conference is the Johnnie Lee death penalty. And as I'm sure you are aware, assistant district attorneys are precluded by statute from discussing any pending case or investigation. Perhaps your questions would be better addressed to the New Orleans Police Department."

The D.A. nodded his approval and ended the conference.

The captain called Shep from the doorway and indicated for him to sit.

"Chapetti, were you watching the press conference?" The captain reached into his desk and pulled out a stress release ball.

Shep nodded.

The captain started torturing the rubber ball while looking at the framed photographs on his desk, focusing on one of Ryan. She was fifteen years old at the time, dressed up for her first high school dance. He recalled the argument they had gotten into about her curfew right after the picture had been taken, moments before her date had arrived. As his children got older, it seemed he simply traded in one set of worries for another one.

The captain looked up at Shep, trying to gauge his reaction. "What do you think about what that Halley kid said?"

"That Ryan might be linked to the two murders? That's a bunch of bullshit."

The captain paused for a moment. "She did prosecute both of the victims. And lost both cases."

"She didn't actually lose the cases," Shep pointed out. "They were dismissed."

"Same thing to her." The stress ball flattened in the captain's grip.

Shep scratched his chin. "Cap, are you saying you think she had something to do with the homicides?"

The captain slammed the ball on the desk top. "Chapetti, don't be an idiot, of course she didn't have anything to do with them." He put the ball back in his desk drawer and blew out a long-drawn breath. "My mother had a stroke. I'm leaving for Grand Isle tonight. I don't like being out of town with Ryan still going to these crime scenes. And I particularly don't like leaving knowing that a pretty-boy reporter is trying to connect up dots that don't connect."

Shep shifted in his seat. "I think Halley may have just been trying to get Ryan to notice him. He asked about her the night of Smith's murder."

The captain looked at him sharply. "Why didn't anybody mention this to me?"

"It was no big deal," Shep answered quickly. "Sean and I handled it."

"Yeah, I can see that by the way Halley pointed the finger at her on TV. I just don't like him for some reason." The captain's caustic expression faded into a look of solicitude. "Chapetti, do you think I've got something to worry about with this punk?"

"I doubt it," Shep said, shaking his head. "But with Ryan, you never know. She could find trouble at Sunday mass."

The captain had to smile at that. She could. And he would take whatever steps necessary to keep her safe, regardless of whether Ryan liked it or not. "Chapetti, find out where Halley's getting his information. And make sure that little prick stays away from my daughter."

Shep shifted in his seat again, obviously uncomfortable with the requested task. "Uh, Cap, I can dig around a little on Halley, and I have no problem keeping an eye on Ryan at the crime scenes, but are you asking me to interfere with her personal life? I mean, what I am supposed to do if he asks her out?"

The captain picked up the dance picture. "Make sure he doesn't. Give him a friendly warning to stay away from my kid. And don't mention this to Sean. He'll handle Ryan all wrong and she'll end up doing the exact opposite. You got this?"

"I'll do my best, sir."

The captain returned the picture to its original spot, and pulled the stress ball out of his desk again. He wondered if it would work better if he chewed on it. Shep stood up and turned toward the door. The captain squeezed the ball as hard as he could. "And Chapetti, you do know better than to try anything with my daughter, don't you?"

Shep nodded. "Absolutely, sir."

After the press conference, Ryan was on her way out of the office when she was called to the office of the Chief of Trials.

Rick Martin didn't wait for her to sit before he held out a large expandable file and said, "If you want the Gendusa case, it's yours."

Ryan nearly snatched the file from Rick's hand. "Of course I want it. But what about Christina?"

"Don't worry about Christina. The case is yours," Rick said and sat down, offering no further explanation. "If there's not too much on your plate already."

Ryan shook her head vehemently. "I'm good."

Rick leaned back in his black leather chair. "What do you think about co-chairing with Bo Lambert? He's got the time on his hands now that Smith fell through, and he asked for the case as soon as he heard we were reassigning it."

"Bo knew before me?" The expression froze on Ryan's face.

"You know the rumor mill." Rick seemed unaware of the effect his answer had on Ryan.

She tried to keep her expression impassive. "I don't have a problem with Bo, but you know, Judge Jackson doesn't really care for him that much."

Rick looked surprised, obviously unaware that Ryan was lying. "I didn't know that."

"I think it has something to do with Bo's father." At least the lie was credible. A whole lot of people didn't care for the elder Lambert's courtroom style. "I think

Mike could use the experience. And the judge really likes him."

Rick nodded. "You can have Mike, then."

Clutching the file to her chest, Ryan started to walk out of the office.

Rick stood up. "Who knows, if everything goes well, Gendusa might just wind up being your first Strike Force trial credit."

She paused in the doorway. "Really?"

"Nothing official yet, of course, and it's a really close call. You're one of three still in the running, but so far, you're ahead. I'd say it's looking pretty good."

Ryan walked out of the building and to her Jeep, deep in thought. She didn't like that part about being one of three. One of two she knew. One of three could only mean that Kellie Leblanc was still in the running, not that Ryan had much doubt about what Kellie was doing to stay in the race.

She pushed the thought aside. Kellie couldn't possibly compete with her and Bo. And between Ryan and Bo, Ryan should win.

Her thoughts bounced around in her head like Mexican jumping beans as she drove home. She had just been handed the Gendusa case. She was moving to Strike Force. And she couldn't even tell anybody, because it wasn't official. She wondered how long Bo had known Gendusa was up for grabs. Not that she would have expected him to mention the case. After all, he was trying to steal it from her. All that talk about the camaraderie he felt with her was all a bunch of crap. She was glad she had never trusted him.

Five minutes later she pulled into her driveway and found Sean parked in front of her house.

"Jimbo doesn't believe we're related," Sean said without so much as a hello. "You need to talk to him for me."

Ryan gave him a smug look. "I'm kind of busy right now."

"Ryan, don't make me call dad," Sean warned. "I'm sure you don't want him to know about that tattoo."

"You don't even know about my tattoo," she said, and realized too late she had just provided him the ammunition he needed.

"I do now," he said with a laugh. "Come on, I'll buy you a Coke when we're finished."

She reluctantly got in his car, annoyed that she didn't at least get the chance to make Sean beg a little.

He drove down St. Charles and turned on Carrollton Avenue, stopping in front of a three-story house that had been converted into several offices.

Ryan rang the bell next to the bright yellow door of Suite B.

A second later, the door buzzed and they were inside, the smell of recently-burned marijuana inundating the air. An overweight, bearded man with unkempt long hair, his arms and neck covered with tattoos, was sitting at the counter reading an Archie comic book. A smile spread across his face as he looked up, revealing large, slightly overlapping yellowed teeth.

He rushed around the counter, and with a voice full of gravel said, "My favorite customer. Long time no see." He picked up Ryan and swung her around, squeezing her in a full body hug before he put her down. "Can't believe you're related to L-7."

"Sometimes I have trouble believing it myself," Ryan said, smiling back.

"So what you been up to?" Jimbo sat back down. "I saw you on TV. You got any problems with that fag reporter, you just let me know. I got lots of friends don't like reporters."

Before Ryan could answer, Sean shoved Devon's sketch in Jimbo's face. "Does this look like one of yours?"

"Still can't see how the two of you are related." Jimbo held the sketch out a foot-and-a-half away from his face and stared at it for thirty seconds. "Yeah, this was one of mine, but I haven't used that design in years. I update the devils every six months or so. People don't want to have the same art as anyone else. But that one's old. I don't recall who got it."

"What about cops?" Sean asked.

"Don't care for them too much," Jimbo answered with a shrug. "Anything else?"

"No, I mean, would you remember if you did one of these on a cop? A white cop?" Sean's eyes darted around the room and he sniffed the air. Ryan hoped he wasn't going to try to sweat Jimbo over the marijuana.

Jimbo thought for a second. "You know, that does sound kind of familiar, some years back, a cop asking for a devil on his arm. It was sort of funny. Why would a cop want a devil on him? But hey, who am I to judge? Can't remember his name, though. Maybe if I think on it a while something will come back to me."

"Is there anything I can do to help jog your memory?" Sean pulled out his wallet. He must have realized that the threat of busting Jimbo for marijuana wouldn't get results.

Jimbo shook his head. "I'm not hitting you up for money. I would do anything for this lady. Even if she is related to you." He turned to Ryan. "I have your number in my palm pilot. If I remember anything, I'll call you."

"Exactly what have you done for him?" Sean asked when they were outside.

"I made a phone call to a judge to get his mama out of jail."

"Why was she arrested?" Sean started the car.

"Marijuana. No big deal."

"Pecan doesn't fall far from the tree," Sean said, and shook his head sadly. "Smelled like Jimbo may have burned up a few too many brain cells smoking dope himself to be of much help to us."

"His mother is seventy years old and got caught smoking after her chemotherapy treatment. Even Judge Jackson didn't think it was necessary to keep her in jail."

They rode in silence for a minute.

"Do you have any leads on the homicides?" Ryan finally asked.

"I wouldn't tell you if we did. You seem to forget that your involvement is limited to viewing the crime scenes, not solving the crimes." He turned onto St. Charles.

"It's not like you couldn't use some help. Look at how successful you were with Jimbo." Sean had a lot of nerve. Sometimes he annoyed her even more than Shep did. Then, remembering her conversation with Shep the night before, she asked, "So what's the deal with Shep's family?"

"Why are you so interested in Shep all of a sudden?"

She ignored his question. "I said something last night to the effect that he should worry about his own family. He got kind of put out. Then I started thinking, wasn't there something wrong with his family?"

Sean gave her a severe look. "I would say so. Shep's father used to beat the crap out of him and his mother. One day Shep finally got sick of it and fought back, and ended up putting his father in the hospital. His mother thanked him by kicking him out on the street. He was fourteen at the time."

"What happened?" She bit her lip, feeling a little bad about the family remark now. That was definitely not cool.

"His dad died of a heart attack a few weeks later. Shep's mom moved away with his little sister, and left him behind. Lucky for Shep some cousins took him in. You don't remember any of this?"

Ryan shrugged casually, but was appalled, as much by her own comment as by Shep's family history. "I never would have said anything if I had known, you know."

"Well, maybe it would be a good idea if you thought before you shot off that big mouth of yours," Sean said and shook his finger at her. Ryan slapped his hand away and didn't speak again during the rest of the brief ride, feeling a mixture of anger at Sean for being right and shame at herself for being wrong.

Two hours later, Ryan was finishing her third glass of wine and reading through the Gendusa file. Her father had stopped by after Sean left and told her about Gram. While Ryan was worried about her grandmother, she was equally upset at her father's level of distress. Instead of focusing all of his attention on taking care of his ill mother, he had concerns about not being around to watch out for his defiant daughter. He seemed to calm down only after Ryan swore to watch how she dressed, spoke, acted, and pretty much lived while he was out of town. When he got back, however, all bets were off.

Ryan tried to focus on the file in front of her. While the tape of Marcelo Gendusa was the stuff of a prosecutor's wet dream, the rest of the file was dry and boring. She decided to give up for the night and was pouring herself a fourth glass when the phone rang.

"Yeah."

"Did you see Conchita Beliza?" Her best friend, Edie Guilliot, was on the other end.

"You must have Conchita Beliza radar," Ryan said. "Every time that woman is on TV you manage to find her."

"That bitch stole my boyfriend. Quick, put on Channel Nine."

Conchita was reporting live from the St. Thomas. "With multiple murders in the St. Thomas Housing Development, the citizens in this neighborhood are asking what they can do to protect themselves against this wave of violence. Residents of the St. Thomas feel that the police aren't taking the rash of criminal activity seriously enough, and wonder how many more people must be killed before the Superintendent reassigns full time officers to the development. Calls to Captain Kelly Murphy of the Sixth District were unreturned this evening. More information will be provided as it becomes available. This is Conchita Beliza, reporting live for WVUE News." And then she flicked her tongue over her lower lip, the famous Conchita Beliza trademark.

"That ought to put daddy in a good mood," Ryan said, turning the TV off. "You're right. Conchita Beliza is a bitch. Although Grant wasn't exactly your boyfriend." Grant was a reporter Edie had dated for a month last year.

"He might have been if Conchita Beliza and her tongue hadn't gotten in the way. What are you doing tonight? Feel like going out?"

"Don't you have a trial tomorrow?"

"Yeah, so what, I'm just going to lose anyway." Edie never seemed to care about winning. In fact, occasionally she would forget she had a trial scheduled and would wing it the best she could.

"Well, I have a trial tomorrow I plan on winning. And I've got crime scene duty. I promised daddy I would behave. At least until he gets back in town."

"Ooh, and you've got Detective Yummy don't you?" Edie smacked her lips over the phone, and Ryan could picture Edie's bushy black eyebrows arched over her green eyes. "Girl, if you don't try to break yourself off a little piece of that, you are crazy."

"I'm a little too busy working on the Gendusa case." She told Edie how she had manipulated Rick into letting Mike sit on the case with her instead of Bo.

Edie didn't seem impressed. "All I know is that if I was looking for a little action, Anthony Chapetti is definitely the man I would go to. Gendusa will be waiting for you in two weeks. Chapetti is in your grasp right now."

"I'm not looking for action," Ryan said, annoyed that Edie was more impressed with the fact that Ryan would be working with Shep than she was with Ryan landing the big mob case. "Or in grasping Chapetti. Oh, you know what I mean."

Edie let out an cackle. "Yeah right. Anyway, I'm going out somewhere. If you change your mind, call my cell."

Ryan decided now was a good time to take a long, hot bath, finish her glass of wine, or maybe even the whole bottle, and then catch up on her sleep before the inevitable call came.

WEDNESDAY

1:30 A.M.

Several hours later, Ryan heard the voice again.

Does it hurt yet? The man loomed over her, a sardonic grin on his face.

And it did hurt. She tried to scream, but no sound came out.

Well, does it? Answer me, bitch.

She opened her eyes, heart pounding, in a panic. Her eyes fervently scanned the room. The clock was on the dresser. She knew she was out of the nightmare when she saw the clock.

She tried to go back to sleep, but the cruel smile and stony eyes taunted her from inside her closed eyelids. She fumbled on the night stand for the remote control and clicked on the television. She surfed, not really focusing on anything, willing her mind to slow down enough so her body could get the sleep it desperately craved. She did this for an hour, her eyes going back and forth between the television set and the clock until the phone rang.

"Yeah."

"There's another gift waiting for you," the distorted voice said.

"You must have the wrong number," she answered, and then felt stupid for some reason.

"Ryan, the gifts are for you."

The phone trembled in her hand, but her voice was steady. "Gifts?"

"I thought you knew." Silence. Ryan didn't know if he was still on the line or not. "You'll understand tonight."

Ryan stared at the phone in her hand as if it was alive, until she heard the operator's recorded voice, "If you would like to make a call, please hang up and dial again."

She clicked the talk button on the cordless handset. The phone immediately rang back. She saw Sean's cell number on the caller ID.

"Yeah."

"Thirty in the St. Thomas. I'm outside."

Wonderful. Not even five minutes to get ready this time.

She hung up without a word and quickly dressed, settling on a clean T-shirt and a pair of capri jeans. No matter what she promised her father, she still refused to dress up to visit another dead body. She hurriedly brushed her teeth and reached for her keys and tennis shoes on the way out.

As soon as she opened the car door, Sean started in on her.

"Your number was busy. Who were you talking to at this time of night?"

"You must have been dialing at the same time as my prank caller," she answered casually as she sat back and buckled the seatbelt. "Some loser with a voice distorter can't seem to get enough of me."

Sean's knuckles turned white as he clenched the steering wheel. "I don't like the sound of that." He carefully looked both ways at the stop sign on St. Charles before crossing the intersection.

"At least he doesn't say anything nasty. Not yet, anyway. So, what do we have tonight?"

"The victim is a woman, probably a hooker, probably raped." Ryan saw him watching her from the corner of her eye, but wouldn't turn to face him.

"Do you know the cause of death?" She wondered if the scene was going to be gruesome. This would be her first female victim crime scene.

"Strangulation."

They rode in silence the rest of the way to the St. Thomas.

Sean stopped the car at the intersection of Chipewa and St. James, the two streets converging to a point at Felicity.

The police cars were parked near the same side of the development as the previous night, but two blocks down and around the corner. Several uniformed officers were standing under the street light. Sergeant Mitchell, the homicide sergeant, was on his phone as Sean and Ryan approached. Ryan lit a cigarette. Sean gave a reproachful look but said nothing.

"Coroner and crime lab are on the way," Sergeant Mitchell said as they walked up. The sergeant was more than a few inches shy of six feet, with a stocky build and thinning brown hair, just starting to gray at the temples. He rubbed the side of his broad face and then pinched the bridge of his nose. "Hooker, I'm presuming, looks like she was choked with something, like a cord or a rope, maybe. She has a ligature mark around her neck but no finger marks."

Behind him, a black woman who appeared to be in her twenties sat propped against an orange and white striped traffic barrel. The barrel had originally been placed in front of a section of the street that had collapsed two feet into the ground, making for one of the city's better-known potholes. Instead of repairing the street, the barrel had been placed in front of the hole to warn drivers to go around it. A prankster had moved the barrel years ago, presumably to watch cars lose their tires, and it had sat on the sidewalk ever since.

The dead woman had bleached white hair, cut close to her head, and full red lips, her lipstick unmarred by death. She was naked, her legs open and her knees slightly bent, with one hand placed between her legs in a lewd, masturbatory gesture. The only noticeable injury was the ligature mark. Angry red sores covered her body, and what appeared to be a piece of plastic dangled from her mouth.

Ryan stared, recognizing the woman.

Before Ryan had a chance to say anything, Shep walked up from the direction of the nearest apartment building. "I've got a little girl in building 40."

"Son of a bitch." The sergeant's fingers went back to the bridge of his nose. "Is she hurt?"

"She's dead." Shep's eyes were so dark the pupils were indiscernible from the irises. "She has the same mark around her neck."

The sergeant cursed again and started off in the direction of the building. "Is she posed like this one?"

"No."

"Well, that's something at least," the sergeant said.

Ryan followed behind, stepping outside of Sean's reach as he tried to stop her. She rubbed her arms, feeling an inexplicable chill. She looked around at the surrounding buildings, the same feeling of unknown eyes watching from behind red brick walls.

"I recognize that hooker," she said as they walked. "Charmaine Reynolds. She was a defendant on a homicide last year. I didn't like her, but I certainly never thought I'd be looking at her out here, like that."

Building 40 was only twenty yards away from the woman's body, but faced the opposite direction. Two uniformed officers were kneeling in the open doorway at the top of the steps. The body of the little girl was seated on the top step, leaning against the wall, her eyes wide open.

The tiny form was emaciated, with the same ugly sores as her mother. She was shoeless, clothed only in an inside-out T-shirt and a pair of dirty jean shorts.

Ryan's voice threatened to shake as she looked into the vacant eyes of the child in front of her. "Charmaine's daughter, Jasmine. She should be around six. Charmaine bonded out of OPP, and when she came to court she'd bring Jasmine with her and leave her in the hallway alone. It came out during motions that Charmaine tricked in front of her, and I suspected she also tricked the kid out to perverts that like them young, although I couldn't prove it."

"How did Charmaine bond out?" Sean asked with a frown. "Didn't you say it was a homicide?"

"She was charged with manslaughter, not murder. Judge McAllister gave her an ROR. Apparently he didn't have a problem with Charmaine killing her pimp. But then again, I heard rumors that McAllister had a professional relationship with Charmaine, if you know what I mean."

The sergeant shook his head. "He released a homicide suspect on her own recognizance? Somebody should have done something about that." He walked back to Charmaine's body, still shaking his head.

"What happened with the case?" Shep asked, removing his gloves.

"Street Crimes picked Charmaine up for solicitation and got a confession to the pimp's murder. McAllister threw it out. Charmaine's statement was the only link to the murder, so I had to dismiss the case."

"Was the confession good?" Sean asked.

Ryan shrugged. "I'd confess to crucifying Jesus if Danny Di'Franco was kicking my ass." Di'Franco was a detective with Street Crimes, well-known for his questionable interview techniques.

Shep frowned.

Ryan shrugged again. "I'm not saying Charmaine didn't kill the pimp. She had a very volatile relationship with Marco Bouvier. But she had the crap beat out of her while she was in custody. Whether she killed him or not, her confession was not exactly voluntary."

Sean knelt next to Jasmine's body, feeling in her pockets with a gloved hand. The dead child's empty pockets were depressingly symbolic.

Ryan looked back at the hooker's body. "I called Social Services on Charmaine twice. I guess they were backlogged."

Suzie Chin and Larry Davillier from crime lab arrived together, and, a second later, Doug, the deputy coroner, pulled up in the coroner's station wagon.

The sergeant led Doug to Jasmine. "Anything you can tell us right now to give us any kind of a lead? I've got a dead six-year-old. I need to find this bastard fast."

Doug did a cursory exam of the child's body. "I'm not going to be able to tell if she was sexually assaulted until I get her on the table. The cause of death appears to be strangulation, no finger marks, no patterns. From the smooth line I'd say most likely a belt or a piece of cloth. I'm sure I'll find the same on the woman. Is that her mama?"

The sergeant nodded.

Doug then inspected Charmaine's body. "Condom in the throat looks like it's full of DNA. Maybe we can get a match on that with something in the system. Also looks like a condom in the vagina, probably full of DNA as well."

"A rapist wouldn't likely leave DNA if he knows his is on file," Ryan said. "And why use a condom if he was just going to leave the evidence behind?"

"See these marks?" Doug pointed to the dark sores on the woman's body. "Kaposi's sarcoma. That's why he used a condom."

"AIDS?" Shep walked up to get a closer look. "Kid has the same sores."

"Kid could have been born HIV positive, if mama didn't get any kind of treatment when she was pregnant. Then again, mama might have been tricking the kid out for heroin — see all these track marks?" He pointed to the dead woman's arms and legs.

"Where's the patrol unit that's supposed to be out here?" Sean asked. Ryan hoped for Sisko and Malette's sake they hadn't screwed this one up as well.

"Right where it's supposed to be, two blocks away and around the corner, barely out of the line of sight. This guy's got balls of steel," the sergeant answered. "Sean, go with Doug, get the details, start the report." The sergeant walked away.

Sean nodded and turning to Shep, pointed at Ryan.

Ryan walked to Shep's car and sat in the passenger seat, trying to compose herself as she waited for him to finish talking to Sean and the sergeant.

When Shep got in, he turned to Ryan and lightly squeezed her shoulder. "You okay?"

She shook her head, not trusting her voice to speak. They drove down Jackson Avenue in silence.

At the left turn on St. Charles, Shep finally spoke. "I don't care how long you do this, you never get used to the sight of a dead child."

"How can something like this make any kind of sense at all?" Ryan asked, blinking back tears.

He didn't respond, but reached over and squeezed her shoulder again. Ryan knew he couldn't give her an answer, and they didn't speak the rest of the way to her house. She had wanted to apologize to him for her comment about his family, but since worrying about her own lack of matters seemed petty right now, she kept her mouth shut.

Shep started to get out at Ryan's house.

"I'm good." She put her hand up to keep him in the car. He obeyed, as if he didn't want to infringe on her sorrow. But at the front door, Ryan fumbled with her keys, and watched as they dropped to the porch. Instead of picking them up, she pressed her forehead against the front door, as tears started rolling silently down her face.

"You okay, babe?" Shep's voice was uncertain from the bottom of the steps.

She nodded, but didn't try to reach for her keys. She heard Shep's steps on the concrete, and then felt his hand on her back, steadying her. He picked up her keys and opened the front door, guiding her to the sofa. He wrapped his arms around her, and pulled her head into his chest, letting her cry on his SID shirt.

Ryan instinctively held onto him, inhaling his woodsy scent, trying to control her sobs.

"Just let it go," he spoke soothingly, caressing her hair. "It's okay."

After several minutes, she finally got to the point where no more tears would come. She took a deep breath, embarrassed by her breakdown, but not entirely ready to lose physical contact with another body. She wiped her nose on his shirt, and finally sat back. "Sorry about your shirt."

"It'll wash." He wiped a tear from her face with his knuckle. "Maybe you should call your dad."

Of the many times she didn't want her father around, the one time she needed him, he wasn't there. "No. Daddy's got enough of his own problems right now. I'm okay. Really." She stood up and stepped away from the sofa. "I'm fine. That scene back there was just — difficult."

Shep nodded sympathetically. "That scene would have been tough for anybody to take, but especially for you."

She could tell his words held no deprecation, but she didn't like what she suspected they did hold.

"What's that supposed to mean?" She put her hands on her hips to avoid the temptation to bite her thumbnail.

"Ryan, I know about your mother. I've been friends with Sean too long not to."

Her thumb went into her mouth as she nervously began nibbling the hangnail anyway. "My mother has got nothing to do with it."

"Ryan, there's no way you weren't thinking that little girl could have been you."

"You don't know anything about what I'm thinking," she said, avoiding his eyes.

"Well, why don't you tell me then?" He took a step toward her.

She quickly strode to the front door and opened it. "I really don't feel like talking about this. You can go now."

"Ryan, I'm only trying to help."

She gestured to the door. "I don't need your help. And I certainly don't need your pity."

He stared at her for what seemed like forever, a look on his face she couldn't read. "Pity? Babe, you really don't have a clue, do you?"

And then he crossed the threshold and walked out.

Ryan watched him get in the car, and finally shut the front door when she realized he wasn't going to drive off as long as she was in the doorway. She poured herself the last glass of wine from the bottle, and fell asleep sitting up on the sofa, only halfway through drinking it.

JACOB

Jacob was not pleased. The cop had screwed up. He was supposed to kill the hooker and wrap a bow around her head. Instead, he killed the child, raped the hooker, and forgot the bow. The only thing he did right was kill the hooker. But without the bow, killing the hooker was pointless. The bow was the key. Everyone was supposed to think the dead hooker was a gift for Ryan, and no one would even be able to guess that without the bow.

He shook his head in disgust. Jacob wasn't bothered by the rape of the hooker, or in theory by the murder of her AIDS-infested child. But while the gift-wrapped hooker would have sent the proper message, the dead child might cause Ryan to start thinking about her own past, and that was something Jacob didn't want Ryan to delve into quite yet. Not that he really thought she was smart enough to figure out his plan.

The extraneous crimes also wasted time. Time the cop should have used to put the fucking bow around the hooker's head.

As much as he wanted to, he couldn't get rid of the cop yet. A few more people had to be killed before he could move on to phase two of his plan. And at this point, he couldn't take the risk of doing the murders himself. When everything was ready, when it was time, Jacob would kill the cop himself.

Jacob had watched when Ryan first got out of the car, waiting for her to recognize the hooker. Any normal woman with feelings would have been devastated at such a scene, a dead child, her mother raped and murdered. He wasn't surprised to see Ryan's lack of emotion for a common whore and her bastard child. As if her own mother had been any better. She had to know where she came from, and yet she still couldn't empathize, further proof to Jacob that he had made the right decision. Past inequities had to be resolved. Soon he would make Ryan realize that.

9:45 A.M.

Ryan tapped her ink pen on the table nervously. She had chosen the jury for the trial of Tyrone Cleeves, and was waiting for Shep and Monte. Mike was doing a motion hearing, and as soon as he finished, the trial would begin. Ryan never relaxed until her cops were in the courtroom. Not that she thought Shep or Monte would skip out, but the judge wouldn't be happy if the state's witnesses were late. And after the way last night had ended, Ryan wasn't exactly sure what to expect from Shep when he did show up.

Voir dire had taken less time that Ryan had anticipated. She thought she had chosen her jury well, but she wouldn't know for certain until the verdict came back. She felt comfortable with her choices, with the exception of a young black guy she couldn't strike. She was out of challenges, and a vote of ten of the twelve was all that was needed for a conviction, so she felt she could take the chance.

Ryan heard the back door open, and looked up to see Shep and Monte together in the doorway. She went to the back of the courtroom and led the two men into the hallway.

Monte smiled at her. "We ready to hook this gangsta up?"

Ryan pointed over her shoulder to the courtroom door. "As soon as Mike finishes his hearing. Maybe five minutes."

"I'm going to let section K know I'm over here," Monte said. "I'll be back by the time the jury's up."

"Do you need the police report?"

Monte took the report and walked down the hall.

Ryan turned to Shep. "What about you?"

He held his hands up. "Before we start talking police reports, I want to make sure we're still friends."

She looked at him dubiously. "I didn't realize we were ever friends." Shep's apology was the last thing she expected, not that she was complaining.

He tilted his head, looking down at her, his gray-blue eyes questioning through his lashes. "You're not still mad, are you? I'm sorry if I crossed some boundary last night."

"It's fine. I'm not mad. Do you need a police report?"

He held up his copy to show her.

"Good." She turned to go back into the courtroom, when he grabbed her arm.

"Is something up with you and Carlson?" His eyes locked hers, making her heart race slightly.

"What's it to you?" Her response was a force of habit, fast and defensive, without any thought given before she said it. She immediately regretted it.

"Nothing. Sorry. I didn't mean to get into your personal life again. Never mind." He looked away and walked into the courtroom ahead of her.

Shep's words stayed in Ryan's mind while the public defender questioned Tyrone Cleeves. She tried to stay focused on the trial, but she didn't need her full attention on a case this easy anyway.

The state's case had lasted less than an hour, and Ryan thought it was a lock. Shep and Monte had both done well on the stand, not that she hadn't expected them to. They both knew how to testify, looking directly at the jurors as they recalled the events of Tyrone Cleeves' arrest in almost identical detail.

Monte had received a tip that a reluctant witness on one of Shep's open homicides was hiding out in the St. Thomas. The detectives were looking for him when they saw Tyrone Cleeves on the corner of Felicity and St. Thomas, showing off an AK-47 to a group of black men. Monte and Shep had jumped out of the car and identified themselves as police officers. The group scrambled, Tyrone Cleeves throwing down the AK in the melee that ensued. Shep retrieved the gun while Monte chased Cleeves, catching him just past the first building in the project. The testimony was consistent and entirely believable. Ryan didn't see how the jury couldn't be convinced.

After she introduced her evidence, a dangerous looking AK-47 machine gun, the state had rested and Pablo Martinez, Cleeves' attorney, had called him to the stand. Naturally, Cleeves told a completely different version of events than Shep and Monte. According to Cleeves, another man had the gun. The detectives were putting charges on him for some reason he couldn't explain. His story was completely ludicrous, and it didn't appear that the jury was buying it. Ryan could hardly wait to cross-examine him.

Pablo smiled at the jury, and then his client. "Mr. Cleeves, please answer the state's questions."

Ryan stood up. "Mr. Cleeves, how many felony convictions do you have?"

The best part about a 95.1 was that the defendant usually testified. In cases where the accused didn't testify, the state couldn't bring up his prior convictions without causing a mistrial. Thus, in most cases, if the defendant had a prior conviction, he simply didn't take the stand and the jury would never know how bad a guy he really was. But with the felon in possession of a firearm charge, the jury automatically got to hear about the priors, being that a prior conviction was one of the elements the state was required to prove. Consequently, since the jury would learn about the prior convictions anyway, the defendant almost always testified. And he almost always tripped himself up.

"Six or seven," Cleeves answered. "But I just pled guilty to those so I could get out of jail."

Ryan nodded. "I see. So you lied so you could go home faster?"

"Yes ma'am, I did."

Ryan walked in front of the jurors. "Like you're lying to this jury right now, isn't that right?" She pointed to the jury box.

"No, miss, I is not lying right now. Them cops is lying. I never had that gun. You just want to put me in jail for fifteen years. I got a brand new baby girl that's going to be growed by the time I get out. Fifteen years, that's almost her whole life."

"You should have thought about that before you tried to sell an AK-47 machine gun on the street," Ryan said.

"Objection," Pablo said, standing up. "That's not a question."

"Withdrawn," Ryan said quickly. It was a trick she had picked up from watching *Law and Order*, completely improper and generally frowned upon in real life, but the judge let it slide with a warning look. "So, Mr. Cleeves, exactly what were you doing on that corner then?"

Cleeves smiled. "I was just hanging out."

"So you're saying another man had this gun, and not you?"

"I never even touched a real gun in my life."

"Well, Mr. Cleeves, what's that on your forehead?" She pointed for emphasis.

He shrugged. "It's just a tattoo."

"That's actually a tattoo of a gun, isn't it?" She didn't wait for him to answer. "Do you think the automatic machine gun tattooed on your forehead looks like the automatic machine gun I gave to the minute clerk? The gun the police officers retrieved from you? The AK-47 you claim you never touched?"

Cleeves shrugged again.

"The state requests the defendant stand in front of the jury box so the jurors may view his tattoo and decide for themselves."

Pablo stood up. "Objection. The jurors are not qualified to identify tattoos."

Thank you, Ryan thought, but aloud said, "Your Honor, I think the jurors are intelligent enough to decide for themselves if the gun I'm holding is similar to the gun tattooed on the defendant's forehead, despite defense counsel's opinion to the contrary."

The judge glared at her. "Ms. Murphy, that was out of line. Do it again and you'll find yourself in contempt of court. Mr. Martinez, your objection is overruled. Get up and stand in front of the jury, Mr. Cleeves."

Ryan walked to Donna, who held the evidence that had been admitted, and picked up the AK-47. Cleeves stood up and slowly walked in front of the jurors, giving them a view of the tattoo on his forehead. Ryan walked behind him with the weapon, stopping at the state's table.

She held the AK-47 out in front of her, so the jury could compare. The gun bore a striking resemblance to Cleeves' tattoo.

Cleeves took a single step toward Ryan. "This tattoo don't make that gun mine."

"Sit down now, Mr. Cleeves." The judge stood up behind the bench.

Cleeves ignored the judge. "I never had that gun and I ain't going to jail and never see my baby again." And then Cleeves did something Ryan had never seen before in her four years at Orleans Parish Criminal Court. He made a run for it.

Cleeves ran past Ryan, who jumped behind the table, and moved the gun out of Cleeves' reach. But Cleeves wasn't going for the gun. He was going for the door. At the first row of benches, Monte and Shep were waiting for him. The two men took him down in half a second and passed him back to Mike, who passed him to the bailiff, who brought him into the holding cell in the back. Nero quickly led the jury back to the jury room.

Cleeves was searched, and when the court deputy determined he didn't have any weapons hidden in any of his body parts, was brought before the judge.

"I do not tolerate that type of behavior in my courtroom," Judge Jackson said, looking down sternly at Cleeves from the bench. "I'll decide how to penalize you after this jury returns a verdict. But make no mistake, you pull something like that again, and you'll be sitting in Orleans Parish Prison for the rest of your trial. Nero, cuff his hand to the defense table."

The jury was brought back in.

"No further questions from the state," Ryan said, giving the jury a smile.

"The defense rests," Pablo said uncertainly, then sat next to his client.

As far as Ryan was concerned, between the tattoo and the escape attempt, she should have been able to stand there with one finger in her nose and her other hand scratching her ass and still get a conviction without even opening her mouth. And put herself one step closer to Strike Force in the process.

Shep and Monte stayed in the courtroom during the brief closing arguments, as well as for the jury instructions. Some of the prosecutors didn't care if the police officers left as soon as their testimony was over. Ryan always tried to make her officers wait, keeping them in front of the jury as long as possible. She also always requested they at least stayed on beeper so she could call them back for the jury verdict. She wanted the jury to have to look the police in the eye if they were going to return a not guilty verdict, in effect saying the cops were lying. Not that she was worried about that on this case.

When the jury left to deliberate, Ryan grabbed a cigarette and lighter from her purse. "Shep, would you mind walking me down the hall?" She thought the time was finally right to apologize to him for the comment about his family. And maybe to find out exactly what sparked his question about Monte.

"Uh, sure." He seemed surprised as he followed her out.

Smoking was not allowed in the courthouse, even in the hallways. At the opposite end of the second floor, an unlocked door led to a set of outside stairs, and to what the regulars in the building considered an unofficial smoking area.

As they walked down the hall, Shep spoke first. "So what do you really want? I know you're not scared to walk the halls of criminal court."

"Honestly, I was kind of freaked out by that. No one's ever tried to escape on me before." She was conscious of Shep walking next to her, their elbows almost touching.

"I didn't think you were scared of anything." Gilbert's smiled appeared.

"See what you get for thinking?" She waved at Edie down the hall. Edie gave her a thumbs up. Ryan ignored her, hoping Shep hadn't noticed. "So, any leads on the homicide from last night?"

Shep cut her off, opening the door at the end of the hall. "Sorry, babe, I got strict instructions not to let you in on anything with this investigation."

She walked through the door in front of Shep. They went down four steps to a second door that led to a full flight of stairs. The full flight descended into a fenced-in courtyard with a locked gate, where the inmates would be brought if the building caught fire, a security measure to ensure nobody escaped if somebody got cute and pulled the fire alarm. The deputies responsible for transporting the inmates through the courthouse each had a key to the gate.

"What brought this on all of a sudden?" Ryan frowned, thinking of Sean's comment to the same effect the day before.

"I think Sean told the captain about your role in assisting him with Jimbo."

"And I think Sean's an ingrate. But you'll still let me know what's going on, won't you?" The stairway was hot and sticky, even more stagnant than the inside of the building. Ryan took off her suit jacket and put it over the railing at the top of the landing. She climbed on the rail and sat on her jacket, and then finally lit the cigarette.

He shook his head. "Captain's orders." He paused for a second, and then said, "And I can kind of see up that short skirt with you sitting like that."

Ryan took a drag on the cigarette and exhaled before she spoke. "Daddy's out of town. What if I talk to Sean and he says it's okay? I did help you, after all. And while I know you're not accustomed to women who wear underwear, if my panties are offending you, you don't have to look at them."

"I wasn't complaining," he said quickly, not bothering to avert his eyes. "Let me talk to Sean. But I really don't want to go against the captain, especially where you're concerned." He stood facing her in silence for a few seconds while she waited expectantly. "I said I'd talk to Sean."

Ryan decided to try to soften him up. "I'm sorry for being such a bitch last night," she said, flicking an ash behind her. "Look, I know we don't always get along, but I realize you think you were helping."

"If that's your idea of an apology, I guess I accept. But don't think I'm going to change my mind. I'm not that easy."

She tried again. "See, I wasn't thinking that I could have been Jasmine. It was more like I was wondering why Jasmine couldn't have been me. Why do things work out for one kid and not another? You know what I mean? What did that little girl ever do to deserve a mother like Charmaine?"

"I do know what you mean. Exactly." He leaned against the rail next to her.

"I'm not really comfortable talking about my biological mother." She watched an ash slowly dancing its way to the ground beneath them.

His eyes followed the ash as well. "I can relate to not wanting to talk about your mother." He glanced up at her suddenly. "I don't like talking about mine either. People with crappy moms don't."

Good segue. She was going to have to suck this one up eventually. She might as well apologize now.

"While we're on that subject, I'm also sorry about that comment I made the other night about you worrying about your own family. I didn't realize your family was so screwed up." Seeing the look on his face she quickly added, "No offense."

"None taken," he said, but shifted away from her slightly.

"This isn't working, is it? Apologizing is one of the few things I'm not good at. Let me try again." She pushed several loose strands of hair away from her face.

He smiled then, but not Gilbert's. "Don't strain yourself, babe, I know what you mean."

"So, you never worked things out with your mom?" Ryan threw the cigarette to the ground, watching it float to join the wasteland of butts in the courtyard below.

He shook his head. "I never spoke to her again. I heard she died a while back. Some kind of cancer. I wasn't even invited to the funeral. So now that you know my life story, you want to tell me about your mother? And if you don't, that's cool."

She climbed down from the rail, picking up her jacket. "There's really nothing to tell," she said after a moment. Shep took her jacket and held it out for her. "Mama's sister, Patti, was my biological mother. She was caught buying heroin when she was pregnant with me." She thought for a second. "I was born while she was still in jail, so she gave me up to mama and daddy. Then when I was four, she showed up at the house and stole me. I don't really remember it."

"Do you want to?" he asked, holding the first door open for her. They walked up the four steps to the second door that led back into the courthouse.

"Sort of. I mean, I've always sort of been curious about Patti and why she came for me. Seeing Jasmine last night reminded me of how much I don't know."

"Have you tried asking your parents? Or one of your brothers?" He paused at the second door.

"They refuse to discuss the whole thing. It makes me wonder what really happened."

"Don't you think the captain or your mom would have told you if anything bad had happened to you?" He finally opened the door leading into the hallway.

"Not if they were trying to protect me." She focused on the exit sign at the opposite end of the hall as they walked back in the direction of the courtroom.

Shep stopped and took out a small notepad from his pocket. "What was your biological mother's name?"

"Patricia Ryan. Why?"

He scribbled the name down. "Do you know her date of birth?"

Ryan shook her head.

He put the notebook and pen back in his pocket. "I'll see if I can find out anything for you."

"Thanks," Ryan said, surprised that Shep was helping her with something the captain would obviously disapprove of. "That's actually kind of sweet."

"Good. Sweet is exactly what I was going for. Just do me a favor and don't mention this to anyone. God only knows what would happen if the news got out that I did something nice for a woman I haven't even slept with yet."

"Yet?" she asked, raising her eyebrows. "You have some mighty high aspirations."

"Slip of the tongue," Shep answered, Gilbert's smile reappearing. "And that's an expression, not an offer, so don't get your hopes up."

She tried to come up with an indignant response, but an attorney called to Shep before Ryan could think of anything.

"I'll be back before the verdict," Shep said and walked away quickly.

Ryan started back to the courtroom, feeling a little overheated. She glanced back over her shoulder and caught Shep looking back at her, and smiled to herself.

In the courtroom, the staff was discussing Tyrone Cleeves.

"I can't believe that jackass tried to escape," Donna said. "Where did he think he was going?"

"He ain't here because he's a Rhodes scholar," Monte pointed out. "What can you expect from a dude who stands on the street corner trying to sell a machine gun?"

They shook their heads in unison. Monte walked over to the state's table and sat next to Ryan.

"So what's going on?" His tone was casual, but the look he gave her made her blood race.

She tried to sound nonchalant. "Same old."

"You into Chapetti now?" He looked over her head, in the direction of the doors.

"I'm not into anybody," she answered, feeling her face turn red.

"I kind of got the impression you were into me the other night."

She was saved from responding by Donna's voice calling, "Jury's back."

Ryan looked at her watch. Nice. The jury had only been out for twenty minutes. She was about to call Shep when he walked in.

The jury filed down the stairs from the jury room, and back into the jury box. The attorneys stood.

"Madame Foreperson, what is your verdict?" the judge called from the bench.

The foreperson stood up, looking down as she unfolded the verdict slip. "On the sole count of possession of a firearm by a convicted felon, we find the defendant not guilty."

The courtroom was eerily silent.

"The state requests a polling of the jurors," Ryan announced too loudly, not believing she had heard right. She needed to know which jurors voted guilty, if any. The rest would not be chosen by any of the state attorneys for the rest of the jury month.

Jurors served two days a week for a month in Orleans Parish. Each prosecutor had a list of all the jurors, and would jot down notes next to the jurors' names, in particular the way they voted during the trials. The lists would be disseminated to the rest of the prosecutors by the trial secretary, so the assistants would know which jurors to strike from their own juries.

"Members of the jury," Judge Jackson said, "when I call your name, please stand and tell me if this is your verdict."

One at a time, the jurors stood up and said if they agreed with the verdict. There were two guilty verdicts, one middle-aged white woman and the young black man.

"I find that the verdict is legal and in proper form. Thank you ladies and gentlemen for your service. Please return to the jury lounge downstairs and the clerk will give you further instructions. You will need to report back for service on Monday." The jurors started filing out.

Ryan stood with Mike and thanked the jurors for their service, shaking their hands as they walked by, although what she really wanted to do was grab them by their hair and shake their heads unmercifully. Juror number 29, the young black man, mouthed the word sorry as he walked by.

"Thank you for your service," she said, and shook the man's hand.

"I hope none of them ever need me for anything," Monte said when the jurors were out of the courtroom.

"Nothing like a little jury nullification," the judge commented from the bench, slightly out of character for him. "Mr. Cleeves, because you were out on bond for this charge, you are free to leave. However, you will be getting a subpoena to come back in two weeks for a contempt charge for your behavior during this trial. If you fail to appear, a warrant for your arrest will be issued. I suggest you hire an attorney or the public defender will be appointed, as you are facing a maximum of six months without hard labor in parish prison, and I will tell you right now I am feeling inclined to give you the maximum. Do you understand me?" He stared at Cleeves for a second.

Cleeves nodded, a toothy grin on his face.

"Good. Get your subpoena from the minute clerk. Court is adjourned." The judge pounded the gavel and walked back into chambers.

"This verdict is just so wrong," Donna said, filling in the blanks of a subpoena, ignoring the fact that Cleeves was standing right in front of her desk. "At least he'll get six months for the Houdini attempt."

Cleeves took the piece of paper when Donna handed it to him. "Thank you," he told her. "And six months ain't nothing. I could do that standing on my head."

"Don't let me catch you out there, bra," Monte warned, putting his hand on Cleeves' shoulder. "I didn't have anything against you before, but I sure do now. I'm gonna be keeping an eye out for you."

"It's all good," Cleeves told him, and knocked Monte's hand off his shoulder. He nodded at Ryan and Mike. "You two better than my free lawyer, but the truth will always set you free."

"Then you should still be locked up," Ryan answered. "You're just lucky there were ten people stupider than you in the jury pool."

"Watch what you saying, Miss D.A.. I eat bitches like you for lunch." He took a step in Ryan's direction. "I might even see you around later."

Shep and Monte quickly stepped in front of Ryan. Shep pushed Cleeves roughly with two hands, causing the other man to stumble backwards into the podium.

"You can bet on seeing me again," Ryan said, determined not to let Cleeves get the last word. "I give you a week before you get yourself arrested again."

"I'd give you a day if you're going to be hanging in the St. Thomas," Shep added, pushing him again. "It's not nice to call the prosecutor names. You could have an unfortunate accident off of something like that."

"I'll take my chances," Cleeves said. He looked at Ryan again before stepping away from Shep, and walking out of the courtroom.

Shep and Monte stalked out after Cleeves without a word.

Ryan gathered her files and walked out of the courthouse with Mike, wondering if the defective logic of the world's stupidest jury had just screwed her out of the Strike Force spot.

Ryan was back at the D.A.'s Office by four, and didn't plan on staying long. She was tired and aggravated, and the thought of a nice long nap was appealing. She would just check her docket for tomorrow and then call it a day.

Bo was getting off the elevator at the first floor as Ryan got on.

"How was your trial?" she asked.

"Not guilty," he said, pushing the glasses back up on his nose. "I don't know what happened. How could I lose a third class crack possession?"

"I feel you," Ryan answered, and waited until the elevator doors closed to smile. Losing a crack possession technically wasn't as bad as losing a 95.1, but a loss was a loss when counting statistics.

She put Cleeves' file face down on her desk so she wouldn't have to look at it, and pulled her files for the next day. She tried to imagine how she would react if Bo, or worse yet, Kellie, got the promotion instead of her. Fortunately, the phone rang, snapping her back to reality. No way. That Strike Force spot was hers, Tyrone Cleeves or no Tyrone Cleeves.

"Ryan Murphy, Trials."

"Ryan Murphy, this is Chance Halley, from WDSU News. How are you today?"

She was more than a little intrigued about the purpose of his call, but she gave Chance the standard press response. "I'm fine, thank you. But all requests for statements have to go through Miss Vera, the D.A.'s secretary. I'll transfer you."

"Wait, I don't want a statement. I just wanted to say I was sorry. I'm sure you heard about my gross error in judgment." He was too slick, but at least he was apologizing.

"Oh that's right. You called me a hooker. Oh, and accused me of murder."

"I never accused you of murder. I just said you had a connection to both victims, which is true, isn't it?"

Ryan ignored his question. "But you did call me a hooker. And I thought you were supposed to be apologizing. It sounds to me like you're still after a statement."

"I'm a reporter. I can't help myself. But I do truly regret the hooker remark."

Ryan was sure he did. Especially after Sean's warning. "Is that because you're sorry you said it, or because you don't want to get your legs broken?"

"A little of both. I thought one of those cops was going to hurt me." Chance Halley's tone was suddenly serious. "When I asked about you, the tall one told me to suck his dick. And the redhead told me I'd better not even look at you or I'd find myself underneath Orleans Parish Prison."

"The redhead is my brother," Ryan told him.

"Ouch. No wonder he was so mad. But I can't help asking questions. I learned a long time ago that the only way to find out anything is to ask. You would understand if you had any reporter in you."

"Well, Mr. Halley, I can't relate. I'm an attorney. I don't happen to have any reporter in me."

"Would you like to?" His lascivious response was fast enough that Ryan realized it was a set up, and one he probably used frequently. "And by all means, call me Chance."

"Do you ever get lucky with that one?" she asked, wondering where Chance got his nerve. She figured it was probably from looking in the mirror every morning.

"You'd be surprised. But now that you've accepted my apology, would you like to go out with me some time?"

"I didn't say I accepted your apology. And why would I go out with you? So I can give you information on the cases I'm working on?" She drummed her fingers on the desk, slightly irritated. He was cute, but she wasn't stupid enough to go out with him when he was clearly only after a story.

"Well, not just that. I was thinking we could have sex, too."

His answer didn't brighten her mood. "Why don't you call me after the homicides are solved. I wouldn't want anyone thinking you were consorting with a murderer."

"I will call you back. I felt a spark when you looked at me. I swear, I'm not just about getting information."

"I know. You're also about getting laid." She hung up the phone and decided she'd had enough for the day. Now she would go home, hoping she could forget about lost cases, hidden agendas and dead defendants long enough to catch up on some much needed sleep.

Ryan couldn't keep her thoughts from drifting back to the homicides on the short drive home. L'Roid Smith had been killed in a way common among gang members—beaten, shot in the head execution style, and left naked. It was the ultimate humiliation, and the same way he had committed his own gang murders, including the one Ryan had tried to prosecute. And Jeremiah had been beaten, the same way he had beaten his wife on the case Ryan had handled. She thought about Charmaine Reynolds, but couldn't remember how Charmaine had killed her pimp.

As soon as she got home, Ryan pulled out the file where she kept her copy of the nolle prosequi forms, the paperwork that had to be completed and approved by the supervisors to dismiss a case.

Charmaine had waited until her pimp, Marco Bouvier, had passed out from taking too many Soma tablets, and then choked him in his sleep with her scarf, tying it around his neck and pulling until he quit breathing. There was no doubt that Bouvier had taken the Soma himself, and Charmaine had just waited until he lost consciousness to kill him.

Ryan nibbled her thumb. All of the victims had been killed the same way that they had committed the crimes that Ryan had dismissed. Could this really have something to do with her? Was Chance right? She remembered the feeling of being watched at the St. Thomas, and thought about the prank phone calls.

There's another gift for you. The gifts are for you.

She picked up the phone and dialed Sean.

"What?" His tone suggested he knew it was her.

"Sean, I was thinking about the last three homicides, the ones I prosecuted —"

"Why?" Sean interrupted. "Didn't I tell you once we don't need your help?"

"I know what you said, but Chance Halley mentioned —"

"Why are you talking to Chance Halley?" Sean interrupted again.

"That's none of your business. Do you want to know what I was calling to tell you?"

"If it's about my homicides, no, I don't. You've got no reason to be putting yourself in the middle of this investigation. Unless you're thinking of getting information for your new boyfriend."

Ryan hit the button on the cordless phone, hanging up on Sean. Still seething, she threw the phone across the room, and felt a slight release when it took a chip out of the paint on the wall with a thud. So she wouldn't get her damage deposit back when she moved some day. At least it made her feel better.

She couldn't believe Sean was ignoring her information, especially since he should have been kissing her feet after her help with Jimbo. While Ryan wasn't a hundred percent sure she was right, she thought somebody should at least check out her theory. She picked up the phone from the floor and dialed Shep's cell.

He answered on the first ring. "Hello, Ryan. To what do I owe the pleasure of this call?"

"You're talking to Sean on the other line, aren't you?" She was glad he couldn't see her expression.

"I just got off with him. He told me to hang up on you."

"Sean is such a wiener. Would you just listen to me? I think these homicides have something to do with me."

"And Sean thinks Chance Halley put some crazy idea in your head."

Ryan bit back a host of insults about Sean. No sense showing her ugly side. "Sean thinks I'm a mindless idiot," she said instead. "I prosecuted all three of the victims. And all three were killed the exact way that they committed the crimes I prosecuted. L'Roid Smith was killed gang style, just like he killed Willie Paz in the case I had to dismiss. Both were beaten, with a single GSW to the head, then left naked. They're identical."

"That's how most gang hits are done," Shep said, obviously unconvinced. "And you've prosecuted hundreds of people."

"And Jeremiah was beaten just like he beat his wife."

"That could still just be a coincidence." Shep seemed less sure of himself now.

"Charmaine Reynolds was choked with a piece of material. She killed her pimp Bouvier by waiting until he passed out from taking too much Soma, and then choked him." She paused for dramatic effect. "With a scarf. Which is also a piece of material."

She heard Shep make a small noise before he said, "I don't know."

Ryan thought he might be starting to believe her, so she continued. "And some freak with a voice distorter keeps calling me and asking if I like the gifts. At first, I thought they were just really lame obscene phone calls, but last night I told the caller he had the wrong number, and he said my name, and that I would understand. Then Sean called and said we had another body."

Shep was silent on the other end.

"You can hang up now if you want," she said, knowing she finally had his interest.

"Did you tell Chance Halley any of this?"

She rolled her eyes through the phone. "Do you think I'm stupid? I know what Chance Halley is about, regardless of whether you and Sean give me credit for that or not. You know, I'm not so desperate that I would spill my guts to a reporter just to get a date."

"I never said that."

"Well, Sean did. And he sort of hurt my feelings."

"Babe, don't take it personally. Sean just doesn't like reporters."

"Then he doesn't have to date one. Shep, do you think I'm right? Do you think these are all coincidences, or do you think somebody thinks he's doing me a favor by killing the defendants on the cases I lost? Because if that's true, I'm not going to mind losing Tyrone Cleeves quite as much."

Shep blew out a long breath before he answered. "I don't know. Let me talk to Sean. If you're right, if you are the link to these homicides, we need to figure out who is killing these people. And we need to do it fast."

She hung up, pleased that somebody was finally taking her seriously, but also concerned about Shep's remark. He was right. Knowing the link between the homicides wasn't enough; finding out who was committing them was the important thing.

But Ryan didn't feel like thinking about that right now. Instead, she turned off the ringer on the bedroom phone and cranked the A/C unit to high, and then crawled into bed, her gun sitting on the nightstand in reaching distance.

THURSDAY

2:00 A.M.

At 2 :00 a.m., the ringing of Ryan's cell phone woke her up. She read Sean's number off the cell's caller ID before she answered.

"Yeah."

"Why aren't you answering your house phone?"

"I turned it off to sleep," she answered. "What the hell do you want?"

"Another 30. I'm on the way."

Ryan got out of bed and shivered. She peered through the slats of the cheap plastic window blinds and saw that it had rained while she slept, considerably cooling things off. She turned the air to low and changed into a T-shirt and jeans. After slipping into her tennis shoes, she went into the living room to wait for Sean, and noticed the light flashing on her answering machine. She tucked a pack of cigarettes and a lighter into the pocket of her jeans, and then hit the play button.

The distorted voice floated through the air. "I forgot the bow on your gift last night. Please forgive me. I won't do that again. Wait until you see your new gift. Ryan, you should be very happy." As she checked the caller ID, she heard the unmistakable plunk of slow, fat rain drops hitting the metal on the outside of the living room A/C unit. Unknown number. Time of call, 1:05 a.m.

A horn honked. Ryan grabbed her keys and tried to run between the rain drops as she got in the car with Sean. The air smelled like hot, wet cement.

"Looks like another banger," Sean said as she got in the car. "This is getting old, isn't it?"

Ryan refused to look at him, instead watching the pattern of the rain pelting the windows of the Crown Vic. She had to ride in the same car with her brother, but she didn't have to talk to him.

He made the left on St. Charles, and after a few seconds tried again. "So you called Shep today?"

She couldn't keep quiet any longer. "You know I did, so why are you asking as if you don't already know? And I thought you weren't interested in what I had to say."

"I've got a lot on my mind, Ryan, okay? I'm sorry if I didn't jump up and down because you had a thought."

She decided to plead her case again. "Sean, I'm right. The prank caller left another message on my machine when I was sleeping."

Sean glanced over at her. "What did he say?"

"Does it matter? You don't want to listen to me anyway."

"Ryan, maybe you're onto something, but maybe you're not. And what's up with you calling Chapetti?"

"Shep was the only one who would listen me."

"Well, Shep called dad and dad told him to look into your old cases. So, as usual, you got your way." The corners of Sean's mouth turned down slightly. Ryan thought he was jealous.

"Maybe you could use me as bait, and lure the killer out." Ryan's eyes lit up at the prospect. "I could wear a wire."

Sean snorted disparagingly, and gave her a mocking smile. "You're getting way ahead of yourself, Nancy Drew. You need to quit watching those cop shows. Even if we had a suspect, which we don't, there is no way you're going to be involved in the investigation. Dad would kill me."

"And would he leave your body in the St. Thomas?"

Sean's smile dissolved. "Why did you say that?"

She tried to stifle a yawn and failed. "Chill, loser, I was joking."

"With all the murders in the St. Thomas, how can you possibly think that's funny?" Sean's knuckles were white on the steering wheel.

"It may have been a little tasteless, but yeah, I did think it was funny. What's got your drawers in a knot?"

Sean shook his head and drove in silence, accelerating the car, the tires squealing as the car skidded on the wet street.

She grabbed the handle above the passenger door. "Sean, you don't have to explain yourself if you don't want to, but please slow down. I don't want the next dead body daddy sees to be mine."

Sean took the left on Magazine and pulled over in front of an antique store that used to be a Woolworth's. He hit both of his hands on the steering wheel, and then looked at Ryan, as if debating whether to tell her or not. She pulled the lighter and a cigarette from her jeans.

He pointed at the cigarette. "You're not smoking that in here."

"Fine." She lit the cigarette and opened the car door to get out. At least the rain was slackening.

"All right, shut the door. You can smoke in here, but crack the window for God's sake." He was preoccupied, and Ryan knew if she waited him out he would tell her what was wrong. A few seconds later he answered. "PID is investigating dad. I saw the letter in his desk. Dad hasn't told anyone that I know of, and I wasn't planning on telling anyone either."

"For what?" The cigarette sizzled as she took a long drag.

"L'Roid Smith. He tried to run when they brought him to the station for questioning. Dad happened to intercept him and Smith won a trip to the ER for his trouble. I'm betting he filed a complaint against dad, and PID is just now getting to it."

"Coincidentally right after Smith's dead body was found in daddy's district," Ryan finished. "You're really worried about this, aren't you?"

"A PID investigation is nothing to play around with."

Ryan agreed. The Public Integrity Division couldn't be taken lightly. For more years than most people realized, the Internal Affairs Division of the NOPD had been a really bad joke. The head of IAD, Andre Villevegas, had not only ignored the crimes of other officers, but was himself one of the slipperiest criminals in the city, using byzantine methods to create a drug trafficking empire governed by rogue cops.

Eventually, an FBI investigation resulted in his indictment on various charges, prosecuted by the U.S. Attorney's Office. Then, it was like a row of dominoes falling, starting with Villevegas, who gave up the names of fifteen other officers involved, in exchange for concurrent life sentences on all counts, and ending with three politicians, two judges, and a former governor, all involved in crimes ranging from money laundering to murder.

In the aftershock, the division had lost so much credibility that the name was changed to the Public Integrity Division, and the entire system overhauled. The FBI had stepped in to supervise, and eventually the new entity responsible for policing the police grew into the typical pain-in-the-ass internal affairs that most police officers knew and despised.

Ryan blew a stream of smoke out of the window. "Are we going or not?"

Sean pulled back onto Magazine Street. "We're going. Ry, what I said, strictly on the D-L, okay? The complaint might turn out to be nothing, and I don't think we need dad's name showing up on the morning news as a suspect for Smith's murder."

"Oh, so that's your problem with Chance Halley?" Ryan asked, mildly amused. "You think he's going to get me all sexed up and I'm going to spill my guts?"

"I really don't need to hear that, Ryan, okay? Just stay away from Halley. He obviously wants a story, and if you don't watch your big mouth, you're going to wind up giving him one."

Ryan pinched her brother's arm hard, her amusement waned.

"What was that for?" Sean asked, rubbing his arm.

"For insinuating I'm either stupid or desperate. And if I want to go out with Chance Halley, I'll go out with him, whether you like it or not."

"And do you want to?"

She ignored his question. "I don't see how PID could be looking at daddy for Smith's murder when you've got an eyewitness who's pointing you to a suspect."

"The suspect is a fat white cop. Dad is a fat white cop."

"Daddy's more big-boned than fat. And Devon didn't identify him."

"Devon refused to make an identification, remember?"

She wanted to smack the superior look from her brother's face, but decided it would bring her greater pleasure to make him feel like an idiot. "You didn't think I'd let Devon off the hook without making sure the fat white cop he saw wasn't one of the fat white cops playing around at the Jeremiah scene, did you, Matlock? Even my two boyfriends were eliminated as suspects."

"Your two boyfriends?"

Ryan smiled. "Sisko and Malette."

"Ryan, that's not even funny. Who else did Devon look at?"

She took a final, long drag and then threw the cigarette out of the window. "I eliminated everyone at the crime scene while Devon was there. Except crime lab. They weren't outside."

"I wish you would have told me all this before." He gave her a chiding look. "I just wasted a lot of time making lineups of uptown cops for Devon to look at, including the ones who were at the scene."

Ryan threw her hands up in the air, in a decidedly captain-like gesture. "Nobody bothered to tell me that Devon was willing to look at lineups now. And you make it your mission in life to ignore me. Why should I bother to tell you anything?"

"When it's something useful I listen. And Devon hasn't actually agreed to look at lineups yet. But I'm sure we can convince him. When we find him, that is." A hint of red crept into Sean's cheeks. At least he had the decency to be embarrassed. Ryan decided to take advantage of Sean while his defenses were down to see if she could find out anything about the case.

"So, did you run the sex offenders in the area, just in case? For Charmaine and Jasmine?"

"Yeah. And Doug confirmed Jasmine wasn't raped, just strangled." Sean's face was still flushed, but his knuckles were back to their normal freckled state.

"Wasn't she lucky. I never thought I'd see the day when you'd be happy a six-year-old was only murdered."

Ryan was about to light another cigarette when Sean stopped the car near the corner of Felicity and St. Thomas. Four marked units were blocking the street, as well as an unmarked Taurus and a black Corvette Ryan recognized as belonging to Shep.

"The case I lost yesterday happened right here." The words popped out before she thought about them. A second later she was racing through the drizzling rain to where the uniforms were standing.

She stepped through the circle of damp officers and stopped when she saw the body of Tyrone Cleeves, propped up against a wall, his body riddled with dozens of gunshot wounds. An AK-47 and a single piece of paper rested in his lap. His torso was adorned with a big red Christmas bow, already saturated with blood. The rain had caused the blood to form small pink rivulets on the uneven ground beneath his body. The drizzle increased to a patter as Ryan stared open-mouthed at the dead man in front of her.

Shep ran up from around the corner, his normally perfect hair plastered to his head from the rainfall. "We had a witness who saw the body get dumped, but she took off."

"Shep, did you see who this is?" Ryan asked, pointing at the body.

Blood normally turned dark, nearly-black, when it dried, but Cleeves' blood retained its bright red hue as it commingled with the rain. The end result was the grotesque illusion that the dead man was still bleeding from his wounds.

Shep squeezed her shoulder lightly. "You sure called this one."

Sean looked at them and put his hands out. "What?"

Ryan hugged herself, trying to rub the chill from her wet arms. "I tried this guy's 95.1 yesterday. Shep and Monte were the officers. I lost."

"This is where we saw him with the gun," Shep said, and then turned and looked back into the development.

"What does the note say?" Ryan asked, biting her thumbnail. "Are we waiting for crime lab, or can one of you just read it?"

Sean picked up the wilting page with a gloved hand and read it silently, his face ghostly pale.

"The note is for me, isn't it?" Ryan felt a chill creeping down her spine. She glanced around, trying to ignore the ominous feeling of evil pervading the air. "Read it."

Sean held the letter up for her to see.

Ryan read it out loud. "*Ryan, Here is your gift. I hope you like it.*" She dug in her pocket for another cigarette.

"You're going to have to answer some questions at the station," Sean said.

The cigarette fell from her fingers to the wet ground. "You don't think I had something to do with this?"

"Of course not," Shep said quickly, and put his hand back on her shoulder, frowning at Sean.

"We have to follow protocol, Ryan," Sean answered, and frowned back at Shep.

"That means getting a statement at the station."

Ryan pushed her dripping hair back from her face. She had thought she would have been happier proving Sean wrong.

"You better call Carlson," Shep told Sean. "We both exchanged words with Cleeves after the trial."

"Great. Just what I need. Let me call the sergeant." Sean made the call from his cell as Suzie Chin walked up, soaking wet.

"Thought Cooper was on tonight," Doug said as he walked up behind her.

"So did I." The tiny Asian woman's dark eyes flashed. "He called in sick and didn't have the decency to call me and let me know."

"Don't look now but looks like the press got wind of this," Puddy said, pointing to three news vans stopped on the street. "You want me to chase them away?"

Sean shook his head. "Just keep them back. I don't want them seeing this note." His eyes held a look of warning as he glanced around at the other officers. "If this note gets out, somebody's losing their job, you all got that?" The officers nodded, watching as the reporters tried to get closer to the crime scene.

For once, Ryan wasn't thinking about the press. She was thinking about the note that Suzie Chin had started to bag. She was also thinking about Cleeves' numerous gunshot wounds and the AK-47 sitting on his lap. She peered through the crowd starting to form. The killer could be out here, right now, watching.

"What about the witness?" Sean asked Shep.

Shep pointed in the direction of the complex. "Crack whore. She told Puddy she might have seen the body getting dropped off. Puddy got me, but when we went back she had already disappeared into the development."

Sean began barking orders to the officers. As the others dispersed, he added, "Shep, the sergeant wants you and Ryan at the station."

Shep pointed to the street where his Corvette was parked. Ryan heard her name as she walked behind Shep to the car. She looked up to see Chance Halley waving at her from the opposite side of the street. Ryan acknowledged him with a nod, too absorbed in her own thoughts to pay him any attention.

Shep stopped and blew Chance a kiss. Chance stepped back quickly behind a cameraman.

"Isn't Halley the one that gave you the idea that you might be connected to this?" Shep opened the door for Ryan, squinting in Chance's direction.

She shivered and immediately began trying to dry her arms and legs with her hands. Shep grabbed a towel from the trunk space and handed it to her.

"Chance asked one question at the press conference. I put the rest together myself."

"Did he say where he got his information?" Shep asked as he backed out onto the street.

"No. Why?" Ryan put the towel over her head and began squeezing the water from her hair.

"He comes up with this idea out of the blue connecting you to two homicides, and then someone leaves a note for you proving his idea was right." He turned left on Magazine.

"You think Chance is the killer?" She stopped drying her hair long enough to laugh.

"Maybe he's tired of trying to get on the news. Maybe he's trying to make it now. Where did he get his information?"

"You're the detective. You figure it out." She handed him the towel. "And you don't really believe Chance Halley is a killer."

"No, not really." He tossed the towel in the back and then glanced over at her. "I just don't like him for some reason. And what kind of a sissy name is Chance anyway?"

"He's a little slick, but I don't think he's a killer."

"Slick?"

"Yeah, kind of like you." She smiled faintly, anticipating Shep's reaction.

"He is nothing like me," Shep answered, his lip curled almost in a snarl.

Sergeant Mitchell was waiting for them at the front door of the station. Ryan followed him into the interrogation room and sat in the center chair at the table. The sergeant sat across from her, and a moment later, Lt. Powers joined them.

Lt. Powers was a towering, dark-skinned black man, somewhere in his early fifties. He had large features and exceptionally white teeth. He reminded Ryan of a bull, so much so that she secretly called him El Toro.

Looking around, Ryan could see how a suspect might be nervous in a similar situation. The walls were stark white and bare. The floor had plain gray industrial carpet, which Ryan knew was more to prevent a suspect's head from cracking open if it should somehow happen to hit the floor than for its aesthetic value. The two men across the table from her worked for her father, yet they still managed to appear threatening. She could only imagine what it would feel like to be an actual suspect.

"Chapetti, you can sit in on this for now, unless I see a reason to make you leave," the sergeant said, pointing to a chair at the end of the table. Shep nodded and sat.

Lt. Powers leaned down on the table with both hands. El Toro was getting ready to charge. Ryan would have confessed had she committed a crime. "Sean filled us in on his theory about the other murders this week being connected to you. He said that the body tonight had a note addressed to you, and you got a call from somebody who might be a suspect."

"He left a message on my machine," she told him, wondering when Sean had started calling her theory his own.

"Good. Maybe we can pull something from it to figure out where he called from." Lt. Powers glanced doubtfully at Sergeant Mitchell.

The sergeant jotted something down on the notepad in front of him and asked, "Anybody you prosecuted particularly nasty lately?"

"Just Tyrone Cleeves. And you saw what happened to him."

The sergeant continued to write. "Are you dating anybody right now?"

She raised her eyebrows. "You're a little old for me, Sarge. And I don't think my father would approve."

The sergeant's cheeks turned red. "We'll see if anybody you prosecuted got released recently, but we also need to rule out the possibility that this is a domestic situation. I need to know if there's anybody you can think of that might want to impress you — somebody who might think he's doing you a favor by killing the defendants on your old cases."

She lit up a cigarette, contemplating her answer. Lt. Powers looked at the cigarette in her hand and then at the No Smoking sign on the wall across the room. She followed his eyes.

"Oh, sorry. This is a no smoking building, isn't it?" She looked around nervously for a place to put the cigarette out.

"We won't tell if you don't," Lt. Powers said and then pointed at Shep. "Get an ashtray."

Ryan waited several seconds before she answered. "I'm not seeing anybody. My last relationship ended three months ago."

"Who was that?" Sgt. Mitchell resumed the questions while Lt. Powers began pacing behind him.

Shep walked back in and set an ashtray down in front of her.

She took a long drag of the cigarette and then answered. "Chad Lejeune."

Sgt. Mitchell nodded. "He's that personal injury lawyer, isn't he? He's got those rap commercials on TV."

"That's him," she answered, and then sang the chorus of the rap jingle. "*When you get hurt bad, just call Chad.*" The jingle had been performed by a local rap artist so famous he had already been murdered by the time the commercial aired.

The sergeant looked her as if she was crazy. "Yeah. Okay. So, did you break up on good terms?"

"Not really." She exhaled and flicked an ash. It missed the ashtray and landed on the table. Lt. Powers frowned slightly. Ryan blew the ash to the floor.

Powers reached across the table and Ryan jumped. The lieutenant patted her hand in a way he must have thought was comforting. "Ryan, this may be difficult, but we've got to ask these questions. Anything you can think of might help."

"I can't think of anything." She took another drag from the cigarette and hoped none of the men would mention her smoking to her father.

"Was Lejeune ever violent?" The sergeant leaned forward slightly, as if inviting Ryan to confide in him.

She shook her head. "Chad wouldn't do this."

"Why not?" Lt. Powers asked, crossing him arms across his chest, looking down at her. While it wasn't exactly Good Cop/Bad Cop, Lt. Powers and Sgt. Mitchell had a system that was effective.

Ryan wondered which answer she should give them. Chad preferred slapping and punching to shooting and strangling? Chad only had the balls to go up against women? She shook her head and finally answered, "It's just not his style."

The sergeant looked at Lt. Powers, who nodded back at him.

The sergeant continued. "Whose idea was the breakup?"

"Mine." She flicked another ash. This one made the ashtray. "I broke up with him."

"Why?"

"I caught him with his paralegal." She looked up, directly at the sergeant. "And this was an hour after he couldn't rise to the occasion with me, so to speak. So it's difficult to imagine why he would be killing people now to get back in my good graces. I mean, sorry I couldn't get it up, but here's a dead body to make up for it? That doesn't make sense." She crushed the cigarette violently into the ashtray.

"We have to check him out," Lt. Powers said, not quite meeting her eyes with his own, "but I don't want to overlook any other potential suspects. Have you dated anyone since then?"

She shook her head. "Not exactly."

"Have you been, er, intimate with anyone?" Sgt. Mitchell asked delicately, and Ryan knew then that news of her social life had hit the gossip circuit. Lt. Powers finally sat down next to Sgt. Mitchell. Ryan was relieved. His pacing and hovering were disconcerting.

She sighed, knowing how the recitation of her late night activity over the previous three months was going to sound to the men. She didn't expect them to understand. "In February I saw Anthony Espinito for a couple of weeks."

"From PID?" Shep asked.

Her eyes darted to Shep. "PID?"

"Espinito is with PID," Shep said. "He's been with them for at least two years. You didn't know that?"

"No," she answered softly, feeling stupid. "I thought he was in robbery in Mid City."

"He was. Until PID took him. Did he also tell you he was married?" Shep asked.

"No, although I did find that out. As a matter of fact, I answered his cell phone when he was in the bathroom and it turned out to be his wife." She stopped for a second. "PID, huh? Well, that would explain his bizarre interest in daddy." She propped her chin on her hand, her elbow on the table, and sighed again. She had been fooled twice by Espinito. Being exposed in front of her father's men gave her a feeling she didn't like.

"Babe, we really don't need to know the details, but what happened with the, uh, relationship?" Sergeant Mitchell asked.

"After I talked to his wife, I kicked him out. Literally. He probably still has the bruise on his ass to show for it."

The sergeant scribbled on the pad again. "Did he try to contact you after that?"

"For about two weeks. He called a bunch of times, apologizing, asked if we could get together and talk. I kept hanging up on him and he finally stopped."

"Put him on the list," Lt. Powers said, his eyes almost glowing.

"He is a white cop," Shep said, leaning his chair back on two legs.

Ryan frowned at Shep, unsure of why she felt compelled to defend Espinito. "But he's not fat. He actually has a very nice body."

"Way too much information," Shep answered, letting the chair fall forward.

Lt. Powers glanced at Shep, but continued with his questions. "Have you dated anybody else since then?" Ryan could tell he was hoping the answer was no. She was mighty sorry to have to disappoint him.

"Well, I wouldn't say we actually dated, but I did kiss Joel Marks last month in his car after he gave me ride home from Dominick's."

"Marks, the homicide detective from the Third?"

She nodded again.

"And by kiss, you mean a quick good night peck?" Lt. Powers asked. Again, Ryan could tell he was hoping for a different answer than she was about to give him.

"More than a peck. Nothing under clothes, though. We didn't get naked or anything like that, but we did make out, I guess. And same thing with Bobby Taylor two weeks ago. He also gave me a ride home from Dominick's."

"Taylor from Robbery?"

"Yeah, unless of course he's really PID, too. And then last weekend, Monte Carlson. Also a ride home from Dominick's."

"Where do I sign up to give you a ride home from Dominick's?" Shep asked.

"I take it Chapetti's not going to be on this list," Lt. Powers said, sounding relieved, as he patted her small hand with his huge paw again. His attempt to soothe her was no more comforting the second time. "What about somebody you've turned down? Maybe you hurt somebody's feelings?"

"I turned down Chance Halley yesterday. But I seriously doubt he has the balls to kill anybody."

The sergeant jotted something down. "Might not hurt to check him out. After all, he is a reporter."

"And Big Mike asked me out a few weeks ago, but he was pretty drunk at the time."

"Big Mike?" the sergeant asked.

"You know, Boudreaux, the ex-Saints player," Shep said, his tone barely short of disdain.

Ryan scowled at him. "He took it like a gentleman and hasn't mentioned it since."

"Nobody else?" Lt. Powers asked. "Nobody bothering you, nothing like that?"

She shook her head. "I know that I annoy a lot of people in the courtroom, but I can't think of anyone in particular."

The sergeant stood up. "That should be enough to get us started. I'll be questioning Lejeune and Espinito. We'll talk to the others to potentially exclude them. I'm going to get a printout from the phone company of all the calls made to your house this last week, to see if we can get a number to trace. The caller's number shows up on the phone company's list, whether it shows up on caller ID or not. And there's going to be a marked unit following you, so don't be concerned when you see it parked outside your house. Now, would you mind waiting in the hall while we get Chapetti's statement? He'll bring you home afterward."

"Can I wait in daddy's office?"

The sergeant looked at Lt. Powers again, who nodded. Ryan got up and glanced at the sergeant's notes on the desk. She wondered how long it would be until her father saw them and went ballistic.

She sat in her father's chair and looked through his desk, hoping Sean had left the PID file where she could find it. A few seconds later, she found the unlabeled file. It contained the police report from Smith's arrest, including the medical reports from Charity Hospital, where Smith was treated for minor scrapes and bruises. Some big takedown. Ryan had suffered worse injuries stumbling down the sidewalk after a late night at the Hole.

A letter from PID was behind the police report. The letter didn't say much, just that a complaint had been made by L'Roid Smith.

She put the file down and her mind went back to Anthony Espinito. She had met him at Cooter Brown's, an uptown bar she frequented with Edie. Espinito claimed he recognized Ryan from court, and when he showed her his badge, she hadn't doubted him.

She had been so desperate to get past the disastrous relationship with Chad that she had been an easy mark. She thought Espinito's interest in her family, particularly her father, was a little unusual, but figured he had ambitions of climbing the ranks one day.

She was hesitant to get involved with him, especially when she thought he might be using her just to further his career. She was just so drunk, and he was so good looking, she couldn't seem to tell him no. And they hadn't had sex, just fooled around a little, and then he left.

She was surprised to hear from him two days later, and they spent several evenings together over the next couple of weeks. She should have been suspicious that he never tried to have sex, and was never able to stay the night. She had assumed he was taking things slow because he respected her, or, at the very least, feared her father.

Until his wife had called and busted him. She remembered the look on his face when she had handed him the phone.

Ryan wondered what information Espinito could possibly have thought she would have given him about the captain that would have been useful to PID.

She looked through her father's desk to see if there was another file, some PID investigation that would solve the mystery of exactly what Espinito had been after. A minute letter she had her answer.

Inside a second file was a letter from PID, advising that the captain was being investigated for a battery on Chad Lejeune. A week after Ryan had broken up with him, Chad had been attacked in his home, the intruder leaving him with a permanent limp from a torn ACL and fractured right kneecap.

Ryan wondered why Espinito or PID would suspect her father of having anything to do with Chad's beating. She had intentionally not told her father, nor anyone else in her family, what Chad had done to her. Not that she remembered it all, but she recalled enough that she knew what they would do to Chad if she mentioned even the small part she could remember. And in the end, Chad had been taken care of without the intervention of her father or brothers.

So PID thought her father had beaten Chad, and that was the reason Espinito had pretended to be interested in her. She had felt bad enough when she thought he was just cheating on his wife. She felt even worse now, knowing that Espinito had only pretended to like her so that he could extract information from her about her father. Especially when she knew one-hundred percent her father had nothing to do with Chad's beating.

She heard voices down the hall and quickly put the files back in her father's desk. She wondered how effective an investigation against Chad was going to be when her father was being investigated by PID for beating the man.

A second later, Shep walked in. "Sean brought the witness in. She saw a man get out of a black car, but she took off before the guy could see her, so she only saw him from a distance. Her description matches what we already have. Sean's cutting her loose, unless you want to talk to her."

Ryan shook her head. "Would you mind bringing me home now?" She needed time to contemplate the fact that PID was after her father for Chad's beating. And to determine what, if anything, she was going to do about it.

She followed behind Shep to the front desk, and stopped when she saw the witness, a hooker she had previously prosecuted. She was a stout woman, and looked more like the checkout girl at the Wal-Mart than a prostitute. She smiled a silver-toothed grin when she saw Ryan.

"Ms. Ryan, I didn't know you was the po-po now. How you been, baby?"

Ryan shook her head. "No, Cherry, I'm still with the D.A.'s Office. You saw the body get dumped?"

Cherry continued smiling. "Yes ma'am, I sure did. And if that body was Tyrone Cleeves like everybody saying, whoever shot him up did the whole project a big favor. That man one crazy son of a bitch."

"Did you see the guy?"

Cherry nodded. "But just for a second. I was out looking for a little business, and he pulled over. First I thought he a customer and I was about to go to the car. But he look real nervous and start dragging something out the trunk. I knew he wasn't looking for no Big Cherry, so I got my happy ass out of there. Sorry I can't tell you no more than he was a white man, short and sort of chunky. There was another girl out there might have seen something. I think she stay in my building. If somebody could give me a ride back, I could maybe help you find her."

Sean nodded and turned to the sergeant. "I'll get Jackson to ride with me."

Ryan walked down the hallway toward the front door of the station, disappointed that Cherry hadn't seen more.

Shep stepped in front of her and held the door open. "You're friends with a hooker named Cherry?"

"We're not friends. I reduced her charges a couple of times." She started down the steps of the station, walking in the direction of Shep's car.

Shep followed behind her. "I don't believe you gave a hooker a deal."

She stopped at the corner, next to Shep's Corvette. "My goal in life is not to put everybody in jail. Dangerous criminals and drug addicts belong off the street. I don't care so much about wasting jail space on hookers."

He opened her door. "I just always thought of you as a rule follower."

"I guess you don't know as much about me as you thought." She pulled out a cigarette and frowned into the pack. It was nearly empty. She put the cigarette back in.

"Maybe you're right." He shut her door and got in on the driver's side.

Ryan pulled out the cigarette and lit it anyway. She could always buy another pack tomorrow. If she had to.

They drove in silence back to her house, Ryan not sure whether she was more embarrassed about the personal information she had just revealed to the men at the station, or more worried about the fact that her father would soon hear all about it.

"We're going to find out who's doing this," Shep said finally, breaking the silence as they turned on her street.

Ryan sighed. "I'm more worried about what daddy is going to do when he sees the Sarge's notes on me. I mean, how would you feel knowing about your daughter's sex life?"

Shep stopped the car in front of her house. "You're blowing this way out of proportion," he said, opening the door and getting out. "You're an adult. He must know you have sex."

Ryan felt her face turn red. "But some of that stuff, especially the stuff about Chad, no parent wants to hear that."

Shep was quiet as he walked her up the front steps to the door.

She unlocked the door and started to walk in.

"I think your dad is just going to be worried about you, Ry. I don't think he's going to be mad," Shep said. "And for the record, I think Chad Lejeune is the biggest fool in the world." He stepped away quickly, almost running down the front porch steps.

As Sean and his crew made their way through the project, calls of, "Five-O!" rang out, warning everyone in the vicinity of the police presence. Nevertheless, the six officers knocked on every door of Cherry's building, unable to find the second hooker. They then tried the three buildings immediately adjacent to the corner where Cleeves was found, talking to the few people who would talk to them, getting absolutely no useful information. No one heard the gunshots, and no one saw anything.

Sean was ready to give up, and wished the press shared his sentiment. He couldn't understand why his sister enjoyed playing up to them. But then, even as close as they were, he always had a little trouble understanding his sister.

Suzie Chin was still at the crime scene, and Sean went to check on her before he left. Suzie had carefully kept the note from Cleeves' body hidden from the press, but the bow couldn't be bagged before the press had seen it, the news cameras greedily recording the blood-encrusted decoration. The only positive thing was that the press hadn't learned that Ryan was the intended recipient. Sean hoped they would catch a break before anybody outside of the circle of police found out.

Cleeves had been shot twenty-five times, and it was apparent from the stippling or pattern of gunpowder on his clothing that the shots had been close range. Doug seemed doubtful that the ammunition could be traced. Ammo for AK's could be bought at any one of the numerous gun stores or pawn shops in the metro area, not to mention gun shows and the internet. And of course, ammunition was frequently stolen during the course of robberies.

At Sean's car, he and Suzie were stopped by an elderly white woman who could only be Eulah Mae Simpson. Stoop-shouldered, she was nearly as tall as Sean, who was 6'0", and easily outweighed his 185 pounds. She had a shock of white hair, cut in a masculine style, beady black eyes with tortoiseshell cat-eye glasses, and wore a thick purple terry cloth house robe with bright yellow galoshes.

Without preamble, she began her story. "Officers, the young man who lived in the apartment down the hall was murdered a year ago, and that place had been empty ever since." She peered closely at Suzie. "You know, this isn't exactly the kind of place for a little Asian girl. Some of these people are animals." Eulah Mae spoke with a deep, masculine voice that matched her physique.

"I've got that covered," Sean said, gently prodding her along. "Maybe you could tell me more about your problem."

"Well, a few months ago, one night after I went to bed, curtains went up in one of the apartments in my building, like somebody was moving in. I'm the only one left in the building, which is exactly how I like it, although I think the housing authority is just waiting for me to die or get murdered so they don't have to relocate me. Anyway, I called the housing office to see who moved in, but they refused to tell me. Said it's none of my business, if you can believe it. So this phantom is living in my building, but I've never seen him during the day. Sometimes he plays music real low at night, but that's it. I keep calling the housing authority, but they still won't tell me anything."

"So your problem is that the new person doesn't come outside during the day?" Sean asked. "You're not afraid of vampires, are you, Ms. Simpson?"

Eulah Mae's eyes went dark. "No, I am not afraid of vampires, young man. But anybody that doesn't come out during the daylight is certainly up to no good. I haven't seen any indication of drug dealing like the last fellow that lived there, but it's probably just a matter of time. I've knocked on his door a couple of times, planning on finding out exactly what he thinks he's doing there, but he never answers."

"Ma'am, unless you can point to some criminal activity you've actually seen, there's really nothing I can do," Sean said. He tried to be nice, but he had a murderer to catch and didn't have time to worry about some poor schmo who had the bad luck to live in the same building as Eulah Mae. "And it's probably not a real good idea to knock on somebody's door you don't know."

"Well, I'm just warning you, if that bastard gives me any trouble, you're going to find him sprayed all over the walls of the breezeway," Eulah Mae said, shaking her finger.

Sean was taken aback. "Excuse me?"

Eulah Mae opened her robe, revealing too much age-spotted wrinkled skin and a .45 caliber pistol strapped around her waist. "You didn't think I would walk across the project without protection, did you, Five-O?" she asked, with a dry, cackling laugh. "And I have a concealed handgun permit, in case you're wondering." She closed her robe and walked away.

Sean wasn't planning on making a report, but he jotted down a note to pass along to Shep, just to keep him informed.

11:00 A.M.

Later that morning, Ryan tried to figure out how she was going to make it to the weekend without getting more sleep. And she knew sleep would be hard to come by. Every time she tried, she saw images of the dead bodies, even the gang bangers she didn't care about. And when she did finally drift off just as the sun was rising, her father was in her dreams, handing Jasmine to Chad Lejeune with a smile, a bright red blood-soaked Christmas bow tied around her torso.

At least the morning had been uneventful so far. No press was waiting outside the courthouse, so no one had connected her to the homicides yet. The docket was almost complete and Ryan was thinking about going home during lunch for a nap when a clerk walked in and wordlessly handed Judge Jackson a file.

The judge glared at the clerk. "Why are you bringing me an add-on at eleven o'clock in the afternoon?"

The clerk shrugged, unconcerned. "It was transferred last week by Judge McAllister."

"So why wasn't this case on my docket?" the judge asked. "And why is it just being brought to me now?"

The clerk shrugged again. "We were going to put it on the docket for tomorrow but his attorney came in and said the 701 runs today."

While the judge began chastising the clerk for the late add-on, Bo Lambert walked in, followed by a young black woman. She sat in the first row while Bo walked up to Ryan.

"My rape case," he explained. "Durrell Wilson. His attorney came in screaming about his case not making the docket over here because the clerk's office was sitting on the transfer. I called for a jury so I could try it because the 701 runs today, but the jurors were released already."

Bo appeared nervous, and Ryan almost felt sorry for him. Even though the error technically wasn't Bo's fault, he should have realized the defense attorney would manage to get the case on the docket the day the 701 ran. And regardless of how she felt about Bo, she didn't want a rapist to get a second shot at his victim because of an administrative screw up.

The judge waved them up to the bench. "State, how are we going to handle this?" He looked at Bo.

"Your honor, I was just waiting for the case to make your docket. I'm ready to try it right now," Bo said.

"Not if he wants a jury trial," the judge said. "The jurors are gone. Why was this case transferred?"

"McCallister represented the defendant's sister on something in civil court years ago," Bo explained.

The judge glared at Bo. "So why did he wait almost two years to transfer the case?"

Bo shrugged. "I don't know, judge. I was just waiting for the clerk's office to put it on your docket so I could try it."

"Except that it didn't make the docket," the judge muttered. He turned to Donna. "Make sure Durrell Wilson gets brought up. Five minute recess."

When the judge went back into his chambers, Ryan grabbed Durrell Wilson's file and began thumbing through it. A second later, Rick walked in and began talking to Bo in a hushed tone. Ryan sat down at the state's table, trying to overhear what Rick was saying, but his voice was too low. Bo then went over to the young black woman, apparently the victim on the case, and began explaining the situation to her.

Rick walked over and sat down next to Ryan. "I heard one of your defendants took a hit this morning. I got called into a meeting with the D.A. about it first thing this morning."

"Oh yeah?" Ryan asked, wondering exactly where this was heading.

Rick lowered his voice. "I was going to tell you later today, but since I'm here now you might as well know. We're going to delay a decision on the Strike Force position until we see what's going on with Cleeves' murder."

Ryan stared. "Exactly what does Tyrone Cleeves have to do with the Strike Force spot?"

"Nothing," Rick's answer came quick. "But if it gets out that he was killed because you lost his case, well, it's just probably better for us to wait. It's not imperative we decide this week."

Ryan tried to keep the anger from her voice. Pissing off Rick would not help her. "So if this somehow makes the evening news, I'm going to get screwed out of Strike Force?"

"Ryan, you've still got my vote. You're doing good work." A compliment from Rick was rare, a highly prized commodity in the office. "It's just a timing issue. It shouldn't change anything in the long run."

Bo walked up, cutting off any response Ryan might have had. "The victim's upset. She understands that the clerk's office is at fault, but she's nearly hysterical knowing Wilson might get released today."

"I don't know what took so long to get this case to trial," Rick said with a harsh look at Bo. "I know McAllister is a slow section, but the state should never let a rape case get to the point of a 701. Come see me in my office when you get back."

Ryan tried not to feel smug about Bo's predicament. After all, she had just received praise for her work, while Bo had just gotten a lecture, albeit a short one.

Ryan opened Bo's files on Durrell Wilson again, noticing that Bo hadn't even bothered running a current rap sheet for the file. Every case was supposed to have an updated rap for each court date. On a hunch, Ryan used Donna's computer to access the NCIC system. The first thing listed on Durrell Wilson's rap sheet was a warrant for an open traffic violation. This was good news for Bo and his victim, and bad news for Durrell Wilson.

Ryan kept the discovery to herself. No sense letting Bo off the hook yet.

The judge took the bench after Durrell Wilson was finally brought up from the prison. "Mr. Wilson, where is your attorney?"

"Mr. Klegg in the hallway," Durrell Wilson said and looked over at the victim with a smile, displaying a sparkling diamond chip. "We ready for trial."

"Well, we can't call your case with him out in the hallway, can we now?" The judge waved his hands around impatiently. "Nero, go get Mr. Klegg."

A few seconds later, Bill Klegg walked in, a tall, round man with a receding hairline and an extravagant red nose. He looked like an alcoholic Humpty Dumpty.

"Your honor, the defense is ready to proceed to trial," Klegg said and put his briefcase down loudly on the defense table.

"Mr. Klegg, your case didn't make my docket today because of the negligence of the clerk's office. As a matter of fact, it wouldn't have made it as an add-on had you not personally gone into that office and had them pull the file. While I commend you on your diligence in representing your client, the jurors were already released for the day by the time the clerk alerted me to this case. Since there are no jurors tomorrow, the only thing I can do is set it for trial for Monday, when the jury will back. Unless of course you wish to proceed by bench trial."

"I don't mean to be a hard ass, your Honor," Klegg began, "but my client's 701 runs today. The law is clear that if a continuance is due to the court, the 701 is not interrupted."

The judge scowled. "You expect me to release your client on a 701 for a charge that carries a mandatory life sentence?"

"I not only expect it, I must insist upon it." Klegg wore a sly smile.

Bo had a look of panic on his face, as did his victim.

The judge looked at the victim as he spoke. "While I loathe doing this —" the judge began, but Ryan stood up.

"Judge Jackson," Ryan stopped him, waving the printout of the rap sheet in the air. "I have the defendant's rap sheet in my hand." She felt very *Law and Order* as she announced, "Mr. Wilson has an attachment for a traffic violation."

Klegg stared at the file, the smile frozen on his face. "What's that?"

"An attachment is similar to an arrest warrant, Mr. Klegg," Judge Jackson spoke slowly. "It's an order to hold a defendant until he appears before a judge, in this case, in traffic court."

"No, I know what an attachment is," Klegg sputtered. "Of course I know that. I meant, what's the violation?"

Ryan circled the open attachment on the rap sheet in red marker and held the page up for Klegg to see. "Mr. Wilson failed to appear for his traffic court date three months ago."

"Your honor, my client was incarcerated three months ago," Klegg began.

The judge interrupted him. "That's not my problem, Mr. Klegg."

"My client still gets released on his 701, right?" He didn't sound quite as confident now, and the smile was beginning to show strain at the corners of his mouth, twitching slightly.

"Well, Counselor, regardless of whether your client is released on the 701 today, he'll still have to wait in jail for the traffic warrant."

"I can make bond on the traffic," Klegg said, more to his client than the court.

The judge looked at Durrell Wilson. "I'm sure you can. Mr. Wilson, I'm going to have you transferred to traffic court at the convenience of the sheriff's office so they can deal with the attachment. When the traffic division is finished with you, they'll bring you back so I can rule on the 701."

"Your honor, that could take until tomorrow afternoon," Klegg argued. "You'll be gone by the time the traffic court handles the matter."

"Assuming that's true, then your client will remain in jail over the weekend and make my Monday docket. The 701 will become moot when the case is tried then."

"Your honor, my client is entitled to bond on the traffic violation," Klegg argued.

"In case you haven't noticed, Mr. Klegg, this is not traffic court. The traffic court judge can set the bond when he's transferred. And then your client will be sent back here. We'll rearrange the whole docket Monday to try this rape. This should resolve the 701 issue."

"But your honor, my client should be released today for this charge." Klegg looked around the courtroom as if trying to find someone who would agree with him. "I have to insist you set a bond on the traffic violation and then rule on the 701."

"Oh, you insist, do you?" The judge glowered. "Okay, Mr. Klegg, I didn't realize you were the boss. I'm going to set a bond on his traffic violation. What's the charge?"

"DWI," Ryan answered.

"And what are his priors?"

"You can't consider his priors on a traffic violation," Klegg stated.

"I am setting a bond in criminal district court. That means I can."

Ryan read off the rap sheet. "Nineteen arrests, ten felony, nine misdemeanor. Prior convictions for forcible rape, indecent behavior with a juvenile and cocaine possession."

"And, Your Honor," Bo spoke up, "the defendant has made repeated threatening calls to the victim from jail, calls which are recorded and have already been ruled admissible at trial by Judge McAllister. "

The judge nodded slightly. "I see. Well, you are absolutely right, Mr. Klegg, your client is entitled to a bond on the DWI. If you can make bond on the DWI in the next three hours that I will be in this building, then we'll get everybody back over here and I will be forced to rule on the 701." The victim gasped, and the judge held up his hand, pausing for a moment. Ryan had a feeling she knew exactly where he was going. "Bond is set at one million dollars for DWI."

Ryan smiled. She couldn't stop herself. At least she didn't laugh out loud.

"Your Honor, I strenuously object!" Klegg jumped up and slapped the table. "That bond is outrageous and excessive, and there is no way my client can afford that."

"Do not beat on my furniture, Mr. Klegg." The judge shot him a dour look. "And if your client cannot afford the bond, then he stays in jail. That doesn't happen to be my problem or concern. And I'm putting a hold on the bond so that it can not be reduced by another judge until your client appears before the traffic court judge. And then I am personally going to call over to traffic court and get your client a court date for the end of next week. In the meantime, your client will be tried in here on Monday."

"This is a travesty of justice!" Klegg was used to being theatrical, but he had never tried a case in front of Judge Jackson. Ryan sat on the edge of the desk, wishing she had popcorn to munch while this scene from the Living Theater played out.

"Two million dollars," Judge Jackson said. "Bond is now set at two million dollars. Cash only. No property, no ROR."

"What?" Klegg yelled, slapping the table again, and now Wilson was standing as well.

"Ten million dollars!" Judge Jackson pounded his gavel several times. "Bond is set at ten million dollars!" The judge stood up and leaned over the bench, pointing a crooked finger at Klegg. "And one more word from you, Klegg, and you'll be joining your client in jail. You never should have pushed me to set that bond. Your client can thank you for that."

"I ain't getting out?" Durrell Wilson asked, turning to Klegg. "Mother fucker, you was paid five thousand dollars to get me out."

"Mr. Wilson, I suggest you invoke your right against self-incrimination and save your comments for when you are out of this Court's presence," the judge warned him. "Anything you say in this courtroom can be used against you."

"Fuck you," Wilson yelled. "My time ran today, you got no right to keep me in jail. Klegg, you better fix this shit right now."

"Mr. Wilson, you will appear back in this courtroom in two weeks for a contempt hearing." The judge scowled fiercely. "This is not the 'hood', young man, this is my courtroom. And I demand that everyone who sets foot in here behaves with decorum and respect. Deputy, give him a subpoena in case he bonds out before Monday."

Ryan did laugh out loud this time.

Wilson pointed to the judge. "You fucked up, judge." He then turned to Ryan. "And you too, Ho. You should have stayed out of my business. You both gonna be sucking my dick when I get out of here. Ain't no bars strong enough to keep this nigger down." Wilson continued ranting, and Klegg suddenly looked scared. Wilson tried to move, but was stopped by three deputies, who had no trouble subduing a man in shackles and handcuffs.

"That's another contempt charge, Mr. Wilson," the judge said. "Mr. Klegg, you would be wise to warn your client to control himself in my presence. And I am going to personally speak to the District Attorney about charges for the threat against me and Ms. Murphy."

Wilson had his face pressed into the fluffy carpet and couldn't have spoken if he wanted to. The deputies finally picked him up from the ground and carried him to the courtroom holding cell.

"Mr. Klegg, if I ever hear another outburst from you in my courtroom, you will become a guest of the state for as long as the law allows. Am I making myself clear enough for you? Now, if there's nothing else, court is adjourned." The judge pounded the gavel and stalked back to his chambers.

"You really saved me on that one," Bo said and pushed his glasses back up with a relieved smile. "Why don't I treat you and your junior to lunch? It's the least I can do."

As much as Ryan didn't want to break bread with Bo Lambert, lunching with Bo would give her the opportunity to rub the Gendusa case in Bo's face.

"I'll put my car on Tulane," Bo said, waiting for an answer.

"We'll meet you out front," Ryan answered as Mike began packing up the files.

Ryan had just walked into Della's, a soul food restaurant across Broad Street, when her cell phone rang. The caller ID showed Sean's cell. She turned to Bo and Mike. "Excuse me, I've got to take this."

"Yeah." She walked outside to escape the noise inside the small restaurant.

"Did you see the twelve o'clock news?" Without waiting for a response, he continued, "Conchita Beliza did a story about Devon Jones."

"How did she find out about him? And what did she say?"

"She didn't give his name, only that there was a witness to Smith's murder and that the witness was the juvenile brother of a drug arrest made the following night. And I was about to ask you how the press had gotten the information."

"How should I know?" Then she realized what he was getting at. "You think I leaked something like that to the press?"

"Not that many people knew about it, and you do have a relationship with Halley."

"Go to hell, Sean," she said and hung up on him. As if she would tell Chance anything about the case. And Conchita Beliza was Chance Halley's competition. Even Sean should have known that the two reporters worked for competing stations. If Ryan had given the information to Chance, Conchita wouldn't have been the one doing the story. Sean should have checked out his own facts before accusing people. She wondered if this was how some of Sean's suspects felt.

She was about to walk back into Della's when her phone rang again.

Thinking it was Sean calling back, she answered and said, "I hope this is your apology."

"What did I do?" Shep asked. "Or should I apologize in advance for something I'm going to do?"

Ryan didn't try to hide the disappointment in her voice. "Oh, it's you."

"Glad to hear your voice too, princess."

She sighed. "I thought you were Sean. We just had an argument."

"Sean will get over it. Where are you? I looked for you at the office, but they said you were still in court. Then I walked over to court and they said you had just left. I have something for you. Are you on your way home?"

"I'm at Della's."

"I don't suppose you're alone? I could meet you there."

"No. I'm having lunch with Bo." She peered through the plate glass window and saw Mike already talking to the waitress.

"Oh." Shep didn't say anything for a moment. "I can call you later if I'm interrupting something."

"You're not interrupting anything, trust me. I'd rather be eating alone. What do you have? And if you're calling to accuse me of giving the press information on Devon, Sean already did that. And as usual he doesn't know what he's talking about."

"That's not what I'm calling about. But what are you doing with that douche-bag Lambert? I thought you had better taste than that."

"Mike's here too. Bo's treating us because I saved his ass on a 701 today." She explained to him what happened with Durrell Wilson.

"I fail to see how having lunch with Bo Lambert is reward for saving his ass. First he gets you threatened in court by a rapist, then you get stuck eating with him? Doesn't seem like a fair trade to me."

"You're not jealous, are you, Chapetti?" she asked, an involuntary smile springing to her lips.

"No. I'm sure I can have lunch with Lambert whenever I want," he answered. "Can you meet me at your house?"

"Now? I didn't even order yet."

"Eat at home, unless you're really in the mood for chitlins and pig's feet. That stuff will kill you anyway, clogs your arteries."

"You'll have to pick me up. My car's still at court."

"I'll be there in two minutes."

Ryan walked back inside. "Sorry guys, I gotta bail. Got a detective on the way about a case."

"Which case?" Mike asked. "Not Gendusa, huh?"

Ryan looked for a reaction from Bo, but he had none, the usual blank expression on his face.

"No, just Chapetti. He needs to talk to me about the case from last night," she lied. "Some new information just came in."

"Anything important?" Bo asked, seeming interested.

Ryan gave him a bored look. "Nothing earth shattering."

"Rain check, then?" Bo asked.

"Oh, most definitely," Ryan answered with a fake smile.

Ten minutes later, Shep finally pulled up.

"It's about time," she told him, just as he had told her four days ago. Had it only been four days? This had been the longest week of her life.

"Here," he said, and he threw a po-boy wrapped in white paper to her as she got in the Vette. "Fried shrimp, dressed. I was going to eat it myself, but since you're missing lunch, I figured I'd let you have it. I know how mean you are when you're hungry."

"Thanks," Ryan said as she opened the wrapper and tore into the sandwich. The outside of the French bread was warm and crusty, the inside soft, filled with crispy fried shrimp and crunchy lettuce and tomatoes. There was just enough Tabasco to give it a kick.

He handed her a fountain Coke. "I had fries, but I ate them on the way."

She took another bite of the po-boy, realizing for the first time that she hadn't eaten anything substantial in days. She took a sip of Coke as her eyes watered from a glop of hot sauce. "I thought you didn't like Tabasco on your shrimp."

Gilbert's smile appeared. "I don't. I really ordered it for you."

She couldn't help but smile back. Shep could definitely be charming when he wanted to be. She took another big bite, wiping ketchup off of her chin with the back of her hand.

Shep handed her a paper napkin. "You look sort of cute when you're attacking food. You get that same look on your face when you're going after a defense attorney."

She blushed slightly, remembering his comment last night about Chad. After all, they were on the way to her apartment, where they would be entirely alone. She looked at the body underneath the badge. She wasn't made of steel. "So, what do you have to show me?"

"Be patient. You'll see when we get to your house. Any trouble ditching Lambert?"

She shook her head. "But I feel sorry for Mike. He got stuck eating with Bo by himself. I think he was hoping I was going to invite him along."

"I'm glad you didn't," Shep said, and then added quickly, "This isn't something you would want anyone else to see." He refused to tell her anything else, and a few minutes later, they were in front of her house.

Shep carried an expandable file up the front steps. As soon as Ryan opened the front door, he handed it to her.

She could tell from the case number on the file that it was an older file from the D.A.'s office. Patti's name was typed on a label under the number.

"Shep?" She slowly looked down at the expandable, afraid to look at the documents inside. "What is this?"

He made no move to walk further into the house. "The story of your kidnapping, everything that happened to you, is all in there."

"How did you get this?" she asked, not quite believing him. "This is a D.A. file."

"The police file was missing. Your father probably has it stashed somewhere," he answered. "But the closed file from your office was in the D.A.'s storage facility out by the airport. I made a phone call to have it pulled and then I picked it up. You could have done that at any time, you know."

She looked down at the file in her hands. Finally, she said, "Do I really want to know what's in here?"

Shep seemed to understand what she was really asking. "I don't know if you do or not, Ryan. But I can tell you that your family isn't keeping anything bad from you. I promise."

"Can you leave this with me?" She walked inside and put the file on the coffee table, leaving Shep behind in the doorway. "I want to take my time looking through it on my own, if that's okay?"

"It's been closed for twenty-four years. Nobody will even care that the file is gone." He turned to leave, but stopped and asked, "You want a ride back?"

She shook her head. "I'll get a ride back later." She walked back to the front door and touched his arm gingerly, not quite sure what to say. "Thanks. I really do appreciate this."

"If you want to talk later, give me a call." He looked down at her hand on his arm, and brushed a strand of hair away from her face, touching her cheek in an intimate gesture. For the first time, she noticed his hands, big and wide, with long fingers and short, neat nails. And then, with his hand still on her cheek, he brushed his lips lightly across her forehead, before saying, "Take care of yourself, okay?" He walked quickly to his car, leaving her in the doorway with her heart racing.

Ryan watched as Shep drove off, wanting to contemplate what had just occurred, but also wanting to find out about what had happened to her all those years ago. Finally, the past won out over the present, and she went back to the file. Breathe, she ordered herself, waiting for her heart to start beating at a normal pace, the whole while thinking about what Edie always said about men with big hands. She closed her eyes for a second, still feeling Shep's lips on her forehead, and exhaled loudly.

When she finally opened her eyes, she forced herself to focus on the contents of the brown expandable in front of her. Inside was a green file, indicating it was a second class felony, which meant the crime charged was punishable at hard labor. Ryan grabbed the police report from inside the file.

She skimmed the report quickly, authored by now-retired Detective Ribson. A call had been made by NOPD officer Kelly Murphy that his sister-in-law, a known heroin addict and prostitute, had kidnapped his four-year-old daughter, Victoria Ryan Murphy, known as Ryan, from her uptown home. Patricia Ryan had gone into the home under false pretenses of discussing a medical problem with her sister, Kelly Murphy's wife Angela Murphy, who was a registered nurse.

When Angela left the room to make coffee, Patricia Ryan grabbed the child and left the residence in an older model blue Chevy station wagon. Seven-year-old Sean Murphy immediately alerted Angela, who observed the car as it fled the area. Angela wrote down the license plate number and called her husband. A warrant was immediately issued for the arrest of Patricia Ryan.

Ryan's memory was jogged by the report. She recalled running out of her parent's house with Patti, and Patti saying it was going to be a funny joke on her mama. And then she started to feel that something was horribly wrong when Patti made her get into the car and then drove away. She had started crying, and had fallen asleep in the back seat.

That was the end of the initial report. There was one supplemental report, also authored by Ribson, and contained the same item number. The item number on the police report was assigned as soon as a crime was reported, and indicated the month of the crime by a letter, A through L corresponding with January through December, a dash and then a two-digit number indicating the year, and then a unique number assigned for every crime committed that year.

The supplemental report was longer. Two hours after the kidnapping, an anonymous tip was called in that a child matching Ryan's description was seen with a woman inside an apartment in the St. Thomas Development. The tip gave the building number, but not the apartment number. A task force went to the building, and searched every apartment until they found the child in one of the units. Patricia Ryan was present in the apartment as well.

Ryan was painfully jolted back in time, sitting on a lumpy gold sofa, shrinking back into the worn cloth, trying to avoid the roaches scurrying around her.

She was crying, because she was afraid of the nasty bugs, because she thought she was going to be in trouble with her mama, and because she knew the man talking to Patti was a bad man, the kind her mama and daddy had always warned her about. He was scary, even though he was smiling, and sat so close to her she could smell his stinky breath.

In the corner of her eye, there was a flicker. Somebody else was there, somebody who didn't scare her.

And then she was back in the present, wiping tears from her face. She found her place in the supplemental report, deciding she needed to find out what had happened to her back then more than she needed to have a breakdown right now. There would always be time for a breakdown later.

Patti told the police that she was Ryan's biological mother, and insisted that she was only trying to get her daughter back, claiming that Kelly Murphy had planted heroin on her when she was pregnant, so that she would be forced to give the child up to him while she was in prison.

A neighbor, however, disputed the story, reporting that she had been sitting on the stoop in front of the apartment when she overheard Patti arguing with two drug dealers about trading Ryan for heroin.

Ryan put the police report down and picked up the medical reports. They indicated the victim was four years old, alert and active. A rape kit was performed, with no evidence of trauma or sexual abuse found. The hymen was still intact, and the victim indicated no sexual or physical abuse had occurred. A lab report in the file indicated no evidence of semen or any other unknown fluids was found.

Ryan remembered the rape kit well. She had thought she was being punished for playing the joke on her mother. Why else would they have done that to her? Even today, her gynecologist had to talk her through pap smears and pelvic exams so she didn't panic.

Ryan looked at the back of the file, which contained notations made by the various prosecutors who handled the case. The tracking indicated Patti had received twenty years for second-degree kidnapping.

Well, at least some of Ryan's questions were answered now. She had been missing for several hours, not abused or molested, and all so that her prostitute biological mother could score heroin. She refused to add Patti's allegations to the equation. Nobody would have ever had to plant heroin on Patti. And clearly the woman was lying about why she had kidnapped Ryan. The neighbor who called the police had no reason to fabricate a story, and Ryan recalled the other men being present, although at the time she hadn't been aware that they were bargaining for her.

She decided she would hold onto the file for a while, look through it more carefully and maybe listen to the taped statement when she felt better able to focus. She started to put the file away when she noticed a yellow sticky note stuck to the inside of the expandable. The note was in Shep's handwriting, and said *Patti Ryan, Upperline Convalescent Home, Rm. 111, South Hall.* Interesting, since Patti was supposed to be dead.

Ryan reached for the phone and called Shep's cell, which had somehow managed to find its way to number five on her speed dial. He answered on the first ring.

"Shep, Upperline Convalescent. What does that mean?"

"That's where Patti lives. I'm sure you have questions that the file doesn't answer."

Ryan let his words sink in for a second. "Would you want to ask your mother questions if you had the chance?"

"Ryan, it doesn't matter what I want or what I would do. This is a choice you should get to make."

"Did you know that mama volunteers at Upperline Convalescent Home every Saturday? Do you think that's some crazy coincidence?"

"I don't know, Ry. That's something you need to talk about with her."

She started to hang up, and instead asked, "You can't get in trouble for getting this stuff for me, can you?"

"Only if your dad finds out."

"You definitely don't need to worry about that. I'll talk to you later."

It was almost 5:00, no point in going back to the office. That was one nice thing about being a prosecutor. Nobody bothered keeping track of the assistants as long as they showed up in court when they were supposed to.

Ryan thought about going to the convalescent home to meet Patti. Shep was right. She did have questions for the woman, for instance, why Patti cared so little for the child she had given birth to that she was willing to trade her for heroin. The captain and her mother had led her to believe that Patti had died in prison, although they had never actually said anything definitive. Meeting Patti now would answer the last few questions Ryan had about her biological mother, and then she could close that book forever.

But then Ryan had a better idea. She would wait until Saturday to go the Upperline home, and show up when Angie would be there. That would teach her mother to keep secrets from her. She was too wired right now anyway to deal with meeting the woman who tried to sell her for drugs, and the tequila bottle was beckoning to her from the kitchen table.

Her mind was racing in too many different directions, full of thoughts she didn't want to face. She wanted to confront her parents for making her believe Patti was dead, but couldn't as long as her father was out of town. She was too afraid to think about Shep, not ready to believe the possibility that he might have feelings for her. Her interest in the Gendusa file had waned for the time being. She tried to contemplate who might be killing people for her, but didn't like the possibility that

119

kept suggesting itself.

Tequila was definitely not going to clear things up, but maybe it would help her forget long enough so she could get some much needed sleep. On her way to the kitchen, she noticed the light on her computer in the study blinking, letting her know she had an e-mail from Ty Crowley.

Ty Crowley was a reporter with the Times Picayune newspaper. Ryan had met him at a fund-raiser she had attended with her family, and was somewhat entertained by the fact that he had dated her mother in high school, making him an instant enemy of her father. But Ryan liked him, and every now and then would clue him into something happening at Criminal Court or the D.A.'s office that she wanted brought to the public's attention. She had been quoted as "an inside source" or "an unnamed source" more than once by Ty. Of course, she couldn't tell anyone she was the guilty party. A privacy clause was part of every prosecutor's employment contract.

Ryan had a separate e-mail account exclusively for contact with Ty. She hurriedly got on-line and pulled up her e-mail, knowing Ty was the type of computer nerd who spent more time online than off. She saw the single-word, URGENT.

Before she could respond, she heard the bling of an instant message. She was right. Ty was on the net. The message appeared on her screen.

Where y'at? How's your dad? No life-threatening illness, I suppose?

Not like Ty to get straight to the point. She typed back. *Still happily married. What's so urgent?*

A minute later, her thumb went in her mouth when she read Ty's response.

I got a call at the station from someone using one of those voice distortion devices. He said those project murders were presents for you, but the police are trying to cover it up. Is this some crack pot or what?

She quickly typed her response.

Or what. You're not going to print it, are you?

A few seconds later she found out.

Of course. He'll go somewhere else if I don't.

She quickly typed back.

When?

She looked down at her thumb and noticed it was bleeding. Damn. Now she would have to get used to chewing another finger until her thumb healed.

Not sure. I have to run it by the editor first.

Ryan took that to mean it would be in tomorrow morning's edition. She typed her response.

I'm going to call the Sgt. and let him know what you've told me. Maybe he can change your mind.

A few seconds later, she got Ty's answer.

I know you law enforcement types consider the Constitution a hindrance, but I worship it like the Bible. And I'm not scared of the police department.

Ryan immediately replied.

I know one member of the police department who should scare the hell out of you. I'll be sure to tell daddy you said hello.

She called the sergeant and told him about the killer's contact with Ty Crowley.

"Why didn't this psychopath just rent a goddamn billboard on Canal Street?" the sergeant muttered. "That's just perfect. An asshole reporter with real news. You got his number?"

Ryan gave him Ty's phone number, knowing he probably wouldn't take the call.

"And incidentally," the sergeant added, "we haven't been able to get Lejeune or Espinito in yet. Espinito is supposedly working on something important and can't be reached today, and Lejeune told us to kiss his ass. Anything you can give us to make either one of them a likelier suspect? Something that might equal probable cause for a search warrant?"

"Sorry, I really can't think of anything. Too bad this isn't televison. On *Law and Order* they would just drag them both to the station."

The sergeant snorted. "On *Law and Order* I could get a warrant for Lejeune based upon that rap commercial. Did you know he has a court date set tomorrow for hitting a girl?"

"No I didn't." The phone started beeping, letting Ryan know the battery was low.

"And Lejeune has had three other assault and battery complaints filed against him in municipal court in the last year. All of them were dismissed by the City Attorney."

While the D.A.'s Office prosecuted misdemeanors and felonies, the City Attorney's Office handled all traffic and municipal violations.

"Of course the charges were dismissed. One of the partners at his law firm is also an Assistant City Attorney," Ryan answered. Unlike Assistant District Attorneys, Assistant City Attorneys were allowed to have private practices. "And maybe you should try bugging one of those girls. If they're mad because Chad pulled a favor to get the cases booted, they'll probably talk. Maybe one of them will know something."

The sergeant didn't respond.

"You still there?" she asked.

"Ryan, I didn't mention that the victims on his municipals were female."

"Well, weren't they?"

"Yes, they were. But I didn't tell you that. Babe, are you sure there's not something you want to tell me about Lejeune?"

"I'm positive."

She hung up quickly, worn out.

She was so tired, in fact, she wouldn't even need tequila to help her get to sleep. And if she showered and went to bed right now, she could get a full eleven hours, providing no homicide or rape calls came in.

She stood under the hot stream of water, and wondered if she should have set the alarm. The cop on duty outside, Dubuc, would catch anybody trying to break in, so she really didn't have anything to worry about. She rushed through the shower anyway, still nervous, and was almost finished when the ringing of the phone made her jump. She stepped out of the shower, shaking her head at her jumpiness, and answered the call on the bedroom cordless.

"Yeah."

"Did you like my gift?" The voice was distorted.

"Who is this?" Ryan asked, her heart speeding up.

"I saw you last night looking at my present. I knew you'd be happy."

"Why are you doing this?" she asked, trying to get him talking, hoping he would say something to give her a clue to his identity.

"You'll know soon enough." He hung up.

Ryan ran back into the bathroom and grabbed a towel, trying to control her shaking. Before she could dress, the phone rang again.

It was Shep. "Busy?"

"Kind of. I was just talking to the killer. He said he saw me last night."

"Shit. At least we might have finally gotten a break on this," he said, keeping his voice low. "Sean told me not to mention anything, but Suzie pulled a print from Jeremiah's wallet. The print belongs to a man named Travis Dalton. If we get Dalton, this thing is solved, even if we have to deal him to get whoever else is involved. I'm going to Magistrate to get warrants signed now."

"Good. Will you let me know what happens?"

"I'll stop by when I'm finished," he answered. "If you want me to."

So much for catching up on her sleep.

An hour later, tired of waiting to hear from Shep, Ryan finally caved in and answered the call of the tequila bottle. She was on the third shot when the phone rang again.

"Ryan, Chance Halley."

"I can't give you a statement when I'm off the clock, either, Mr. Halley. You'll still have to speak to Ms. Vera." The tequila was just beginning to warm her chest. "And how in the hell did you get my phone number?"

"I didn't call for a statement," he said, ignoring her question. "I have something to give you. Can we meet somewhere?"

"What's in it for you?" She tried not to be too suspicious, but she couldn't help but think he was pulling a reporter trick.

"Future information. When this story breaks."

"And if I say no?"

"I'd still give you the tape. Because regardless of how you feel about the press, I really am a nice guy."

"Tape?" Her right eye twitched and her thumb found its way into her mouth. She winced as she tasted blood.

"Videotape. And I promise, I only watched as much as necessary. The second I saw you —"

"What exactly is on this tape?" she interrupted.

Chance hesitated. "It's you and some guy."

It was enough to convince Ryan. "Can you bring it here? I don't have my car."

"I'll be there in fifteen minutes."

Ryan paced in her living room, Chance's words playing over in her head. You and some guy. What guy would she be on a videotape with, and doing what? It had just dawned her that Chance hadn't asked for her address when she heard his car pull up.

She opened the front door and waved at Dubuc as Chance looked around nervously and slowly approached the porch. She couldn't tell whether his hesitation was due to Dubuc's glare in his direction or facing Ryan with the tape.

Chance grabbed her hand at the front door. "You look even more beautiful than the last time I saw you."

Ryan glanced down dubiously at her ripped boxer shorts and stained tank top before grabbing the tape from his hand. She didn't know who had taped her doing what, but she was damn sure going to find out. Chance put his hand on her arm before she could get the door shut.

"I don't know exactly what to say in a situation like this, but if you want to talk later or anything, here." He handed her his business card.

She noticed he had written his home number on it.

"How exactly did you get this tape?" she asked, not bothering to hide her mistrust.

"It was mailed to me at the TV station, no return address. Not that I could divulge a source."

"It's only a source if you use the information. Should I expect to see myself on the ten o'clock news?"

He shook his head. "Not with FCC regulations. The station would lose its license for sure for showing what's on that tape."

She prodded him for more information. She didn't believe Chance was the killer, but he might know more than he was letting on. "How did you get the information that I was linked to the first two victims?"

"Anonymous call," he admitted reluctantly. "Some guy with a voice disguiser called me right before the press conference. He told me to ask the question. But honestly, Ryan, I didn't really think there was anything to it."

"Not to cut this conversation short, but I'm sure you'll understand if I want to watch this right now."

Ryan closed the door before Chance had an opportunity to argue, and put the tape in the VCR. When the picture began playing on the television, she gasped, and then stood spellbound, watching until it ended in a screen of fuzzy static and white noise. She turned the tape off and reached for the tequila bottle, tears streaming down her face.

At 11:00 p.m., Ryan woke up on the sofa to the sound of the phone ringing, a burned out cigarette hanging from her fingers.

The cigarette slipped to the floor as she reached for the phone. "Yeah." Her head was throbbing, and for a second, she couldn't remember what had happened, or how she had come to be sleeping in the living room.

"Ryan, it's Bo Lambert. I didn't wake you, did I?"

"No," she lied, not sure why she didn't want to admit to Bo that she was asleep. "I'm reading a file."

"Sorry to interrupt. I just thought you would want to know that Durrell Wilson was released from OPP."

"What?" She sat up too quickly, and tried to ignore the stabbing pain that shot outward from the center of her head. "How did he get out of jail?" She rubbed her temples with one hand.

"They're still trying to figure that out. It looks like some kind of paperwork screw up."

"Does your victim know?"

"Yes. They're putting a patrol car at her house for now. After the scene in court, I figured I should let you know."

"Thanks," she said, and hung up. She noticed the pile of ashes on the floor, and thought it was a miracle that she hadn't set the house on fire.

Her eyes went back to the television, and then to the tequila bottle, which was now empty. No wonder her head was about to explode. Only one cure for that. She went back into the kitchen to look for another bottle of tequila.

Unable to find any more tequila, she started on a bottle of wine. The numbness might take a while to get back, but she would do the best she could. She turned the tape back on again, torturing herself by watching the full twenty minutes. She was in the process of rewinding to watch it again when she heard a car door slam, and a few seconds later, a knock on the door. She turned off the VCR and TV and let Shep in.

Shep was not expecting to find the mess that greeted him at the door. Ryan held a wine bottle in her hand, and had obviously been drinking for quite a while. Her eyes were red and swollen, her cheeks mottled and tear stained.

"What happened?" he asked, starting to panic. "Dubuc said Halley stopped by. Did he do something to you? I will kill that little prick."

Ryan surprised him by laughing a crazy, mirthless laugh. She shook her head at him and opened her mouth to speak, but instead started crying.

Shep put his arms around her just as he had the last time she had broken down in front of him, and led her to the same spot on the sofa.

"Chance Halley didn't do anything," Ryan said, and took a long swallow from the wine bottle.

Shep took the bottle from her hand, noticing the burned out cigarette and ashes on the floor, as well as the empty bottle of tequila on the coffee table. "Would you please tell me what happened?"

"I've got to go to the bathroom," she said suddenly, and stumbled down the hall.

Five minutes later, she was out, her face washed and her hair brushed. When she sat next to him, he detected the scent of Crest.

"Did you know Durrell Wilson was released from OPP?" she asked him.

"No, I didn't," he answered, frowning. "Is that why you're so upset?"

She shook her head.

He pressed his hand against her cheek. "I can't fix it if you don't tell me what's wrong."

"Somebody mailed a video to Chance," she said finally, looking down. "I don't want to discuss the specifics, but the tape involves me and Chad."

He lifted her chin so he could see her face, his heart rate quickening. "Are we talking about a sex tape?"

Her answer was barely audible. "Maybe."

"Shit." He recalled her earlier assertion that Chad hadn't been able to perform during sex, and wondered why Chad would have taped that. "And that's why you're so upset? Because he videotaped the two of you?"

She shook her head. "I'm worried there might be more tapes. I'm thinking about going to Chad's to look for them."

Shep jumped up before he realized it. "Absolutely not. You are not going anywhere near Lejeune."

"I could go when he's not home." She sprung up next to Shep, grabbing his arm. "I could pick the lock, look for the tapes and get out. He'd never know I was there."

"Exactly how many locks have you picked, Ryan? Any?"

"No." She collapsed back on the sofa, tears rolling down her cheeks. "But it can't be that difficult. They do it on TV all the time."

"You really think he's got more tapes of you?" He sat next to her again, wiping the tears from her face with the bottom of his shirt.

"Maybe. I'm not sure." She looked down at the pile of ashes on the floor, a mixture of shame and sadness on her face.

"Babe, you know you can't break into his apartment. It's too risky. Not to mention illegal."

She clutched his arm, a look of desperation on her face. "Shep, the Sarge is looking hard at Chad. It's just a matter of time before he manages to get a search warrant. If Chad does have other tapes of me, they'll be taken as evidence. I can't take a chance that daddy or Sean or the guys at the station would ever see me on a tape like this one."

He nodded in agreement. "You're right. The whole squad would see those tapes, regardless of what your father might think." He scratched his head. "Okay. Is this tape marked or identified in some way? Or the tape jacket?"

She walked to the TV and popped the tape out of the machine.

"The tape has my first name and the date. I assume any others would be the same." She slid the tape back in the jacket and placed it on top of the television. "Why?"

"Powers said Lejeune has a preliminary hearing tomorrow for hitting his girlfriend. I'll go to his apartment and look through his video collection while he's at court."

"But you just said it's too risky," Ryan protested feebly.

"For you," he answered. "Trust me, I've got it covered. Now, does he have any type of alarm system?"

She shook her head. "He doesn't have an alarm, but he does have a security camera outside his front door that's motion-sensor activated. It records to a VCR in the living room. Shep, are you sure about this? If you get caught —"

He cut her off. "I won't. Do you want to hear about Travis Dalton?"

She nodded, a wave of relief washing over her face.

"We found a bloody baseball bat, five thousand dollars in cash and a bag of crack from the evidence room at criminal court. The only thing we didn't get was Dalton. His girlfriend showed up while we were executing the warrant and said she hadn't seen him all day. We explained to her the importance of him getting to the station before the cop he hooked up with gets to him first. She wasn't too impressed."

Ryan frowned. "How did Dalton manage to get his hands on crack from the evidence room?"

"I was going to ask your opinion on that. Who would have access to the evidence once it's logged in at the property room at court? I ran the item number on the bag and got the Docket Master from court. It's a case that was pled three months ago in McAllister's section."

Ryan grabbed the wine bottle and took a sip before Shep could stop her. "Property room guys. Any of the assistants who handled the case could have called up the evidence whenever they wanted. Defense attorneys on the case."

"Don't they have to sign something?"

She shrugged. "In theory. Things get so hectic sometimes that the property room just sends a runner to drop the evidence off. We sign for it when we call them to pick it back up. So if a runner brought the evidence down and no one ever called property to have it picked up, the clerks wouldn't have worried about. Or if the evidence room was closed when court let out, the D.A. would have to hold on to it until the next day. One night I had to bring home an assault rifle and a Schwegmann's grocery bag full of marijuana, because the evidence room was closed and the ad-hoc judge wouldn't let me lock it up in chambers."

Shep thought about that for a second. "So I could look at the prosecutors who were in McAllister's section when this case was open, and the defense attorneys for those cases. And the property people. I can't imagine anybody like that would be involved with Dalton." He squeezed her shoulder. "You going to put that bottle up now?"

"Not yet. I'm still conscious."

"I'm going to call Sean and see what he thinks about Durrell Wilson getting released."

He spoke to Sean for a few minutes and they decided that Sean would come over and spend the night, just to keep an eye on things. Shep didn't mention the tape to Sean, nor his intention to break into Chad Lejeune's apartment the next day and look for any others. Sean wouldn't understand. When Shep hung up, he turned to tell Ryan the plans for Sean coming over, expecting an argument.

Instead, he found her sleeping on the sofa, the wine bottle tipped over, spilling onto the hard wood floor. He righted the bottle, and looked over at the tape still resting on top of the television. It would only take a second to preview it, and Ryan would never know. He stared at the tape for a second, and then decided against it. If she didn't want him to know what was on the tape, he would respect that for now. If he decided later he needed to see what was on the tape, he would find a way.

Thinking Sean wouldn't appreciate finding his sister passed out drunk on the sofa, Shep carried her to her bedroom, and gently placed her in the bed. He covered her with a blanket and then went back into the living room to clean up the ashes and wine mess before Sean arrived.

FRIDAY

10:00 A.M.

Ryan massaged her temples, trying to ward off the headache that was threatening to strike while Mike conducted a motion hearing. The hangover was not as bad as she expected, and recalling the video, she was thankful she had passed out when she did. Otherwise, she would have drank even more.

Until she had seen what was on that tape, she hadn't really thought Chad could be involved in the murders. She knew without a doubt that Chad could be violent. But smacking around his girlfriend was completely different than slaying a bunch of strangers. And killing people to win her back, especially after the way the relationship ended, just didn't make sense. But then, she hadn't realized just how demented Chad was until she saw the tape.

The judge announced a fifteen minute recess.

Ryan took a migraine tablet out of her purse and used the break to go downstairs to buy a bottle of water from the snack vendor. She took the pill, gulping half of the twelve ounce bottle in one sip.

She hurried upstairs and was halfway back to her courtroom when she saw her oldest brother, Patrick, talking to Spence Badon of the day shift SID. She headed in their direction, but stopped and whirled around when she sensed someone staring at her from behind. She caught her breath as she found herself frozen, staring into the most chilling jade eyes she had ever seen.

The man was standing only three feet away, with a superior smile on his face. His blonde hair was fastidiously styled, and Ryan knew that he spent at least thirty minutes in front of the mirror getting his hair so perfect. He had soft features, smooth skin, and a too-long straight nose that didn't detract from his captivating good looks. His only imperfection was a slight limp, evidenced by the cane in his hand.

Patrick turned to hug her, said something she didn't make out, and then stopped in mid-sentence. Ryan just stared, recalling the last time she had seen the man who was now regarding her with blatant amusement.

"It's been a while," he said coolly, an arrogant smile on his face, and then started walking away, leaning heavily on the cane. His other arm was being held by the hand of a small brunette, who had a black eye and a bandage across her nose. The girl gave Ryan a bemused look.

Ryan stared after them as Shep walked up and extended his hand to Patrick. Patrick, red-faced, ignored Shep and followed quickly behind the man with the cane.

"Patrick," Ryan called after him, wondering what Patrick was going to do.

Shep looked questioningly at Ryan, then at Spence. Ryan turned away quickly and Spence just shrugged. Shep ran behind Patrick, wondering what he had just missed, when Patrick suddenly grabbed the blond man by the back of the shirt and threw him against the doors to the Section C courtroom. The cane fell to the floor with a clang.

"Stay away from my sister, Lejeune," Patrick said in a low voice. "Since your breakup, I've come across a place I could stash a body where nobody would ever find it."

Shep wondered what he should do. He certainly didn't want to defend Chad Lejeune, but he also didn't want Patrick getting in trouble for beating the man in the hallway.

"You can't threaten him like that." The brunette grabbed Patrick's arm in an unsuccessful attempt to pull Patrick off of Lejeune.

"There's plenty of room for two," Patrick said, and then stared hard at her bandaged nose and black eye. "Did Lejeune do this to you?"

"Yeah," the girl said, "with his balls."

Chad Lejeune smiled derisively, and Patrick seemed about to go after the man again until Shep pulled him away.

"Dude, chill," Shep ordered, holding Patrick back as one of the doors opened and a man walked out. Patrick didn't attempt to fight Shep, but continued to stare at Lejeune, an uncharacteristic fury in his eyes.

Shep turned to Chad, whose lips were still curved in a taunting smile. "You might want to take this opportunity to get the fuck out of here, Lejeune."

Chad Lejeune looked back at Shep contemptuously, and then finally picked up his cane and walked into the courtroom, slightly dragging his right leg. The brunette followed closely behind him.

Patrick jerked his arm from Shep's grasp, and walked down the hallway, muttering under his breath, and then continued down the steps of the court, leaving the building without a word.

Shep walked back to Ryan and Spence.

"Patrick almost beat the crap out of Chad Lejeune," Shep told them. "Did I miss something?"

Ryan looked down and played with a button on her suit jacket. "Not that I know of."

"His girlfriend looked like she had been roughed up," Spence said. "I don't know what that would have to do with Patrick."

"She said it was consensual," Shep told him, and then looked back at Ryan. "And I got the impression the smack down wasn't about Lejeune's current girlfriend."

Ryan looked up. "I have a trial." She started to walk towards her courtroom. Shep followed her.

"Do you want to tell me what that was about?" Shep asked, wondering what Patrick knew that he didn't. It seemed unlikely that Patrick was aware of the problems between Chad and Ryan in the bedroom, and even less likely that Patrick would want to kick Chad's ass over it. And while cheating on Ryan would have earned Chad the Murphy's ire, it was hardly the type of thing that would drive Patrick to violence, especially three months after the fact. But maybe there was more to Ryan's story than Chad cheating on her.

Ryan just shook her head and started walking away again.

Shep walked next to her. "Travis Dalton was shot to death early this morning. Looks like another dead end, no pun intended."

Ryan closed her eyes and rubbed her forehead. "That was not the news I needed to hear right now."

"Babe, are you feeling okay?" Shep asked, concerned.

Instead of entering the courtroom, she detoured to the bench across the hallway and plopped unceremoniously on the seat. "I have a headache," she said, looking away. "No big surprise there. Thanks for taking care of me last night. Sean didn't mention the mess, so you must have cleaned up for me. I guess I owe you one."

He sat on the bench next to her, and nudged her knee with his own. "You don't owe me anything. Unless you want to tell me what that was all about with Lejeune."

She turned her face away. "Not right now, okay? I have a lot on my mind, and I don't really feel like talking about Chad. And after the video —" She cut the sentence off. "I just can't talk about this right now."

He decided to cut her break for now. He had another way to get the information. "I have that errand to run right now anyway. But I'm not dropping this Lejeune thing."

"I kind of figured that," she answered with a sigh, and walked back across the hall and into the courtroom.

As soon as the doors closed behind Ryan, Shep called the D.A.'s office on his cell phone to find out Edie's section of court. The operator told him section L, a slow-moving section where the judge was constantly getting off the bench to take phone calls in his chambers and chat with the endless line of attorneys and politicians that seemed to stop in his section on a regular basis. Sometimes, the judge would just leave court, for hours at a time, leaving the court staff and attorneys sitting around doing nothing, wondering if the cases were ever going to be heard. It was a really fun section of court. But at least Shep would have ample opportunity to talk to Edie.

He walked in and found Edie sitting at the state's table with her head on the desk, sleeping so hard she was snoring, a small spot of drool at the corner of her mouth. Shep walked to the front of the courtroom, smiling at the people he knew and winking at the minute clerk out of habit. He sat in the chair next to Edie.

Without lifting her head, Edie said, "Tomas, you smell good enough to eat today. New cologne?" Tomas was Edie's junior.

"No, just my regular stuff," Shep said. He couldn't see how somebody like Ryan ever became friends with somebody like Edie. Edie lifted her head and opened one eye. Her frizzy hair was secured on top of her head by a hodgepodge of paper clips and brass fasteners.

"Oh, no wonder you smell so good. You're not Tomas." She smiled back at him, out of one side of her mouth, wiping the corner with drool. "What brings you to my little neck of the woods? And if you've heard I've been checking up on you, it's strictly for a friend. I'm taken, sorry." She laughed at her own joke.

"Do I know this friend?" Shep asked, starting to like Edie a little bit more.

She raised a bushy eyebrow and gave him a crooked smile. "Can't betray a confidence."

"Fair enough. I don't know if you can help me then." He waited, baiting her.

Edie was curious, and bit. "What do you need?"

"Information. About Chad Lejeune."

"What makes you think I'd know anything about that turd?" She sat up straight, both eyes open now.

"Because you're Ryan's best friend. And I think you know what kind of information I'm after." He leaned on his elbow, staring at her.

Edie stared back at him, seeming to weigh her words. "Anything you're thinking about him is probably too good."

"How exactly was their relationship?" He glanced around quickly to make sure no one was listening.

"She went out with him for three months. He just wasn't very nice to her most of the time, not even in front of other people."

He waited, knowing there was a lot more to the story.

Edie lowered her voice. "I think he hit her."

"What?"

She shook her head. "I know. It's hard to believe Ryan would let anybody get away with that. They had been together for about a month when they went to a fund-raiser together. Chad's father kept making passes at her all night. Ryan was upset and embarrassed, but Chad was laughing about the whole thing. They got in an argument and finally left.

"I called her the next day to see what happened, and she said they had it out when he brought her home. Chad blamed her for the whole thing, saying if she hadn't dressed like a whore his father wouldn't have been playing grab-ass with her all night. She didn't come out and say it, but I got the impression it got physical. That Monday at work she wore a lot more makeup than usual. I think she was hiding a black eye."

"This happened just the one time?" Shep strained to subdue his anger.

"She told me about a few other big fights, but she never told me he hit her. I guess I assumed he might have. I didn't know why she was staying with him."

"What happened when they broke up?"

Edie leaned closer to him. "I don't know for sure. She went to her parent's house and told Angie to get her dad and brothers to pack her stuff, that she was never going back to her apartment again. She refused to explain what was wrong. Her mother even called me to see if I knew what happened. They thought maybe somebody had broken in and attacked her. All I could tell her was that Ryan caught Chad cheating on her and broke up with him."

He grabbed Edie's arm. "What do you think happened, Edie?"

"Ryan wouldn't talk about it, but a few days later, I saw all these horrible bruises and welts all over her. She tried to hide them from me, but there were so many I couldn't help but see them. She made me promise I wouldn't tell anybody." She stopped, and then lowered her voice. "I told Angie anyway. I couldn't help myself. I had to let her know what I thought Chad had done to Ryan."

Shep sucked in his breath. "And nobody went after Chad for this?"

Edie shrugged. "I'm sure her dad or one of her brothers did. I mean, look what happened to Chad a few days after I told Angie."

Shep frowned. "Why wouldn't Chad have pressed charges?"

"Tit for tat. Ryan didn't report him, so Chad didn't report the captain. Or whichever of her family members maimed him."

The judge suddenly appeared from chambers, talking to two city council members.

"Thanks a lot, Edie. I owe you one." He stood up and squeezed her shoulder.

"Just don't tell Ryan I told you, okay?"

"No problem, babe." He left the courtroom, giving tight-lipped smiles at the people he knew without realizing he was doing it. No wonder Patrick wanted to kick Lejeune's ass. Shep only wondered why the captain hadn't killed him.

He hoped he would find something to implicate Chad in the homicides. Or maybe he'd get really lucky and Chad Lejeune would walk in on him while he was searching his apartment, and give Shep the chance to finish what Patrick had been about to start.

Big Mike looked earnestly at the officer on the witness stand. "Sergeant, what first drew your attention to the defendant?"

Ryan was barely listening. She should have been, but Mike was doing a good job, and it was only a bench trial, and a simple case at that. While her headache had finally dissipated, her mind, unfortunately, was still drawn to Chad Lejeune.

Even though she knew he would be here today, she hadn't been prepared to see him again. It was bad enough she had to watch him on the tape last night. She couldn't believe he was actually here, in her courthouse, acting as if he had every right to walk around like a normal person.

The more she thought about it, the more she had to know if he was behind the murders. If Chad was the killer, he would probably get the death penalty. It wouldn't matter that the victims were criminals and he was a lawyer. A rich white boy who murdered a bunch of black folks from the projects would be an automatic jury target regardless.

She just needed to find a way to let Chad catch her alone. If Chad was guilty, he would say something to implicate himself. He was obviously dying to tell her about what he had done. Why else would he have been making the calls to her? If she could get just one witness to overhear him confess, she could get a search warrant. Chad was bound to have something in his apartment that would link him to the murders.

She knew that Shep was on his way there now to look for the videotapes, and wouldn't have time to search Chad's whole apartment. And even if Shep did happen to run across something that linked Chad to the murders, he couldn't use it as evidence without being charged with burglary, not to mention anything he found during the illegal search would be suppressed. No, she had to find a way to legally get the police into Chad's apartment, and the only thing she could think of was an admission by Chad.

"Did I miss anything?" Mike whispered to her, and Ryan felt guilty because she hadn't been listening.

"No, you did great," she whispered back, and patted Mike's arm.

The defense didn't put on a case, and while Mike did the closing argument, Ryan wondered how much trouble she would be in if her plan didn't work out the way she hoped.

The judge called another fifteen minute recess. When he left the bench, Ryan walked over to section C to see if Chad Lejeune was still in court.

She waited at the back of the courtroom, taking stock of the audience. She finally honed in on him. He had the same cocky look on his face, as if the court proceeding was a joke.

"That taste good?" Spence Badon was sitting on the bench in the last row, his arms stretched out along the back of the bench. He stood up and pointed to the thumb she was chewing.

Spence was a big man, tall and broad, somewhere in his late thirties, with a short, military style haircut and a forbidden goatee. He spoke with a slight Cajun dialect, having grown up in Cut Off, a town seventy miles south of New Orleans. He was a country boy at heart, and had been reprimanded more than once for finding new ways to relieve his boredom, both on and off the clock. He always said the city had too many rules, but it paid much better than the Sheriff's Department back home.

Ryan motioned for him to sit back down, and sat next to him, amazed at her good luck. Of all the people who might have been in this courtroom, law enforcement or otherwise, Spence was the one person she knew would do what she was about to ask, without any questions. She paused for a second, giving herself one opportunity to change her mind. Once she enlisted Spence's help, there was no backing down.

"Spence, how busy are you right now?"

He looked at his watch. "The judge just took lunch. I'm free for at least an hour. What you got in mind?"

"I need to check something on a defendant in here. I have this feeling that when I leave, he's going to follow me out."

"You want me to take care of him?" Spence asked, his eyes lighting up with interest.

Ryan put her hands up, hoping to keep Spence from getting too carried away.

The only downside to asking for Spence's assistance was trying to keep him in check. He was not a man easily controlled. "No, actually, I want him to follow me. I also have this feeling he might say something to implicate himself in a crime."

"You talking about that Lejeune guy?" Spence nodded in Chad's direction.

"Does it matter?"

He smiled. "You kidding me? What you want me to do?"

"You need to be close enough to hear what he says so we can use it to get a search warrant, but far enough away that he doesn't realize you're listening. Otherwise, he won't say anything."

"I'll blend into the background like a Ninja," he promised.

Ryan walked to the front of the courtroom, stopping next to the Assistant D.A. handling the case, making sure she glanced back at Chad as she did. "Harry, is Lejeune represented by counsel?"

Harry Stelly looked up. She could see Chad watching intently, the arrogant expression frozen on his face.

"I don't know, let me check. Hey, Lejeune," he called across the courtroom.

Chad stared at him condescendingly.

"Where's your attorney, Lejeune?"

"I won't be needing one," Chad answered, displaying an icy smile.

"Oh, okay. We'll see about that, dude." Harry turned back to Ryan. "You heard him. Why?"

"Is that the victim with him? She's his girlfriend, you know."

Harry pointed to the other side of the room, where a petite red head sat, her face full of bruises, her jaw clenched. A second later Ryan realized the girl's jaw was wired shut.

"Tell Lejeune the prescriptive period for aggravated rape," Ryan whispered, referring to the Louisiana term for statute of limitations.

Harry looked at her with confusion. "Crimes with life sentences have no prescription, do they?"

"You just got an A+ in criminal law, now tell it to Chad."

"Hey, Lejeune," Harry called across the courtroom again. "Did you know aggravated rape has no prescriptive period? That means we can prosecute you whenever we feel like it, no matter how long ago you raped the girl." He looked at Ryan. "Is that good?"

She nodded slightly, staring at Chad, who frowned back at her. Several people in the audience were now looking at Chad suspiciously.

Ryan smiled, and then said loud enough for Chad to hear, "If Mr. Lejeune had an attorney, I was going to tell him to get ready to defend against another rape charge. I've got a feeling an indictment for a 42 is in his future."

Harry smiled back at her and then called to Chad, "Man, you really might want to rethink that not needing an attorney thing." He turned back to Ryan. "You keep adding charges and I'll keep prosecuting them."

Ryan knew exactly what Chad would think. She knew how his mind worked. She looked directly at him as she walked out of the courtroom, challenging him. Spence walked out just ahead of her.

Ryan slowly made her way down the hall, in the direction of her own courtroom. She had to give Chad enough time to follow her. Spence had stopped across the hall from Section C, next to a floor-to-ceiling window that was open, but had metal bars to keep people from falling. Or maybe from jumping. Despite the ban on smoking in the building, he lit up a cigarette and blew the smoke out of the window.

Ryan was halfway back to her own section, thinking the plan was failing, when she got a prickly feeling on the back of her neck. She turned and saw Chad approaching. The hallway was nearly empty. Spence was keeping pace, but true to his word, moved along so casually Chad shouldn't notice him.

"What do you think you're doing?" Chad asked, looking around quickly.

Ryan fought to keep from shaking. "The question is what have you been doing?"

"Look, bitch, you don't even know what pain is yet. Don't fuck with me or you won't know what hit you this time."

"You killed those people, didn't you?" She took a step closer to him, forcing herself into his personal space. "You raped and killed that hooker and her little girl. I know you did, and pretty soon everybody else is going to know too."

What he did next took her by surprise. His hand shot out and he backhanded her across the mouth. Unprepared for the blow, she fell hard to the floor in the middle of the hallway.

"You know there's no such thing as rape." He stood over her, his voice growing louder. "All you bitches like it rough."

Spence darted over and tackled Chad, smashing Chad's face into the granite floor. Chad tried to fight back, but Spence was a lot bigger and had Chad face down.

"You like hitting girls, mother fucker?" Spence punched Chad in the kidney. "Why don't you try hitting a man?" Spence grabbed Chad by the hair and smashed his face into the floor again. Ryan was still down, dazed from the blow, trying to move out of the way.

Three deputies materialized, grabbing Chad, pulling him to his feet. Chad tried to fight them, swinging the cane he had managed to hold on to. The deputies knocked him back to the ground, handcuffing him behind his back, kicking him repeatedly until he finally stopped fighting.

Spence reached for Ryan's hand, still looking at Chad as if he might hit him again.

"Spence, did you hear what he said?" Ryan reached for Spence's hand, tucking her shaky legs underneath her to stand back up. "You think it's probable cause for a warrant?"

"You okay?" Spence helped her up from the ground. "I didn't think he would hit you. Jesus, your lip is bleeding. I am going to be in deep shit with the captain." He drew a handkerchief out of his pocket and blotted her lip. Ryan was surprised that a man like Spence would have a handkerchief in his pocket.

"Do you think he said enough to get a search warrant?" She swiped the blood off her lip with her tongue. "Was that a confession?"

Spence pressed the handkerchief to her lip. "Keep pressure on that. I'll get you your warrant, baby."

The deputies had brought Chad down the hall, where one of them was filling out a report. Ryan started to walk away, feeling relief mixed with just a tad of guilty pleasure.

"Whore," Chad yelled through a mouth full of blood, trying to get away from the deputies. "I'm not going to jail over one lousy fuck."

Spence started in Chad's direction, but a deputy whacked Chad behind his good knee with his baton before Spence made it there. Chad would have been back on the floor if the three deputies hadn't been holding him up.

"Sounds like a confession to me," Ryan yelled back to him. "Just remember what you said, Chad, when your cell mate wants you to be his bitch tonight. There's no such thing as rape."

"Worthless cunt, I should have killed you when I had the chance." Chad fell to the ground this time as one of the deputies hit him behind the knee again.

Ryan smiled, flinching slightly from the split lip. Watching Chad get beaten in the hallway was almost worth what she went through with him. Prosecuting him for murder would even things out completely.

When Ryan got back to the courtroom, Mike was packing up the files, a nervous look on his face.

"We got a guilty on the judge trial. And Rick left a message for you to meet him in his office immediately. He said it was important. Hey, your lip is bleeding."

Ryan hurried across the street to the office, a feeling of dread in the pit of her stomach. She thought Rick was going to chide her about the scene with Chad in the courthouse. But when she walked into Rick's office, he handed her the newspaper. "See this yet?"

Ty Crowley's by-line was on the front page. She skimmed the story. While Ty was not the most inspired writer, the article was attention-getting. The headline read, "Killer Crush: Bodies Presents for ADA." The article was detailed, containing nearly all of the information the police had on the case.

"I have a feeling more is going to come out of this." Rick took the paper back and folded it in half. "The D.A. wants to pull you from the crime scenes. And I know I said you were the front-runner for the Strike Force spot, but this isn't the right time for you to be handling high-profile cases. Especially if you were to lose and this nut job kills your defendant."

Ryan felt as if she got punched in the stomach.

"What exactly are you saying, Rick?" She tried to keep her voice even. If you cried in front of the chief, you could never take it back.

"I'm sorry Ryan, but somebody else is getting the Strike Force spot," he answered. "And Gendusa is being reassigned. I didn't get to make the call, but I can't say I vetoed it."

"Are you moving me out of Trials?" She had a surreal feeling, as if Rick was talking underwater. She would quit rather than be relegated to the ranks of the pencil-pushers and chair-warmers.

"That decision hasn't been made yet. The D.A. wants to meet with you tomorrow morning to discuss your future placement in this office. And this isn't any reflection on you. He was really impressed with the death penalty on the 42. Nobody's trying to push you out."

"Yeah, I can see how impressed Peter was by his decision to give Strike Force and Gendusa to somebody else."

Rick shook his head. "As soon as this situation gets resolved, everything will be back to normal. And we're supposed to be getting a warrant for another Strike Force spot in a couple of months. I know Judge Jackson's out next week. Why don't you take some vacation time? I'm sure the police will have caught somebody by the time you come back."

"And if they haven't?"

Rick didn't answer.

"Yeah, that's what I thought. And I don't need any time off, thank you." She walked out of the office, once again fighting the urge to cry. She would not cry here.

She knew this meant Bo Lambert had beat her. He was going to get the Strike Force spot because some crazy lunatic thought it was funny to kill people and act like he was doing it all for her. She walked back to her office, a sinking feeling washing over her.

For the last four years, her job had defined who she was. She didn't exactly have a personal life. Very few friends. No husband, no boyfriend. Children nowhere in her near future. Her life revolved around the office. And when she missed out on family functions, she convinced herself the lost time was worth it to keep one step ahead. Somehow, nothing else mattered, not as long as she was at the top.

She deserved that Strike Force spot. She knew she did. If Chad was behind this, she was going to do everything within her power to make sure he got what he deserved.

She sat at her desk and checked the clock to determine how much longer she would have to wait to start drinking at the Hole. Too long. She began looking through her cases scheduled for the week after next, trying to pretend as if everything would be back to normal by then. She got lost in working up the files and jumped when the phone rang. She was surprised to see that more than three hours had flown by. At least it was nearly time for the Hole to open.

"Ryan Murphy, Trials."

"Are you okay?" Shep asked. "I heard Chad attacked you at court."

Deflated by Rick's announcement, she had almost forgotten about the scene in

143

the hallway. "Physically I'm fine."

"What in God's name were you thinking, going after Chad by yourself?"

She ignored his critical tone. "Somebody had to go after him. And I got you a search warrant, didn't I? Did you find anything at his apartment, at least?"

"We didn't find anything to connect him to the murders," he said. "And there were no other tapes of you." He paused. "I did find a bunch of videos of Chad with other people, though. When I went back with the SID to execute the search warrant, I took the tapes as evidence."

Chad hadn't taped her doing anything else. That was some small comfort, even if they didn't find anything connecting him to the homicides.

Shep wasn't finished. "A few tapes appeared to be of consensual acts, some even with men. But the rest of the tapes were different. These girls were knocked out, or drugged. If I'm not mistaken, the woman has to be conscious to give consent."

Ryan held her breath, hoping he wasn't going to ask her about the tape of her.

After a second, he went on. "At least if we don't get Chad on the homicides, I'm sure we'll be able to get him on some of these rapes. One aggravated rape conviction and he's gone for life. If we can identify the victims, that is."

Ryan finally exhaled. "Good luck."

"Well, I was kind of hoping you could help me with that," he said, and hesitated. Ryan had the feeling she wasn't going to like what was coming next. "I know this is a lot to ask, but would you want to look at some still pictures from the videos? I wouldn't ask you to look at the actual tapes, but maybe you'll recognize somebody from the stills I'm making. Some of the dates on the tapes overlap with the time you were going out with him."

"Could this day get any fucking worse?" Ryan snapped, and then wished she could take it back. Shep was doing all this to help her.

"Hey, are you sure you're okay?"

"I don't want to talk about it now." She sighed. "I'm going to the Hole the second Dominic unlocks the front door. You can meet me there. If you want to give me a ride home, I guess I could look at the pictures then. You might want to get there as early as possible, because I am without a doubt going to get extremely trashed tonight."

"I'll see you there," he said. "Oh, and one more thing. PID showed up at Chad's before we left. I don't know what they were looking for, but Battaglia made a point to say he'd be at the next COMSTAT meeting. I got the impression it's something to do with your dad."

Ryan frowned into the phone. "Don't worry. I'll take care of Battaglia."

"Uh, Ryan, whatever you're planning, be careful with Battaglia. He can do a lot of damage to your dad if you give him any ammunition."

"I won't. But thanks for the warning." She hung up the phone, too many emotions running through her to control. She felt tears start to form and willed them away. Everything was going to be fine.

First, she would talk to Battaglia, and give him the information that would make him leave her father alone. She just needed to figure out how much she had to reveal. For Battaglia to believe what had happened to Chad was justified, he was going to have to know what Chad did to her. And as much as she didn't want anyone to know the truth, she wasn't going to let PID and Battaglia destroy her father over something she knew he didn't do.

She called the PID office. Battaglia didn't seem happy to hear from her. When she told him she could give him information regarding the attack on Chad Lejeune, he agreed to see her. She grabbed the videotape from her desk, glad she had thought to bring it to the office with her, and walked down the street to Headquarters, where the PID office was located.

JACOB

Jacob looked at the newspaper article and smiled. Everything was going as planned, falling right into place, which was fortunate, since the city council had voted to shut down the St. Thomas. There was a rush on the demolition job, the bulldozers already lining up in preparation for the new Wal-Mart that was coming. Jacob knew the end was near, just as he knew the end had to be at the St. Thomas.

He pulled an old photo with grainy color out of his desk. A little girl on a gold sofa stared back at him, her legs curled up underneath her, looking serious and scared. And next to her, standing on the floor, was Jacob, his legs slightly apart, in a protective stance.

He did not recall the picture being taken, but in retrospect assumed it was the pedophile who had taken it. Jacob had spent a year with him after that day, and the man enjoyed taking Jacob's picture, among other things.

He had thought about that little girl a lot in his life, wondering who she was, and how her life had turned out. And then, after a lifetime of looking for her, he had found her. Justice would finally be served. Unfortunately for her.

FRIDAY NIGHT/SATURDAY MORNING

Ryan was drunk. Earlier, before most of the office had shown up at the Hole, she had been falling down drunk. Now, the buzz was beginning to wear thin. She had been shooting tequila shots for several hours with Edie, trying to forget about how miserable her life had become.

She was devastated enough over not getting the promotion, but an even bigger outrage had come at the trial meeting, when Rick announced that Kellie Leblanc had gotten the Strike Force spot. Ryan had been so wrapped up in her own misery that she hadn't realized Bo Lambert seemed just as miserable as she did. She couldn't even be happy that Bo hadn't gotten the promotion either.

Kellie was flitting around the bar, a big smile on her face, infuriating Ryan even more. When Ryan heard Kellie mention that she was looking for Shep to celebrate with, Ryan made a two-hundred dollar bet with the other woman that Shep wouldn't be going home with her. Ryan knew the bet was unfair, but didn't care.

Ryan sat at the bar, tequila shots lined up in front of her, her eyes watching the door. When the door finally did open, Sean walked in, an annoyed look on his face.

He headed straight to her. "I should have figured you'd be here. I'm leaving in an hour to go to Grand Isle with mom." His pale face was even more washed out than normal. "We'll start packing Gram's stuff tonight and drive back tomorrow. We'll probably need at least two trips, but once I get there at least dad will get a break."

Ryan felt guilty for a second. Her father had called earlier to say that Gram had another stroke and wasn't doing well, and he was bringing her home to New Orleans.

"Sorry I can't help, but I have to go the office tomorrow. So, anything new on the homicides?"

Sean glanced at Bo and Big Mike, sitting a few seats over from Ryan, and shook his head. "No, nothing new."

"Well, you can tell mama I'm going to the Upperline Home to do her volunteer work tomorrow for her. I know she hasn't missed a Saturday in years." Ryan downed one of the tequila shots.

Sean didn't say anything, but gave her a skeptical look as he walked across the room to talk to Suzie Chin. Ryan assumed from his reaction that he was unaware that Patti was living at the Upperline Home. She was equally certain that her mother would have a lot to think about when Sean gave her the message.

"How's it going?" Mike asked, leaning on the bar in front of her. "You must be pretty bummed. If there's anything I can do, let me know."

She shook her head, determined not to break down in front of everybody at the bar, and forced a smile. "Obviously, being a good prosecutor isn't as important as being a good slut in this office." She knew she was being an ungracious loser, but thought she was entitled.

Mike looked uncomfortable, and Ryan's smile came naturally when she realized Kellie Leblanc was standing on the other side of Mike, next to Bo.

Edie walked up and grabbed one of the shots. "You didn't mention to Sean you would be meeting long lost relatives tomorrow, did you?" Her tone was strangely judgmental.

Ryan laughed, even though it wasn't funny, momentarily forgetting about Kellie and the remark. She did another shot, feeling the tequila warmth hitting her chest. "No, for some reason I don't think Sean would approve."

"I still think it's a bad idea," Edie said, uncharacteristically acting as the voice of reason. "If you want to know anything about Patti, you should just ask your mom."

Ryan dismissed Edie's suggestion with a wave of her hand. "It's obvious to me that mama doesn't want me to know anything at all about Patti, or else she would have found some occasion in the last twenty-four years to mention to me that my biological mother is still alive. And second, mama doesn't have the answers to my questions."

"Don't you have enough to worry about?" Edie nodded in the direction of Kellie Leblanc.

"Don't forget your meeting with the D.A.," Bo said, raising his glass to her, and Ryan got the feeling he was getting some satisfaction out of her troubles.

Ryan was trying to think of an answer to Bo when the door to the bar opened again, and Shep waved her over. Ryan bee-lined for the front door, wanting to make sure she got to Shep before Kellie.

His eyes locked on hers as he smiled. "Are you ready?"

She was relieved that he didn't want to hang around. Not that she was at all interested in seeing whom Chad may have violated, but she didn't want to hang around watching Kellie celebrate the promotion that should have been hers. She also had no desire to watch Kellie throw herself at Shep all night, especially considering the level of Kellie's skills of persuasion.

Ryan nodded, and looked toward the bar at Kellie, who had her back to the door. "Let me tell Edie I'm leaving."

Ryan strode purposefully to Kellie. "Put up your money. I'm out of here."

Kellie eyed her doubtfully. "What are you talking about?"

Ryan pointed over to Shep waiting at the door. "He's waiting for me, sweetie. Not you. So pay up."

Kellie handed her a fistful of twenties with a scowl. "Maybe you can count that while I'm working on the Gendusa case."

Ryan snatched the cash from Kellie. "Fine. And you can read your little file while Shep's running his mouth all over my body tonight."

"I've got too many Strike Force cases to keep me busy to worry about Chapetti anyway," Kellie answered with a fake smile.

"Good for you. My only worry is whether Chapetti brought enough condoms for the weekend." Ryan's smile was pure venom. At least she could replace those Ferragamo's, courtesy of Kellie Leblanc.

Ryan walked back to the front door to Shep, who was looking at her intently.

"I'm glad you don't feel like hanging around here," he said, opening the door for her. He put his hand on her elbow, steering her in the direction of his car. "You want to tell me what had you so down today?"

She shrugged. "I didn't get Strike Force." The words left a bad taste in her mouth, so she stopped walking and lit up a cigarette.

"I'm sorry." Shep stopped next to her and grabbed her hand, squeezing it gently.

"And the news gets worse." She kept her hand in his as they crossed Tulane Avenue to his car, hoping her hand wasn't sweating in his. "Kellie Leblanc got the spot instead."

"Ouch. I know how much you wanted this. If I can do anything, let me know." She tried to read his look, but was afraid to give too much credence to what she hoped she saw. After all, she had been shooting tequila for hours. Her judgment could hardly be trusted.

She looked down and swallowed, trying again to combat the tears that were threatening to erupt. "They might put me at a desk. They don't want me handling high profile cases. And the icing on the cake, Kellie also got the Gendusa case."

"Seems like it's Kellie's lucky day," Shep said.

They stopped at his car. Ryan reluctantly took her hand out of his.

"She blew her way to my promotion, I'd say that's a little more than luck." She watched his face for a reaction as she threw the cigarette down to the ground.

Shep opened the car door. "I'm just glad she didn't see me at the bar. I heard I was next on her to-do list."

Ryan stopped, her body halfway in the car. "You know about the list?"

Shep smiled. "Everybody knows about the list. She's very popular among the patrolmen. The ones who haven't caught gonorrhea from her yet, anyway." He shut Ryan's door and climbed in the driver's seat. He pulled onto Tulane, edged into the intersection and ran the red. "You have no reason to be jealous of her, you know."

Ryan felt her face flush. "I am not jealous of Kellie. I just hate her guts. She doesn't even care about being on Strike Force. She just always goes after whatever I want, and not because she wants it, but because she knows I do. I mean first she went after my job, then my case, then my man . . ."

She stopped, horrified, realizing what she had just said.

"Your man?" Shep looked over at her suddenly, stopping for the red light.

"I meant in the past," she said quickly, her heart speeding up. "She's gone after men I wanted. Before, I mean. Like in high school. I'm drunk. I'm not making any sense. You can run this red, you know."

He checked the intersection and ran the light. Gilbert's smile lit up his face. "Oh, I think you're making plenty of sense."

"I'm drunk. I don't know what I'm saying." She knew her face was red. Just like she knew she didn't have a man.

"Babe, you have every right to be angry. You deserved the Strike Force spot."

Ryan was glad he was not going to harp on what she had just said. "The only good part of my day was that Bo didn't get the spot either," Ryan said, and Shep gave her Gilbert's smile again as he pulled up in front of her house.

Inside, Ryan flipped on the light, and handed him the ten twenties.

He looked at her with mock suspicion. "What's this for? Are you trying to bribe a police officer? You know that's a felony."

"Only a third class. I bet Kellie two hundred bucks you wouldn't go home with her."

Shep's eyebrows shot up. "Did you think I would?"

She tried to smooth her hair. "Of course not. I knew you had a boner for me to look at Chad's girlfriends. It was a safe bet."

He handed the bills back to her. "I think the least you could do would be to treat me to dinner one night. Since you won the money because of me."

"I guess that would be fair," she answered, putting the money on the coffee table with a small smile. Was that Shep's subtle way of asking her out?

"And since you just called me your man, we should go out on at least one real date."

"Just give me the damn pictures." She could feel her face turning red again. He was just making fun of her. That was what she got for too many Cuervo shots.

Shep sat down and pulled the pictures out of the file. "Take your time, and tell me if you recognize anybody."

Ryan sat down next to him on the sofa and started looking through the photos. She immediately knew the woman in the first one.

"Norma was Chad's secretary," she said. "She quit right after I started going out with him. I can't say that I blame her, with what he's doing to her in this picture." She looked at the second one. "Oh my, that's the water man."

"The what?"

"Chad's water delivery guy. Gross." She threw the pictures on the coffee table. "And this was going on while I was his girlfriend? I'm glad now I only walked in on him doing the paralegal. I think I've seen enough."

"I'm sorry. I guess I didn't think the pictures would bother you. I mean, after everything, you don't still have feelings for him, do you?" Shep had the same intense look in his eyes as he had at the bar.

"Feelings of hatred and disgust," she said. "But I'm still finding it difficult to accept that my boyfriend was screwing around on me, with unconscious women and water delivery men and God knows who else. I mean, what was wrong with me?" She didn't want to sound so self-pitying, but she couldn't help herself.

Shep touched her cheek lightly. "Babe, there is absolutely nothing wrong with you. Chad's some kind of a freaky deviant. I'm sorry. Your day was bad enough without me putting you through this. I shouldn't have asked you to do this tonight."

She stood up and put the pictures back in his file. "I understand that you want to get him, and this is the only way."

He grabbed her hand. "Ry, there is another way."

She tried to hand him the file. "No, there isn't. I'll press charges for the battery in the courthouse, but nothing else."

He ignored the file in her hand, and looked at her questioningly, still holding her hand.

"What?" Ryan asked. "You obviously have something on your mind. You've got one question, Chapetti. Make it a good one."

He waited a moment before asking, "Did you love him?"

"No," she answered too quickly, surprised by the question. "Most of the time I didn't even like him." She pulled her hand out of his and shoved the file at him, blinking back tears. "I can't look at this right now."

"I didn't mean to upset you. I'll go." He took the file and started for the door.

A wave of loneliness washed over her. She rushed behind him and grabbed his arm. He stopped abruptly, and then slowly turned to face her.

Her voice was a shaky whisper, choked with a mixture of fear and longing. "I don't want you to go. I don't want to be alone."

He looked down at her as she put her hands on his chest and slowly reached up with her mouth, pressing her lips against his. She could feel his heart pounding through his polo shirt as she parted his lips with her tongue.

Shep made a sound in his throat, almost but not quite a moan, before pulling his mouth from hers. "Ryan, I don't think this is such a good idea right now."

"Why?" she asked, keeping her hands pressed against his chest.

"Because you're drunk," he answered, staring down at her through his dark lashes.

"So what?" She reached her arms around his neck and began tracing tiny circles behind his ear with her tongue.

He made another sound, a definite moan this time, and removed her arms from around his neck, holding her hands in his own. "Ryan, what exactly are you after here?"

"I was thinking second base, maybe third, whatever we have time for."

He shook his head, a wistful smile on his lips. "While I have a certain level of appreciation for a woman who starts out at second or third base, that's not really the answer I was looking for."

"What do you want to hear then, Chapetti?" She jerked her hands out of his grasp. "That I'll testify against Chad for making the tape if you have sex with me? Are you really only here to close a case? Do you need an arrest that bad?"

He shook his head. "I just need to be sure what you really want. And that you're not doing this because you're drunk, or because you're feeling sorry for yourself, or because you think this is the way to beat Kellie. I don't want to be with you tonight and have you regret it tomorrow. I don't want to screw this up."

She turned away from him so he wouldn't see the tear that slid down her cheek. "I think you just don't want me. I've seen the women you go out with. Women like Kellie. And Wanda. I can't compete, I guess." She knew she was going to feel like an idiot tomorrow, but she couldn't seem to stop. He was right about one thing. She was feeling sorry for herself. Chad hadn't wanted her, and now Shep didn't want her. And she was out of tequila.

Without a word, he whirled her around and pulled her body against his. His hands traveled underneath her short skirt until they were cupping her bare skin, proving to Ryan that she had made the right choice in the thong versus bikini dilemma.

"I've been wanting to do that since I walked into the bar and saw you in that tiny skirt. And those shoes should be illegal," he whispered in her ear, and then nibbled on her earlobe before bringing his mouth back down to hers. A second later he released her mouth, keeping his body tight against hers. "Do you feel how much I want you?"

She felt his erection pressing against her through her clothes.

"Must be the Prada shoes." She rubbed against his hardness.

He let out a groan. "Shep Jr. is dying to make your acquaintance, I can assure you. As a matter of fact, every time I leave you I have to think about my Aunt Edna to get Junior to settle down."

She kissed him again, their tongues intertwining, and Ryan felt the blood racing to parts of her body that had been dormant for a long time. His hands moved to her tank top, unbuttoning the top two buttons, just far enough to reach her breast with his tongue. A moan escaped her lips as he ran his tongue around her nipple before taking her breast in his mouth.

"I should be leaving now." He moved his mouth to her other breast. "I shouldn't be doing this, but you feel so good."

Ryan pulled Shep's mouth back to her own, feeling like she was melting, until the ringing of his cell phone rudely interrupted her rare pleasure.

He stepped back, a dazed look in his eyes, and a second later answered the phone. Ryan listened to his end of the conversation.

"LaJohnnie Lee? Why are you calling me about this?"

Ryan buttoned her top. What had happened to her ten-year-old rape victim?

"I'll be there in twenty. Don't let crime lab touch anything until the coroner looks at the body, just in case." He hung up and turned to Ryan. "LaJohnnie Lee was found dead. GSW to the head, gun in her hand. But Marks thought it was odd that a kid that age would kill herself, especially by shooting herself in the head, and the mother is screaming murder. He was letting us know what's going on, since she was the victim on the case you just handled."

"So he thinks she's dead because of me."

"He didn't say that," Shep said.

"Why else would he call?" she asked, burying her face into his chest.

"I seem to remember you saying you were friendly with Marks one night. I think he's just keeping an eye out for you."

She looked down at the floor, embarrassed. Well, being a slut wasn't without its benefits.

"Baby, whatever happened to LaJohnnie Lee, it isn't your fault." He kissed the top of her head. "I'll go and see what they find."

"I'm coming with you," she said, reaching for her purse.

Shep grabbed her in his arms, stopping her. "Oh no you're not. After that newspaper article, between your dad and your boss, I'll be in a shitload of trouble if I show up there with you. This isn't even my district, I'm there unofficially. I promise I'll call as soon as I know what's going on." He radioed for a patrol unit to sit outside her house, and waited to leave until it arrived.

Ryan sat on the sofa in the dark. She didn't even try to sleep after Shep left. LaJohnnie Lee was dead. The child had been killed by a maniac because she had the bad luck to be a victim on Ryan's case. LaJohnnie's death was not a suicide. It couldn't be. The timing was too coincidental.

She opened Patti's file, looking for anything to take her mind off poor LaJohnnie Lee. There was a single audio tape in it — Ryan's statement. She had been afraid to listen to the statement before. Now, it would be a welcome distraction. She put the tape in the player in her stereo, and listened to her voice at the age of four. They had let her father conduct the interview, probably because she would be more comfortable talking to him. As the younger Ryan began explaining the story, an image in Ryan's adult mind played along like a movie.

She woke on a gold brocade sofa, disoriented.

"Shut up, she's awake," a woman's voice said. It was Aunt Patti, her mama's sister. The lady who made her play the mean joke on her mama. Her mama must be mad. Her mama hadn't come to get her.

Roaches of all sizes scurried across the floor. Every time one of them moved, Ryan shrank back on the sofa. A little boy stood in front of her. "Don't be afraid," he told her. "I won't let nothing get you. They just bugs, see." He picked up a cockroach and smashed it in his fingers. The roach made a snapping noise, but kept wriggling its antenna and kicking its feet. Ryan started crying.

Patti slapped the boy across his face. He fell to the ground, sending the roaches scrambling. The creature in the boy's hand continued to struggle.

"Stupid little bastard," Patti said. "You make that aggravating little bitch cry one more time and I'll send you away for good this time."

The bad man sat down on the sofa next to Ryan. "You're so pretty. Would you like to stay with me for a while?" He touched her hair. "How old are you, angel?"

She held up four fingers but didn't answer out loud. Daddy said she wasn't supposed to talk to strangers. The man closed his eyes and kissed her fingertips.

Patti looked mad. "Jude, get the hell away from her. You don't pay, you don't play." She then put her hand in the air, as if telling him to wait, and ran to the window. She turned back to the man. "Fuck. Police sirens." Patti tore across the room, grabbing Ryan, digging her nails into Ryan's arm. "If I thought I could get away with it, I'd slit your throat right now, you spoiled little bitch." Patti turned back to the man. "Jude, take the kids. I don't want the police getting them."

He reached down to pick Ryan up from the sofa.

Patti spun to face him and started clawing at the man's face. "Not her, you asshole. The other two."

The man cringed, and ducked, trying to shield himself from Patti's blows.

Ryan scrambled to the other side of the sofa.

The boy ran over to her. "Make them come back for me," he whispered to her. "I don't want to go with Jude." He looked so sad that Ryan began sobbing harder.

Patti turned her attention to the boy, grabbed his arm roughly, and shoved him at the man. "Get out of here. Now."

The man tried to grab the boy's hand, but the boy slipped away from him, and threw his arms around Ryan in a desperate hug. "Please," he whispered in her ear. "Don't forget about me. Make them come for me."

The man grabbed the boy by the arm and dragged him across the room and out of the front door.

A second later, several policemen rushed inside. One of them threw Patti against a wall.

Ryan kept sobbing until her father picked her up, holding her so tight she couldn't breathe. He was crying. Ryan knew she was in big trouble. Daddy never cried.

The memory ended. Ryan found herself back in the present, tears streaming down her face. She could have been killed, or traded to a pervert. But she had been saved.

LaJohnnie had been victimized in a heinous way by her own biological father, and thought she had been saved by Ryan. Only Ryan hadn't saved her. Ryan had helped her go from child rape victim to child murder victim

She made a pot of coffee and sat at the kitchen table, going back through her mind to try to come up with more bits and pieces of what happened to her all those years ago. Who was that little boy? And what was he doing with Patti? Nothing else would come.

Just as the sun was rising, Shep called. Ryan was scared of what he was going to tell her.

"LaJohnnie was definitely murdered, but someone tried to make it look like a suicide."

Ryan felt the air leaving her body. "How can they tell?"

"Besides the fact that in general little girls don't intentionally shoot themselves, several other things were off. She was left-handed, but the gun was found in her right hand. She would never have been strong enough to pull the trigger the way the gun would have been situated. And the note." He stopped.

"What did it say?"

He hesitated. *"I'm sorry I lied in court. I said what Ryan Murphy told me so she could win the case.* Her mama says it's definitely not LaJohnnie's handwriting."

"LaJohnnie calls me Miss Ryan. I doubt she even knows my last name." Ryan frowned. "But why leave a note that makes the suicide more suspicious? That doesn't make sense."

"If this guy is just trying to screw with you, it does," Shep answered. "The press was tipped off and got there before the responding officer. They're going to report LaJohnnie's death as a suicide. Eventually the truth will come out, but things could be hard for you until it does. And he had to know how killing her would make you feel. Not to mention that this could get your death penalty reversed. LaJohnnie's note will call the conviction into question."

Ryan didn't care about the conviction now, or about the death penalty. All she could think about was that another person was dead because of her. The deaths of drug dealers and gang members hadn't bothered her. But this little girl, a child who had done nothing other than to be born from a man who violated her, was different.

"We're going to find him," Shep insisted. "We need Devon. If we could get an ID on the cop, we could get whoever is behind him."

"You don't think the cop is the major player?"

"No. I think he's the hired help. And if it turns out that Lejeune is his boss, he's going to be one sorry bastard."

She didn't mention what she had just remembered about Patti, needing more time to process the information. "So what now?"

He blew out a breath. "I've got some things I need to run down at the station. Unless you want me to come there first."

She knew seeing him would have to wait. "No. That's okay, do what you need to. I have a meeting with my boss, and then I'm going to meet Patti. I think I need to go alone."

"I understand, baby. Call me when you're finished. Or if you need anything."

She got up from the kitchen table and dressed, questions swirling in her head as she got ready to face the D.A.

10:00 A.M.

Her meeting went as well as Ryan could have expected. Since her section of court was closed for the next week anyway, Peter wasn't making a decision about Ryan's fate as a prosecutor at the moment. If the murders weren't solved by the time her judge was back, or worse yet, if anybody else got killed, that could change. But for now, at least, she still had her job.

Peter had also told her that Chad had been released on an ROR. Judge McAllister had signed the paperwork while Chad was still in booking. Ryan wasn't surprised. All attorneys had at least one judge in their corner. She was a little hurt that McAllister would let Chad out knowing Ryan was the victim, particularly with everything else going on, but she couldn't let that get to her at this point. The only significance to Ryan was that Chad could have killed LaJohnnie Lee.

Before leaving the office, Ryan stopped to see Bo, recalling that he was the one who introduced her to Chad in the first place. She had gone to St. Louis Cathedral for Red Mass, a service to bless the Louisiana Supreme Court. Most of the attorneys in the city were there, more to be seen than as a show of respect. Ryan had gotten stuck sitting next to Bo in the last pew because she had arrived late.

Chad had been sitting next to Bo, and Ryan had thought that Chad was the most beautiful man she had ever seen. She had known he was an attorney, and that he came from a wealthy family, but that was all. She had certainly never heard anything to make her suspect he was a sexual deviant. When Mass was over, she had gotten Bo to introduce her to Chad, although Bo seemed a little hesitant at the time. Ryan thought she knew why now.

Bo looked up from his desk with his usual bland expression. "Still got a job?"

"You could say that," she answered, and then got straight to the point. "Bo, was there some reason you didn't want to introduce me to Chad?"

Bo looked embarrassed, but composed himself after a second. "I've known Chad a long time. He was always kind of an asshole."

"Give me a particular."

"He's got a reputation for being a little rough with his girlfriends. I didn't think you were into that kind of thing." He looked away.

"Do you think Chad's crazy enough to kill people?" She watched Bo's face closely.

"You mean those defendants in the projects? I don't know." Bo seemed to perk up. "He's always been a little off. When we were younger, he used to do things like set cats on fire." He pushed his glasses up on his nose. "Do I think he's capable of killing a bunch of people in the projects? Maybe. I just don't know if he's intelligent enough to pull something like that off."

"What do you mean intelligent?" she asked with a frown. "Most murderers get caught because they're actually pretty stupid."

"How would he find out which cases you lost? And even if he was following your career before you started dating him, how would he be able to get your defendants in the St. Thomas to kill them? The paper said the victims didn't even live there."

Ryan dismissed Bo's doubts. "I don't know how he found out about my cases, but he could have paid people to do all the hard work. Chad has enough money. And he's made some obvious mistakes, so he's not that smart."

"He has?" Bo seemed interested in hearing her theory.

Ryan couldn't help feeling a little superior at having inside information on a big case, even if the case did involve her. "Nothing major, but he's left enough clues so the police should be able to find his accomplices. And his accomplices will lead them right back to him."

"Maybe he does some of the things you think of as mistakes on purpose," Bo said. "To let you know it's him. Chad was never exactly subtle. Maybe he's making conscious choices to lead you to him."

"Maybe. He left a suicide note with LaJohnnie Lee that obviously wasn't written by her, to let me know he really killed her. That's what I think, anyway."

"I really hope it's not Chad," Bo said. "He is an asshole, but I've been friends with him for a really long time. You hate to think that someone you know could do something like that."

She nodded, and stood up to leave.

"Uh, and just to let you know, Kellie was talking about you this morning."

"Oh?"

Bo looked uncomfortable again. "I think she had a problem with all the slut comments you made about her last night. Not that I blame you. I wish I had the balls to take her on. But I overheard her saying that the only reason Chapetti has been hanging out with you is because your dad asked him to babysit you while he was out of town. She said that when your dad gets back, Chapetti is going back to Wanda."

"Did she say where she heard this?" Ryan asked, suspicious.

"She said she heard it from Wanda," he answered. "Last night after you left."

"Thanks for the heads up," Ryan said, walking out of Bo's office. She would have to deal with Shep and Wanda later. Right now, she had a biological mother to meet.

Ryan tried to stay calm on the short drive to the Upperline Convalescent Home. She had to put Shep temporarily out of her mind. She needed to focus all of her attention right now on getting up the nerve to talk to Patti.

Upperline Convalescent looked more like a country club than a home for the sick. The palatial building was set back far from the street, and the expansive, well-manicured front lawn had neatly landscaped beds of roses, daffodils and lillies.

Ryan tried the front door, feeling like an intruder, and was surprised when it opened easily. The front desk reminded her of the check-in at the Ritz Carlton. An ornate chandelier was suspended from the cathedral ceiling above the marble floor. A woman with a hundred-dollar hair cut dressed in a Chanel suit looked up and smiled. "May I help you?" Her name tag said Clara Parker. Her shoes said Jimmy Choo.

"I'm here to visit Patricia Ryan." Ryan wondered if she was going to be allowed in. She fought the urge to look down at her own wrinkled T-shirt, frayed jean shorts and shabby tennis shoes.

Clara Parker's face stretched into a pained smile. "Oh my, you must be Angie's daughter. I've heard so much about you."

Ryan was surprised, but tried to act cool. "I don't believe we've met."

"Oh my," she said again, and Ryan got the feeling something was troubling her. "I've been trying to contact your mother all day."

"She's out of town. Is there a problem?"

"Angie told me she would be in Grand Isle, but she's not answering the number she left. I'm sorry to have to tell you this, but your aunt passed away sometime during the night."

"She what?" Ryan grabbed onto the counter top.

Clara obviously mistook Ryan's reaction and patted her hand. "She went peacefully, in her sleep."

"What was the cause of death?" Ryan asked, immediately on alert.

"We don't know yet. The coroner received her this morning. Whenever a guest with a non-fatal illness expires, the coroner has to conduct an autopsy. Your poor mother is going to be devastated. I wish I could tell you more, but that's really all I know. When she couldn't be roused for breakfast, the doctor saw her and determined she had expired."

"I'll be sure to tell my mother." Ryan wasn't sure what she was supposed to do.

Clara smiled with obvious relief. "I am so sorry I didn't have the opportunity to tell her myself. Could you please send my condolences? And ask her to call as soon as she can?"

Ryan nodded, unsure what she should say. So she didn't say anything, and instead went back out to her Jeep and climbed in. She called the coroner's office and finally got Doug. He was surprised to find out that Patti was Ryan's aunt, and said there were no obvious signs of a homicide, but he hadn't had a chance to do the autopsy or gotten the toxicology results yet to determine the cause of death. He also told her that LaJohnnie Lee's death was going to be classified as a homicide. No prints had been retrieved from the apartment, but he had heard that the gun used had been reported stolen. He promised to call Ryan if he found out anything else.

Ryan called her mother next. If she waited, she knew she would lose her nerve. Her mother answered on the second ring.

"Mama, it's Ryan."

"Is everything okay, baby? Your father has been frantic with everything that's been happening there, but Gram's not doing well. I don't know if she's even going to make this trip home. Is something wrong?"

"Uh, Patti's dead." She didn't know how else to say it. "Clara Parker has been trying to get in touch with you. Doug doesn't know the cause of death yet, but he didn't find any signs of homicide." She stopped, wondering if she should offer her sympathy or ask her mother why she hadn't told her Patti had been alive to begin with.

"I got Sean's message." Her mother's voice was distant. "I can't really talk right now."

"Daddy's right there?"

"Yes, he is."

"Are you going to tell him?"

"I don't know right now, Ryan. We'll talk later." Ryan could hear her mother's voice getting shaky, and she felt sorry for her for a second. She wondered if the captain knew that Patti had been living so nearby all this time.

Ryan started the Jeep and was halfway home when Shep called.

"I've got some information. Can you meet me at the station?"

She tried to think of a way to ask him about Wanda, but decided she would be better off asking him in person. She wanted to see his face when he answered her. "I'm on my way. And speaking of Patti, she's dead."

"What?"

"She's dead." She was surprised at how little emotion she felt at the death of her biological mother. "Doug hasn't done the autopsy yet, but he said there were no obvious signs of homicide. Is that too much of a coincidence? Patti dies the night before I go to meet her?"

"I don't know, baby. Did you tell anybody other than me that you were going there today?"

"I have a vague recollection of mentioning it more than once last night. Any number of people might have heard me. I was drunk, remember?"

He was silent on the other end.

"Hello? Oh, I see. It's probably my fault she's dead too."

"I didn't say that. Why don't you wait for Doug to do the autopsy before you jump to any conclusions? And I was just thinking that if Patti was murdered, and it's somehow connected to the other homicides, then whoever killed her was at the Hole last night when you were."

More good news. She was probably being watched by the killer last night, and her biggest concern had been trying to one-up Kellie Leblanc.

"I'm on my way," she told Shep.

Shep was waiting outside the station. Ryan attempted to distance herself from him. He didn't seem to notice, and grabbed her in a hug the second she walked up.

Inside, Shep led her to the SID office and patted the chair next to his desk. He handed her a computer printout as soon as she sat down. "These are the calls that were made to your house over the last two weeks. I highlighted the calls that came in on the days of the homicides. The same number shows up on all of those nights. It traced back to a prepaid cell phone that was logged into evidence at criminal court. The case was assigned to McAllister's section, just like the crack we found at Dalton's." He pulled out a second printout.

"This is a list of all of the people that had access to the cell phone when it was in evidence. I was getting ready to cross-reference this with the list of people who had access to the crack, when I got the information that the gun used to kill LaJohnnie was also part of a case in McAllister's section. So I got a list of everybody who had access to the gun, and cross-referenced it with the list of people who had access to the crack and the cell phone. The list has gotten substantially shorter."

He held up a shorter print out of names. "There are two property room clerks, two defense attorneys and five assistant district attorneys who had access to all of the evidence." He handed her the list.

Ryan frowned. "Why would he leave a gun he got from the evidence room on LaJohnnie? He has to know the evidence can be traced back."

"He's leaving clues so you can try to figure out who he is. He knows how many people are going to be suspects, and how long it's going to take to eliminate the wrong ones. He probably figures he can do whatever he's planning on doing before we're able to pin down his identity."

Ryan read the names to herself. "So he's planning something soon. This list isn't that long." She didn't recognize the names of the property room clerks, but she knew the two defense attorneys, as well as the five prosecutors. "And you really think somebody on this list might be a killer? I just can't see it." She saw these people every day, and as far as she knew, they all liked her. With the exception of Kellie. But as much as she didn't like the other woman, she didn't think Kellie would waste her time killing people to get back at Ryan for some catty feud.

"I'd say it would almost have to be one of them," Shep said. "Or at the very least one of them is an accomplice."

She finally put the list down on his desk, having difficulty believing that one of the people on it hated her enough to kill other people just to ruin her life. "What do you think about Chad being released from OPP yesterday on an ROR? He was out by the time the booking forms were completed. Do you think he had enough time to get processed, find LaJohnnie, and kill her before her mother got home?"

"Yeah, I do. But that doesn't mean Chad killed her. He could have paid somebody else to do it."

"I asked Bo about Chad. They grew up together. He said Chad used to do things like set cats on fire when they were younger. But Bo didn't think Chad would be smart enough to pull off something like this."

"You were talking about this with Lambert?"

"He's known Chad since they were little. He's probably got a better handle on Chad than I ever could."

Shep tapped the list with his finger. "Lambert's name is on this list, Ryan. He's one of the few people who had access to the evidence."

"So is Edie. And Harry Stelly. And Big Mike. That doesn't mean I can't talk to them. And personally, I think Bo is too big a coward to be behind a bunch of murders. You think I'm a rule follower? You should see him. He won't even park illegally in front of the courthouse." And then she added, "And let's not forget about Kellie. Maybe you should investigate her. She certainly hates me enough."

"We're going to check everybody on the list."

"Speaking of Kellie, she said something interesting," Ryan began slowly, refusing to look directly at Shep. "She said the only reason you were spending so much time with me was because daddy ordered you to, and that when he gets back in town, you're going back to Wanda."

Shep didn't respond, and looked as if he was thinking of the right way to answer.

"Did you really tell Wanda that?" Ryan stood up and grabbed her purse.

"Ryan, yeah, I told her that, but it's not how it sounds."

"Good, because it sounds like the reason you didn't want to be with me last night is really because you didn't want to cheat on Wanda. If you want her, you can have her." She jerked her arm away. "Just don't lie to me to suck up to daddy. I felt stupid enough when I thought Espinito was doing it. I certainly don't appreciate you doing it right now."

"Baby, will you please let me explain?" He tried to grab for her again.

She moved out of his reach. "I don't think that's necessary. I can fill in the blanks myself." She started out of the door. "And don't call me baby." His not wanting to have sex with her was explained, at least. There was nothing wrong with her. He just had a real girlfriend he was sacrificing to get ass-kissing points from the captain.

He ran behind her, catching her hand in his, ignoring the looks from the other officers in the hallway.

"I'm going out front to smoke. Just leave me alone for a minute." She tried to walk away, but he wouldn't let go of her hand.

"Will you let me explain when you come back?"

She shrugged. "Just let go of me." She finally pulled her hand out of his grasp and blinked back tears as she left the SID office and walked down the hallway to the lobby area. She could feel him watching behind her, but he didn't try to stop her again.

Ryan lit a cigarette and sat on the stoop outside at the bottom of the steps, thinking about how crappy her life had become. What did she expect? She had been right. Guys like Shep weren't interested in girls like her.

She wondered if she should get in her Jeep and drive off. But Shep would probably just follow her. Maybe he did have an explanation. Maybe he didn't have the guts to break it off with Wanda. Or maybe he really wanted to keep stringing them both along. It didn't matter to her at this point. What Shep had told Wanda hurt, and made Ryan look, and feel, pathetic and stupid. She had felt that way with Chad. She had never imagined she would end up feeling that way with Shep.

She finished the cigarette and walked to the corner, not wanting to go back into the station until she knew what she was going to say. She was relieved when her cell phone rang, thankful for the diversion.

"Miss Ryan, this is Devon," an excited voice said. "I know you at the police station. I seen you on the corner. I'm three houses down, same side of the street. I was coming in when I seen the cop that was in the project that night. I ducked into the bushes. If the cop sees me, he gonna shoot me. Nobody gonna do me nothing if you with me."

"I'm walking right now," she said, glancing behind her. Shep was still in the doorway, but no longer watching her, apparently talking to someone behind him. Ryan quickly made the corner and started down the street.

Devon was going to come in, he was going to look at photo lineups and he was going to pick out the cop he saw in the St. Thomas. When the cop was arrested, he would give up whoever was responsible, whether it was Chad or not, as well as anyone else who was involved. Prison was even more difficult for police officers than it was for regular criminals, and the only way to ensure isolation from the general population would be for the cop to roll over. And then, Ryan would get her life back.

A black Mercedes was parked, trunk open, in front of the third house from the corner. In her peripheral vision, she saw a shadow emerge from the front seat.

"You didn't think I'd find you, did you, bitch?" Durrell Wilson jumped in front of her, the diamond chip in his tooth catching the sun's rays as he smiled. "How you like me now?" He grabbed her by the hair and shoved her, face-down, over the hood of the car. She froze, not quite believing what was happening, until he started pulling at her jean shorts, trying to get them down.

She clawed at his hands with little effect. His grip finally loosened when she brought her foot up and kicked it back as hard as she could, making contact with his shin. Before she could escape his grasp, unseen hands forced a sack over her head from behind, and dragged her toward the back of the car. She felt cold steel pressing against her temple through the cloth.

"Make a sound and I'll blow your head off," a voice said in a barely audible whisper, and Ryan felt herself falling, the back of her knees catching onto metal as she landed in the trunk of the car.

She couldn't move, couldn't breathe. The hands grabbed her frozen legs and forced them into the trunk.

The same voice hissed, "See you in hell, Wilson."

Durrell Wilson's voice rang out. "What you doing, man?"

And then a gun shot rang out, followed by a second of silence as a body landed on top of her. Ryan struggled frantically until she wiggled from underneath him. She heard the sound of two more gunshots close to her ear, and then the unmistakable sound of a car trunk slamming.

The car began moving. Somebody must have seen what just happened, or at least have heard the gunshots. It was broad daylight, and they were right next door to a police station, for Christ's sake. Why wasn't anyone coming after her?

Wilson's body convulsed next to her, and then stopped moving altogether. Ryan pulled the cloth off of her head, but it was too dark to see inside the trunk. The body brushed up against her with every turn of the car, covering her with the Durrell Wilson's bodily fluids. She fought the urge to vomit.

She heard a squawk, like a police radio. Why would he have a police radio in the trunk of his car? And why would he have left it for her?

She tried to remain calm. If this lunatic was going to kill her, he probably would have shot her when he shot Wilson. Unless, of course, he wanted to torture her first.

The trunk was oppressively hot. She wondered how much oxygen a car trunk held, or if she could suffocate before somebody found her. If somebody found her. The car had been driving for a few minutes already. She didn't know where she was, or how far from the station they had traveled.

Then she realized she still had her cell phone, and grabbed it from her pocket. The car hit a bump and she dropped the phone. She reached on the bottom of the trunk, her hand sliding around in something lumpy and wet. The trunk smelled of urine and feces, and she knew Durrell Wilson was definitely dead.

She managed to find the phone and hit number one on the speed dial, the station house.

"Sixth District."

"This is Ryan Murphy. Somebody grabbed me and threw me in the trunk of a car."

"Here's Detective Chapetti."

A second later, "Ryan, are you hurt?"

"No, but I'm in the trunk of his car. I don't know where I am and I think I'm running out of air." She tried to control the hysteria in her voice.

Shep's voice was calm. "There's plenty of oxygen in the trunk. Don't panic, you can't suffocate. Do you know where you are?"

"No, he's been driving around."

"Who is he?"

"I don't know. I didn't see him."

"Did you see the car?"

"No." She began to take big gulps of air. "I did, but I didn't really look at it. It's dark, black I think. A Mercedes." She could hardly breathe. Shep had lied. She was almost out of oxygen.

She heard the squawking again. "I think there's a police radio or something back here."

"See if you can find it. We can find your location if it's an NOPD radio. Baby, keep breathing. You're going to be okay, just breathe."

She felt on the floor until she found a two-way radio. She hit the button. "Somebody help me," she said into the radio. She released the button.

A second later a distorted voice responded through the speaker, "Nobody's going to help you, princess. Tell your boyfriend you're in safe hands now." The car began picking up speed.

"I don't think it's a police radio," Ryan said into the cell phone. "And he's driving faster. What should I do?"

"Stay on the phone," Shep ordered. "We're trying to track your cell phone."

The car screeched to an abrupt stop, and the cell phone flew from Ryan's hands again, hitting the bottom of the trunk with a clank. She frantically grasped for it, but the car started moving again. She could hear the phone sliding from one side of the trunk to the other as the car made a sharp turn.

The radio barked in her hand, the same electronically distorted voice. "Ryan, if you can guess who I am, I'll let you live. For a while, anyway."

"Why are you doing this?" Ryan asked into the walkie-talkie.

"Justice." There was a pause. "You don't remember me. Here's a clue. My name is Jacob." The car started slowing down. He had been driving for no more than ten minutes, and she wished she would have paid more attention to the route he had driven. If she had, she might know where they were ending up, and might have had a better chance of escaping. The car slowed to a crawl. He would be stopping soon. And when he did, he would kill her.

Ryan suddenly realized that her purse was still on her shoulder, and inside it, her gun. She scrambled in the purse for her gun, wondering if she would get a chance to take a shot before he killed her.

The car stopped. Ryan's heart beat so fast her chest hurt. When the trunk opened, she would just shoot, and hope she didn't miss.

But what if he wasn't the one that opened the trunk? What if he grabbed some unsuspecting stranger at gunpoint, knowing Ryan would shoot once the trunk was open?

She waited, pointing her gun. She would have to make sure it was him before she shot. But then, how would she know it was him? What if she thought it was an unsuspecting stranger and she didn't shoot, and it was really the maniac? She was going to lose her mind if the trunk didn't open soon.

Nothing happened. What was he doing? Was he standing outside the trunk? If he shot through the trunk, she wouldn't have a chance. But doing that would be risky. Somebody might see him. Of course, he hadn't worried about the risk when he shoved Ryan into the trunk, or when he shot Durrell Wilson.

She started to feel more nauseated, the smell of blood and bodily fluids overwhelming her. She bit back the taste of bile. The heat in the car was stifling, and she prayed she wouldn't vomit in the hot, confining space.

Still nothing happened. Why was he waiting? Was he trying to get her to let her guard down?

She didn't know how long she had been stopped like this, stuck in the trunk, beginning to feel weak from the heat, when she heard voices. Was it him? And if so, who was with him?

Then the voices were closer.

"Police," a voice yelled. "Get out and step away from the car."

Ryan's adrenaline started pumping. Was it a trap? Or was she being saved?

She felt someone moving around inside the front of the car. She aimed the gun, although she wasn't sure at what.

"Nobody here," she heard a man yell.

She recognized Spence's voice. She dropped her gun and began kicking on the inside of the trunk, screaming for help as loud as she could. The trunk finally popped open and Spence stood on the other side. He quickly holstered his gun and grabbed her from the trunk.

"EMS is on the way. Ryan, you're going to be okay."

"I'm not hurt," she said, confused. And then she realized she was covered with Durrell Wilson's blood. "You can put me down. This blood isn't mine."

Spence set her down on the ground, steadying her as her wobbly legs collapsed. The sun was so bright it took her eyes a second to adjust to the light. She looked around and found herself surrounded by the boarded buildings of the St. Thomas Housing Development.

Sirens screamed in the distance. Ryan's thumb automatically went to her mouth. When she saw the fleshy gray and pink chunks covering her hand, she pulled away from Spence and then vomited on the ground. A minute later, Shep pulled up, jumped out of his car and grabbed her in his arms.

"My God, baby, are you okay?"

She nodded. "You're getting Durrell Wilson's brains on you," she said numbly.

He pulled her closer, holding her tight. "I can't believe he got to you. I am so stupid. I looked away for one minute and you were gone. When I heard those gunshots, my heart stopped."

She believed the concern in his eyes. "I shouldn't have left," she said, unable to control the sobs that were erupting, no longer mad at Shep. She didn't care any longer about what he said to Wanda, or even if he really was planning to go back to her. Ryan just wanted him to comfort her right now, and convince her she was safe.

Spence walked back up, looking as if he didn't want to interrupt. "Uh, the car is stolen," he said. "It was reported two months ago. Crime lab is processing it right now. And Durrell Wilson is dead. Coroner is on the way."

Shep held her tight.

"EMS is here," Spence continued, "in case Ryan needs to be checked out."

Ryan finally pulled back from Shep then and shook her head. "I just need my cell phone from the trunk. And I want to go home and take a shower." She paused, wondering why she was still alive. "He didn't hurt me. He could have killed me, but he just let me go."

Sgt. Mitchell walked up. "Ryan, I need you to answer some questions before you go home."

Ryan told the Sergeant everything she could remember.

"Is there anything about him that was familiar?" the sergeant asked her.

She waited a second, trying to concentrate on what she had noticed about him. "Just his cologne. Somebody I know wears that cologne. I can't remember the brand, but it's something expensive."

"Could it have been Chad?" Shep asked.

She shook her head. "He wears Polo. I just can't remember. Can I go home now?"

"That's probably a good idea," Shep said, pointing to a news van that had just stopped at the corner. The sergeant nodded his agreement

"How did he set this up?" Ryan said out loud, walking to Shep's car, his arm around her shoulder. "How did he know I would be here, or that I would be outside at that particular time? And how did he know Durrell Wilson?"

"He must be watching you, waiting for an opportunity. If he is a cop, he could have found out about Wilson pretty easily. The only thing I know for sure is that you're not getting away from me again."

He grabbed her in his arms and held her possessively. Ryan noticed a flash going off, but ignored it.

They rode to her house in silence, Ryan not wanting to discuss what had just happened and Shep obviously not knowing what to say. She didn't blame him for what had happened, but she knew he would blame himself regardless. And while the maniac terrorizing her was not Shep's fault, she wasn't ready to tell him that yet. Once they got inside her apartment, there was an uncomfortable moment.

"Ryan, I know you just went through something terrible, but I think we need to talk."

"Fine," she answered. "You can talk to me in the shower."

He followed her as she shed her clothes, stopped to throw them in the garbage, and then walked into her bathroom. She turned on the shower and brushed her teeth before she got in.

"I did tell Wanda that I had to babysit you," he admitted. Ryan could feel him watching her, but she refused to look at him. "And your dad did ask me to watch out for you, and to keep Chance Halley away from you. Why do you think the captain wasn't calling you every five minutes to check up on you?

"But I would have watched out for you even if your dad hadn't asked me to. And I only told Wanda that to get her off my back. I tried for three months to explain to her we were through, but she just wouldn't go away. She even made a big scene at the station a while back. I know it was stupid, but it was easier just to put her off for a while.

Ryan frowned at him. "So when my daddy came back, you were what, going to screw her a couple of times before you let her down gently?" She watched the water at her feet turn red, trying not to notice the small chunks that were stubbornly refusing to pass through the smaller holes of the shower drain.

"No. I was going to tell her that after spending so much time with you, I ended up falling in love with you."

"Why would you tell her something ridiculous like that?" Her heart was pounding ferociously as she started lathering her hair with Soothing Lavender shampoo.

"Because it's something Wanda could understand." He took a step toward the shower. "And because it's the truth. Ryan, I knew way before your dad left town that I wanted to be with you."

She stopped lathering and waited a few seconds before responding, her heart still racing out of control while she contemplated her response.

Finally, she said, "You know, I could use some help."

Shep took half a second to strip and join her. He shampooed her hair and scrubbed her body in silence until every trace of foreign blood and tissue was gone.

Ryan stepped out of the shower, her skin pink, and Shep looked at her uncertainly.

"This may sound grossly inappropriate after everything that happened today, but you'll notice I'm not drunk right now," she said, and turned to walk out of the bathroom.

Shep stopped her, grabbing her around the waist from behind.

"Do you think this a good idea?" he whispered in her ear. "You just went through a traumatic experience. Maybe we should wait until things are more normal."

She turned to face him. "Shep, things may never be normal. I just want to forget everything for a little while. I want to forget about dead bodies, and losing my promotion, and somebody putting a sack over my head and driving me around in the trunk of his car. I just want to feel good for a change, even if it's only for a few minutes."

He ran his hands down her naked back. "Baby, if there's one thing I can do, I can make you feel good." His voice was husky. "And for longer than just a few minutes. If that's what you want."

"Is it what you want?"

"What do you think?" He moved her hand to his penis, which was standing at attention. "Shep Jr. has been wanting to come out to play with you for a very long time."

He pulled her tightly against him, and then kissed her neck and shoulders, sending the blood coursing throughout her body. He pressed his lips to hers, his tongue probing deeply, searching urgently, before lifting her up and carrying her into the bedroom.

Her heart raced out of control as Shep nibbled her earlobe, his breath hot in her ear. He placed her gently on the edge of the bed, but remained standing next to her, his mouth engulfing her nipple, and his hands stroking her body. She let out a slight gasp and felt her hips lifting to meet his hand.

"You are so beautiful," he murmured as he knelt in front of her, kissing her belly button, seemingly excited by the belly ring. He buried his face between her thighs, and Ryan suddenly knew why Wanda might find it difficult to give this man up.

Afraid of climaxing too quickly, Ryan pulled back from him and climbed into the bed, reaching in the nightstand for a condom.

He followed her into bed and pressed his face between her legs again. She moaned, and for the next two hours, Shep proved true to his word.

Exhausted, sweaty, and out of condoms, Ryan finally collapsed, her eyes closed, wanting to hold on to the feeling of complete satisfaction forever.

"You okay, baby?" Shep raised himself up and stared down at her.

"Just savoring the moment," she answered, lifting her face to kiss his neck.

He finally rolled off of her, and put his arm underneath her, pulling her close. "You don't have to do that. There's going to be plenty more of them."

She laid her head on his chest and answered, "Not if you don't get some more condoms."

"I'll bring a whole case," he said, nibbling her earlobe. "But four times wasn't enough?"

"It was more than four times for me," she admitted. "God, I never want this to end."

He gave her Gilbert's smile. "I was that good, huh?"

She felt her face turn red. "You were, but that's not what I meant." She stopped, embarassed, and then finally blurted out, "I thought something was wrong with me. You know, because of Chad —"

Shep interrupted her. "I've already told you there is nothing wrong with you, baby. Trust me. The problem was all his."

Ryan swallowed hard, and then forced the words out of her mouth, desperately needing to explain the last few months to Shep. "After Chad, I really wanted to find somebody safe just to be with, to prove the problem wasn't with me. But I kept getting scared, thinking what if the same thing happened with somebody else?" She closed her eyes, slightly ashamed.

"You don't owe me an explanation. And I would have been happy to oblige you at any time," he said, his fingers playing over the cherry-red lips tattooed on her hip.

She opened her eyes and looked away. "Shep, I've seen the girls you get. Tall, gorgeous, skinny blondes, who can probably suck a bowling ball through a garden hose. Why would you have ever thought of me?"

"Are you jealous?" he asked, seeming amused. "You never exactly seemed to be interested."

"I said it before. I never thought I was your type."

"You're right." He held her hair away from her face and kissed her mouth, long and deep. Her heart started racing all over again. "You're too good for me. And you're definitely too good for that asshole Chad. I wish I would have had the nerve to ask you out before you went out with him." He nuzzled her neck. "He would have never had the chance to hurt you."

"Technically, you still haven't had the nerve to ask me out," Ryan pointed out, trying to change the subject. "And do you really want to talk about that loser when we could be doing this?" She brought her head down to his chest and ran her tongue around his nipple.

He closed his eyes and waited a moment before he spoke. "Baby, I could spend the next six weeks making love to you, condoms or not. But even then, I'd still want to know what he did to you."

She sat up. "If I didn't know better, I'd swear you had a thing for the man."

"He's a douche bag," Shep said. "I just want to know what happened."

When she realized he wasn't letting go, she finally gave him a summary. "He hit me a couple of times."

Shep pulled her back down and stroked her hair. "Why did you stay with him after he hit you the first time?"

"I was an idiot. I thought it was a one time thing. He apologized, and cried, and swore he would never do it again." She looked away, knowing how pathetic she probably seemed.

"What about after that? Why didn't you leave him when he hit you a second time?"

She sighed. "I guess because I felt stupid about not saying anything to anybody the first time. I didn't know how to get away from him by then."

"And what happened when you broke up?"

She sighed. "I was so freaking sick of him. We had just tried to have sex and as usual he couldn't. He got mad and blamed his impotence on me, saying I didn't know how to turn him on. I left and called Edie. She convinced me to dump him.

"So I went back to his apartment to break up with him, face to face, which was probably the biggest mistake of my life. That's when I caught him with the paralegal.

He was wearing this freaky leather outfit with the ass cut out, and a mask that had a zipper for the mouth. That weird girl was spanking him with a paddle. I told him we were over. He didn't take it well." She hoped Shep wasn't going to push for more. She still wasn't ready to tell him the rest.

Shep frowned. "And after all that, you still don't think he could be the one behind this? He hurt you and you dumped him, not to mention caught him in his leather fairy outfit. You don't think he could be doing this to get back at you?"

She shook her head. "Why would he call himself Jacob? And why wouldn't he have just killed me when he had the chance?"

"Because it's some sick game to him."

"What about Durrell Wilson?" Ryan asked. "How would Chad even know about him?"

Shep sighed. "I don't know, baby. Maybe crime lab will get something from the Mercedes. They should be processing it now. I'll call over there and see where they're at. And I can call Doug and see if he's found out anything else about Patti for you."

"Speaking of Patti," Ryan said, "when she took me, she brought me to an apartment in the St. Thomas. I really didn't think about it until I found out Patti was dead."

Ryan watched Shep climb out of bed, unable to stop herself from admiring his body, despite the topic of conversation.

"Oh, and it's not mentioned in the file," Ryan added, "but there was a little boy in the apartment. When Patti heard the police coming, she sent him away with a man I'm pretty sure was a pedophile. I only remembered it when I listened to my taped statement. Do you think there's any chance that this could be connected?"

Shep leaned over and held her face in his hands. "I don't know, baby. After I call the crime lab I'll look through Patti's file again. You good for now?"

She kissed him softly on the mouth. "I'm great for now. And we're out of condoms anyway."

MONTE

Monte Carlson sat in a midnight blue, two-door 1987 Oldsmobile Cutlass, knowing he had an important decision to make. The car belonged to one of his sisters, and no one would recognize it or connect it to him. If he wanted to, he could just drive off, without anyone ever knowing he had been there.

He was parked outside the Magnolia Housing Development, the second housing project in the Sixth District. Criminal activity was at an all-time low in the Magnolia, which was probably why Devon Jones was hiding out here.

Monte had known where Devon was for some time— one of his contacts had clued him in to that pretty early on. Monte just had a policy about interfering in what he called SNIM. The acronym stood for Shit Not Involving Monte. And Devon's problem didn't involve Monte, so he should have just stayed out of it. Period.

But he couldn't. He knew there was a hit out on Devon. His sources told him Devon was worth fifty G's to somebody. And Monte didn't see how he could let that happen.

Ordinarily, Monte would just shrug off information like that. For instance, when he heard that L'Roid Smith was going down, Monte hadn't cared. Smith was going to walk one more time, the body count was climbing and wasn't much anybody could do about it. So somebody decided to take him out. Monte didn't so much look the other way as just ignore the information until he had heard Smith was already dead. Not a big dilemma, especially when he heard through triple or quadruple hearsay that a D.A. had paid for the hit.

Then the same thing with Jeremiah. No great love loss there either. Jeremiah was a middle-aged punk who avoided getting caught at least a dozen times for serious crimes nobody could pin on him. And he beat women, not just his wife, but his own mama and his sisters. So Monte ignored the information that time as well. And he heard through the same hearsay network that the same D.A. paid for the hit. So no big deal to him again.

Somehow, Monte didn't find out about Charmaine and her daughter. He might have stepped in for that, gotten the kid to a safe place at least. He liked to think he wouldn't have let an innocent little girl get killed.

Cleeves was a different story. Monte had heard about Cleeves an hour before he went down. Monte had already suspected Ryan of maybe being the D.A. who financed the hits. She hated Cleeves, and she had a connection to all the other victims. Nothing Monte could do. Everything he had found out would have been inadmissible in court anyway, so there was no point in revealing what he knew. And truth be told, if Cleeves was dead, it would save Monte the time and trouble of having to follow him around until Cleeves did something Monte could arrest him for. No way Cleeves was getting away with his little show in court. So Cleeves had been killed and Monte once again hadn't done anything to try to prevent it.

But now he heard that Ryan had been taken on a joy ride in the trunk of a car. Whoever did it could have killed her if he wanted. That bothered Monte more than he would admit to anyone else. And knowing that Ryan wasn't the one behind the homicides, he had to rethink his policy of noninvolvement.

He knew a lot of people were looking for Devon, wanting the money. Wasn't much to some people to kill a kid. Devon was borderline anyway. Any day now the boy would wake up and be a criminal. Today he was stealing bikes to ride, tomorrow he would be sticking a gun in somebody's face who wouldn't give it up. It was the logical progression without some kind of divine intervention.

Call me Jesus Christ, Monte thought, because Devon hadn't crossed that line yet. Monte couldn't just let him get killed. Especially if Devon had the information that could lead to the person responsible for trying to hurt Ryan. Monte decided he wouldn't change his policy — he would just make a one time exception.

8:30 P.M.

Ryan sat at her father's desk for the second time in two days, wondering what he was going to have to say when he got back in town, which would be any minute. She also wondered if they were ever going to be able to find out the identity of the killer. Shep was with Sean in the interrogation room, showing photo lineups to Devon. So far, Devon had recognized many of the cops from the lineups. He just hadn't seen the cop that had been in the St. Thomas the night of Smith's murder. If he wasn't able to make an ID from this set of photo arrays, Shep or Sean would have to compile more lineups. Ryan hoped they didn't lose Devon again in the meantime.

She glanced at her father's inbox and an envelope with the NOPD insignia caught her attention. The return address bore the stamp of the Public Integrity Division. She held it up to the light, trying to see inside the envelope.

Finally, she ripped the envelope open. The captain was going to be so mad at her anyway, one more transgression on her part wouldn't make a difference. She skimmed the letter. The investigation into the beating of Chad Lejeune had been concluded and no disciplinary action would be taken against the captain at this time. The letter was dated this morning, and had been hand-delivered, as evidenced by the absence of a postmark.

So Battaglia had believed her. Whoever sent Chance Halley that tape had done Ryan a huge favor, however inadvertently. She smiled as she folded the letter and put it back in the envelope, sealing it back with scotch tape. Her father would have to be stupid not to realize somebody had opened the letter. She figured when he saw the contents, he wouldn't care. The smile left her face as her cell phone rang, and she saw her mother's home number on the caller ID.

On the way to her parents' house, Shep told Ryan that he had spoken to Devon's aunt, and she agreed to stay with Devon at a motel near the station, on the state's dime, until Sean could put together more lineups.

"How angry is your dad?" Shep asked as they made the turn into the captain's neighborhood.

Crepe myrtle and wisteria battled the black iron gate that surrounded the Magnolia Place Subdivision. The tiny Chinese man that had worked the gate since Ryan's childhood raised the wooden arm with a smile when he recognized her inside Shep's Corvette, and politely bowed as they drove past.

Ryan nodded and waved, and then turned back to Shep with a sigh. "Mama called, so I didn't actually talk to daddy. But I'm guessing that he's pretty mad, especially if somebody told him about us."

"I'm sure somebody did. Well, he was going to find out eventually. It's probably better that the whole thing is out in the open."

Ryan looked out the window. "For some reason I don't find it necessary to tell my father we're sleeping together."

Shep frowned. "Ryan, we're not just sleeping together. I'm not going anywhere. He's just going to have to accept that."

Ryan took a deep breath before walking into the house. She felt like she was sixteen again, caught after curfew on a school night, driving her father's police car to a party she didn't have permission to be at in the first place. Except now she was more than old enough to know better.

The second she walked in, the captain grabbed her in a fierce hug, squeezing her so tight she wasn't sure if he really missed her or if this was some sort of punishment.

"Do you know how worried I was about you?" her father asked in a low, growly voice, as if everything that happened was Ryan's fault. "When they told me somebody snatched you, I thought I was going to have a heart attack. You were four years old all over again." He stepped back, and Ryan could sense his anger building. "And after everything else, this is what I come home to." His voice grew louder and his face started to turn a scary shade of red.

He picked up the newspaper and threw it back down on the coffee table for effect. The front page showed Ryan and Shep in the St. Thomas, Shep's arms around her.

The captain tapped the picture. "What's this, Chapetti? The last thing I told you before I left was to not try anything with my daughter. Did you forget that? Or did you get confused, and think I said jam your tongue down her throat? Or was that just a little lagniappe for your trouble?"

Ryan would have laughed at the joke if her father hadn't been so angry.

Lagniappe— pronounced lan-yap—was New Orleans for a little something extra.

"And you," he pointed at her. "Why were you at the Upperline Convalescent Home? Did you think I wouldn't find out you went there?"

"I was going to do mama's volunteer work," she answered. "How was I supposed to know Patti lived there? Nobody even bothered to tell me my biological mother was still alive. Did you know?"

"What I knew is irrelevant. Patti was nothing to you. Nothing, got it? There was no reason to tell you anything about her. And I can't believe you're standing here telling me you didn't know about Patti before you went to Upperline. Am I supposed to think that you, of all people, were actually going there out of the goodness of your heart?"

"I don't give a damn what you believe," Ryan's voice grew louder. "If anyone had told me Patti was alive to begin with, this wouldn't have been such a big surprise. I see no reason you would have intentionally withheld this information. It seems I'm not the one with all the secrets in this family. My life's an open book."

The captain gave her a look. "So I've heard. I got the pleasure of hearing all about your social activities from my subordinates." He paused again. "Monte Carlson, Ryan? I thought we had that talk."

"The talk was a little after the fact," Ryan said, looking challengingly at her father. "And it's not as if I actually went out with him." Ten seconds later she looked away, angry at herself for not being able to stare her father down. "And my sex life is none of your damn business. I am a grown woman. I can do what I want. And I wasn't talking about me, anyway. You're the one with all the secrets."

"Secrets?" He seemed baffled. "I don't have any goddamn secrets."

"I think Lt. Battaglia might disagree with that statement."

The captain jabbed his finger in the air. "And you'd be just as wrong as him. Battaglia's half-a-prick who couldn't find his own asshole with two hands and a flashlight. And I didn't mention the PID investigation to anyone because Battaglia's got nothing on me because I don't break policy. But we're not talking about me now, are we? We're talking about you, almost getting yourself killed, because you still think it's cute to play cop."

"I thought Devon called me," Ryan continued to argue, even though she knew it was useless. Her father was not going to concede even one point.

"I don't care if Jesus Christ came off the cross and called you. This was a police investigation. You should have let a police officer check out the call, maybe even one of the detectives handling the case, huh Chapetti?"

"I was right outside the police station," she protested. "How was I supposed to know this guy has balls of steel?"

"See, a detective might have known that. That's why you're supposed to be playing lawyer, not playing cop. You know, I want to yell at you for so many things right now, I don't even know where to begin." He looked at Shep. "And you

Chapetti, what the hell were you doing? Talking to some girl while a psycho was trying to kill my daughter? Bad enough I can't trust you to keep your hands off her, but it seems I can't trust you to keep her safe either. You're not stupid, son, but you have a bad habit of forgetting which head to think with."

Shep looked the captain in the eye. Ryan's thumb shot into her mouth. This was not going well at all.

"Captain, I think we'd better wait to have this conversation until you've calmed down," Shep said. "And when we do, maybe you could let me know whom I'm speaking to– Captain Murphy, my boss, or Kelly Murphy, Ryan's father."

"As far as this investigation is concerned, Chapetti, who I am doesn't make one damn bit of difference. Because you're off, as of this moment."

Shep looked as if he had been slapped. "What?"

"You're off this investigation. I don't want to have to worry every time you two have a lover's spat or some pretty girl turns your head that my daughter is going to be an easy target for some homicidal maniac."

"You don't know anything about it," Ryan began, but her father cut her off.

"Trust me, I know enough." The captain pointed angrily at Shep. "I don't need his swinging dick getting my baby killed. And if I have to take him off the investigation or boot his ass out of the whole goddamn department, I'll do it. You are my only priority, Ryan, whether you like it or not."

"This conversation is over," Ryan said and stormed to the door. "You can say what you want about the stupid things I do, but you're not going to screw with Shep because he likes me. When you're ready to discuss things rationally, I'll be more than happy to come back."

The captain followed her to the door. "Where do you think you're going, little girl? I'm not finished. You want to set things right for Chapetti? Move back in here until they catch this guy and quit playing hide the salami with my detectives."

Ryan stopped at the front door, tears of rage welling in her eyes. "Detective, daddy, just one of them. I have not slept with any of your other men, whether you want to believe that or not. And for the record, I'm not playing anything with Shep, so you'd better get used to the idea of us being together."

She started out the door, but stopped and slowly turned back. "And if I had been inclined to stay with you and mama, because maybe I am scared that some freak is after me, and maybe I would like the comfort and support of my family, with me losing my promotion and watching my whole goddamn career going down the toilet, you can just forget that now. After twenty-eight years, you think you'd have at least some small clue on how to handle me."

The captain looked as if he was going to yell again, but instead just turned to Shep and said, "I guess I don't even know my own child, do I?"

"I guess you don't," Shep said. "And you can take away whatever cases you want. But when you think about it, you're going to realize that my time is better spent trying to help you figure out who's after her, before something else happens."

"Are you finished?" The captain had a menacing glimmer in his eye.

"Yes sir."

"You're off this case. You can work whatever new homicides come in, I don't really give a shit. Just don't let me see your face. Now get the hell out of my house."

SUNDAY

11:30 A.M.

Shep worked quietly while Ryan slept. She had fumed about her father for over an hour after they had gotten back to her apartment last night, until Shep finally came up with several inventive ways to calm her down. After that, she fell into the sleep of the dead.

When Shep woke up this morning, he watched the rhythmic rise and fall of her chest as she continued sleeping. Realizing he wasn't accomplishing anything with his borderline voyeurism, he left the room and sat at Ryan's desk, trying to sort through things.

He couldn't find any information in the D.A. file to support Ryan's memory that there was another child at Patti's apartment in the St. Thomas when the police had shown up. So he tracked down Detective Ribson, the detective who had authored the police report. It took a few calls to locate him in Gulf Shores, where he had retired.

After Shep introduced himself and explained that he was working on a homicide investigation, Ribson was happy to talk to him.

"Detective, I just need to know if there was another child in the apartment when you got there. Ryan seems to remember somebody else, but there's no mention in the report."

Ribson hesitated, and Shep knew there was something.

"There were actually two other kids," Ribson said. "A boy inside the apartment, and a girl playing outside. Right as we got up to the door, a man came out with the little boy. The girl was about five or so, and ran up when the man walked out. The man said they were his kids, and he had just come to pick them up. Both of the kids said they were his, and seemed at ease with him, so I took his name and address and let him go. I didn't want the kids around when we were making the arrest. Things can get ugly sometimes, you know?"

Shep nodded at the phone. "Yes sir, I do know that. So what happened to these two kids?"

"I checked the guy's name after everything was over, I don't know, maybe a week later. Turns out he was a convicted sex-offender. I couldn't believe I had done something so stupid. The man gave me his real name like he wanted me to catch him, and I let him just walk out of there with those kids. I hunted him for a year. I thought I was going to lose my mind if I didn't find him. And I finally did, right back in the St. Thomas, almost the same apartment we busted. But he only had the boy. He said he didn't know what happened to the girl, but I figured she most likely got traded to another pedophile."

"What happened to the boy after you found him?"

"He was pretty messed up from being sexually abused. Social Services took over from there. He was adopted a while later by an attorney and his wife, but I don't know the family. Social Services should be able to tell you, if that helps."

"Do you have any idea if either one of the kids was related to Patricia Ryan?"

"I don't know for sure, but it would have made sense. When working girls got arrested they would often hand their kids over to a friend or relative to keep them away from DSS. Although why any mother would think her kids would be safer with a pedophile than in a foster home is beyond me."

"So you don't know if they were the children of Patricia Ryan or if the pedophile really was their father?"

"Sorry. Once Social Services stepped in, I was off the case."

On a hunch, Shep asked, "Do you remember the name of the boy?"

"Hmmm, give me a second. I remember it was an old-fashion name. Joshua, maybe?"

Shep's pulse quickened. "Could it have been Jacob?"

"Bingo, that was it. Jacob. And the girl was Ruth. I remember that because it was my wife's name. And I thought it was odd that two kids with Biblical names would be living with a child molester."

"What about the name of the pedophile?"

"Jude Lightell. It's a name even my old age won't let me forget. But you won't find anything on him. He kicked up a fuss on the way to the station, and ended up getting himself shot by my partner. Died before he made it to Charity."

"I appreciate you giving me this information," Shep said. "If anything else comes to mind, would you give me a call?"

Shep left his number and the retired detective agreed to call him if he remembered anything else. When he hung up, Ryan was standing in the doorway.

"There was a little boy at Patti's that day." He avoided mentioning the little girl. Ryan had enough on her mind. "His name was Jacob. Ribson let him leave with a man named Jude Lightell who turned out to be a convicted sex-offender. Lightell was caught a year later and killed by the police. The boy was eventually adopted by an attorney. Ribson doesn't know the attorney's name."

Ryan nibbled her thumb. "That clears Chad. He's not adopted. In fact, he looks exactly like his perverted father. So that little boy with Patti in the St. Thomas, he's the freak with the voice distorter? What about the nine people who had access to the stolen evidence? I thought you were convinced the killer had to be one of them."

Shep pulled her into his lap and rested his cheek against the back of her head. Her hair still smelled of lavender. "The evidence that turned up on this case isn't the only evidence missing from the evidence room at court. There's a shitload of closed cases that are missing weapons and drugs. And an evidence room key has apparently been misplaced."

"So it could be somebody who didn't make your list then?" Ryan asked.

He nodded. "It could be one of those nine, but it also could be somebody else who had access to the key. The theory is that one of the clerks helped themselves to the evidence and sold it on the street. The Attorney General's Office is taking the case from us."

She leaned back against him with a big sigh. "Are they going to let you know what they find out?"

"They say they are. But the AG's Office is so damn slow, or thorough, as they like to call it, that it could be eighteen months before they figure anything out."

"And by then it could be too late," Ryan finished. "So what's the next step?"

"I'm going to try to find out if Jacob was Patti's son. If I can verify he was, I can get a court order for his adoption records."

"I don't think you're going to have enough to get a court order. Especially to get into sealed adoption records."

Shep grabbed her hand, and kissed her palm before he answered. "Baby, I'll get them if I have to break into Civil District Court in the middle of the night."

"What about me? What can I do?"

"Go make up with your dad."

A shadow passed over her face. "He ought to be trying to make up with me."

Shep traced her lips with his fingers. "He's going to be your dad the rest of your life. No matter what else happens, he's always going to be there for you. And I know how important your family is to you."

She shook her head. "When he's ready to make up with me, he knows my number."

An hour later, after leaving Dubuc outside Ryan's apartment, Shep went back to the station and did a search of Jude Lightell's name in the NCIC computer.

Lightell's prior arrests and convictions popped up, but the molestation of Jacob was not referenced since Lightell had never been arrested for the crime, having been shot by the police first.

Shep then tried to access the actual police report through the station's system, and came up empty. The case was too old to be in the system, and the case file was old enough to be in storage. He decided to stop wasting his time looking for the old report. The police report would not have the information he wanted anyway, the name of the couple who adopted the boy.

He would have to try another course of action. He might be able to find out whether Patti had any other children by looking at her records from Upperline. Spence had caught the case, and would undoubtedly have no trouble violating the captain's prohibition against Shep working on the cases related to Ryan.

His only concern was what Spence might expect from him in return. The last time he asked Spence for a favor, Shep had found himself dodging the Mexican police and the Sinaloa drug cartel in Nuevo Laredo, helping Spence smuggle a narcotics suspect back to New Orleans in the trunk of his Crown Vic. But whatever crazy thing Spence would ask, it would be worth it if Shep could find out who was after Ryan.

He went to Spence's desk, looking around cautiously for the captain. Spence acknowledged him with a nod. "You want to know about Patricia Ryan?"

"What's it going to cost me?" Shep asked.

Spence looked at him thoughtfully for a second. "My little sister needs a date to the prom."

Shep groaned. "What does she look like?"

Spence's face broke into a smile. "Kidding, Chapetti, just kidding. I'll give you a freebie. The captain's being an asshole on this one." He picked a file up from his desk. "Here. Cause of death was an involuntary heroin overdose. The place is locked down every night, but some of the patients keep their windows open, so it would have been easy enough for somebody to sneak in without being seen. And video only covers the front desk and the exits. Nothing on any of those."

Shep flipped through the file, stopping at a copy of Patti's medical records.

"I copied everything Upperline had," Spence explained. "The desk clerk let me help myself."

Shep flipped through the records, finally stopping at the gynecological form. The history listed sixteen pregnancies, including three live births. So Jacob could have been Patti's child. Unfortunately, the form didn't contain the names of the children for the necessary proof. Shep exhaled, wondering what he should do next.

Ryan was right. The evidence wouldn't be sufficient to get a subpoena for records from DSS. The courts were extremely strict about sealed adoption records. Shep tried to think if there was another way to get into the records. One of his ex-girlfriends worked for Social Services, but he doubted Ryan would appreciate him sleeping with the woman in order to obtain the information.

He tossed the records on Spence's desk, wondering what his next step should be.

"You know, the AG isn't coming until tomorrow to jack the stolen evidence case from us," Spence pointed out.

"And you're telling me this why?" Not that Shep really had to ask. Spence wasn't the type to make small talk. If he was bringing up the case, he already had a plan in action. And one that would undoubtedly end in disciplinary action for both of them somewhere down the road, if not sooner.

Spence looked at him earnestly. "I've already done the leg work. I've narrowed the clerks down to the two most likely suspects. All we need to do is go talk to them."

"What happens tomorrow when the assistant AG shows up? He might not appreciate us stepping all over his case."

"If we have it solved for him, he'll get over it. And if we do find the clerk who took the evidence, he'll let us know how the evidence got from him to Travis Dalton."

Shep contemplated the idea. "And how exactly are we going to get this clerk to talk to us? We've got nothing to offer him. No matter what he tells us, the AG is still going to go after him for the stolen evidence."

Spence tilted his head. "The moron won't know that. And between the two of us, I'm sure we can think of some way to persuade the guilty party to tell us what we want to know."

"You're one crazy bastard, Spence. If this wasn't for Ryan —"

"So you're in?" Spence asked.

"What do you think?" Shep answered. "If you're willing to put your job on the line, so am I."

"You worry too much, Chapetti. When have I ever steered you wrong?"

An image popped in Shep's mind of crossing the International Bridge at the Texas border, praying that the border patrol agents didn't ask him to pop the trunk. "You're right, Spence. I'm worrying for nothing. Let's go."

5:00 P.M.

Ryan scrounged through her messy closet for something appropriate to wear to the D.A.'s fund-raiser. She had almost decided not to go, despite the fact that she had paid $200 for the ticket over a month ago. Purchasing at least one seat at the overpriced function was more or less a requirement, an unspoken rule at the office.

Ryan definitely didn't feel like socializing right now, especially in support of the D.A. who might be about to boot her from the office. She doubted Peter even expected her to show up, after everything that had happened.

But on the other hand, she would look good if she did put in an appearance. Peter Berkley paid attention to those types of things, to the point that Ms. Vera insisted that every employee sign in at each function so the D.A. could verify his staff's support. When the murders were solved, Ryan would have brownie points to spare.

Edie had called, begging her to go, promising her that a night out would somehow make her feel better. Ryan debated the issue, and since Shep was busy anyway, agreed to meet Edie at the Superior Grill, the St. Charles Avenue Mexican restaurant where the event was being held.

Ryan grabbed a black Escada dress from the hanger. It was halter-style, but not too revealing, and looked really good on her. She slipped into the dress and doubted that the backless garment would meet her father's approval. Lucky for her she wasn't speaking to him.

She added a pair of strappy black heels that were excellent Dolce & Gabbana knock-offs, and stood in front of the mirror. One more smear of lip gloss over her already made-up lips, and a bit more eyeliner, and she was ready to go. She tossed her powder compact, lipstick and revolver in the matching knock-off purse, and went outside to meet Puddy. Maybe Edie was on to something. Knowing she looked good for a change put a little bounce back in her step.

"Puddy, are you in the mood for Mexican?" Ryan asked, walking up to the police unit.

The chunky cop smiled. "What's her name?"

"Food, Puddy." She laughed, slightly strained, but still a relief. "Superior Grill. Are you my shadow for the night?"

"Better than that. I'm your chauffeur. You need a ride, I'm your man."

In ten minutes they were pulling up outside the trendy restaurant. The music was loud, even from the street, and people were already mingling on the patio outside.

A second later, Edie flew around the corner in her white Camry, and screeched to a stop a foot away from Puddy's car. She parked illegally in front of Puddy and jumped out, grabbing Ryan's arm and leading her into the restaurant. Miss Vera sat at a chair by the front door.

"Sign in, ladies," she said, and handed Ryan a pen. The woman watched carefully, as if she thought they might try to forge someone else's name.

The tables had been pushed against the walls in the casual restaurant, and food had been laid out buffet style. The D.A. was sitting with his wife at the first table, like a king waiting to be hailed by his royal subjects. Ryan made a point of walking up to him, giving him an obligatory smile, pretending as if he hadn't just told her she might need to start looking for a new job. Edie shook his hand with a nervous giggle.

The room was filled with political bigwigs. The mayor, several judges, and a senator made the rounds. Ryan and Edie headed toward the side patio, where the other prosecutors had already gathered.

Bo Lambert and Harry Stelly stood near the doorway, holding Margarita glasses.

"The Margaritas are killer," Bo said, raising his glass in a mock toast with a drunken smile. "Oops. I guess that was a poor choice of words, considering Durrell Wilson."

Mike shot Bo an annoyed look. "Bo, you should just be happy you don't have to worry about losing Wilson's trial now." Mike turned to Ryan. "Ignore him. He's been drunk since Friday when Rick announced Kellie got the Strike Force spot. How are you holding up anyway? That thing with Wilson must have been terrifying."

Ryan tried to smile. "Scarier than that cockroach in the St. Thomas."

"How come you're here by yourself?" He looked around the room for a second. "Shouldn't you have some kind of police escort?"

"Puddy's right outside," Ryan explained, and then ordered a Cuervo Margarita from the waitress. She was digging in her purse for money — the D.A. always had a cash bar at his functions — when she heard her name. She was surprised to see Chance Halley waving to her from across the room.

Mike touched her hand. "I've got this round." He went back inside to the bar to pay for the drink.

"Looks like Big Mike has a little crush on you," Edie said, and then looked Chance over carefully, as if she was checking out a new car.

Chance smiled at Edie and then looked back at Ryan. "Out without your boyfriend?"

Edie raised her eyebrows in Ryan's direction, but remained silent.

"He's busy doing cop stuff. What dragged you out to a boring fund-raiser? Is there a dead body around here I don't know about?"

"Hey, reporters can support a candidate, can't they?" he asked with a hurt look. "But since you are here, any leads on who kidnapped you from the station?"

Ryan rolled her eyes as she shook her head. Edie elbowed her in the side before Chance could ask anything else.

"Edie, this is Chance Halley, soon-to-be-famous television reporter. Chance, Edie Guilliot."

Edie gave him a dazzling smile. "Nice to meet you, Chance. Could you excuse us for one second?" She dragged Ryan to the side. "Boyfriend? So the picture in the paper is for real?"

"Let's just say I didn't shave all the way up to my thighs Friday for nothing."

"Mazel Tov. Here." Edie reached into her purse and pulled out a roll of tape. "You've earned it."

Ryan took the roll from her, confused. It looked like a roll of medical tape, except for the tiny cartoon pictures of people performing sex acts that were printed on it. "Edie, what is this supposed to be? And why in God's name are you carrying it around in your purse?"

"Bondage tape," Edie said matter-of-factly. "Kinky stuff. Chapetti's going to expect something more than missionary position. And I carry it in my purse so I am always prepared for good sex. Now, being that you're with Detective Yummy, do you mind if I shamelessly throw myself at the reporter? Ernie and I broke up."

"Oh, Edie," Ryan began, but Edie was already prowling back over to Chance Halley. Ryan quickly shoved the tape into her purse, afraid somebody would see it.

Mike brought Ryan her drink, and then excused himself, heading to the restroom. Ryan walked around the room making small talk. She almost felt as if things were back to normal until her cell phone rang. She didn't recognize the number on the caller ID, and braced herself as she answered it.

She recognized the gravelly voice immediately.

"Hey, it's Jimbo. I saw the cop who got the devil at Big Who's, looking at an

AK."

"Big Who sells guns at the strip club?" Ryan asked.

"He just opened a pawnshop on Canal Street."

"Oh. Well, who is it?" Ryan realized she was playing cop again, but didn't care.

"Henry Cooper. I told him he looked familiar and he gave me his card. Stupid piece of shit."

"Jimbo, I owe you so big." She tried to absorb the fact that Cooper was the person who had been making her life miserable. She knew he didn't like her, but she couldn't believe he hated her enough to be involved in some master plan to hurt her. In any event, the drama was all about to end. She was about to get her life back.

Ryan hurriedly dialed Shep's cell.

"Hey baby, what's up?"

"I just got a phone call. Jimbo is the man."

"You heard from him?"

"I guess he didn't want to talk to Sean." She couldn't keep the smugness from her voice, not that she tried. "He saw the cop at Big Who's looking at an AK."

"Big Who is selling guns?"

"At his pawnshop on Canal, not the strip club," Ryan explained, as if she couldn't believe Shep didn't know that. "And the cop who got the devil tattoo was none other than Henry Cooper."

"Damn. We didn't even consider the crime lab officers. Stay there, I'll come get you. You see Cooper, you stay by Puddy, okay?"

"Sure. But Cooper's not going to show up here."

"Wait with Puddy anyway. I'll call Sean to pull a picture of Cooper. As soon as Devon makes an I.D., I'll get a warrant."

She quickly found Edie and pulled her aside.

"I have to go. You think Clark Kent can keep you company for the rest of the night?" Ryan tilted her head at Chance.

"I heard that," Chance said. "And Clark Kent was a newspaper reporter, not a TV reporter."

"Whatever," Ryan dismissed the point. "Can you keep Edie entertained or not?"

"I think I can manage that. Something about to break?" He looked hopeful.

"Nah, Shep's finished working so he's coming to get me," she lied.

Puddy walked up. "I can't believe Henry Cooper —"

"I know," Ryan interrupted, shaking her head in warning at Puddy.

"What about Henry Cooper?" Chance asked. "That's the guy from crime lab, isn't it?"

"Yeah," Ryan said quickly. "He got the clap from Kellie Leblanc." Nobody seemed surprised at the news.

"Hey, Puddy, come wait with me out front so I can smoke a cigarette." Ryan grabbed his arm. She led the man through the patio and out the gate, back to the street in front of the Superior Grill.

"Sorry," he said when they got outside. "I wasn't thinking."

"I doubt anybody in there will tip him off. But Devon hasn't even made an ID yet, so I don't think the press needs to be in on it. Shep should have warned you not to mention it."

"Sorry," he said again, and waved as Shep pulled up in the Vette.

JACOB

Jacob walked out to the sidewalk of Superior Grill a second after Shep and Ryan drove away, and dialed Henry Cooper's cell phone number. Cooper's identity had been discovered. In a matter of time, he would be caught. And then he would lead them to Jacob.

Jacob set out the plan as quickly as he could, making sure Cooper understood that he couldn't kill Ryan yet. That was the only rule. When he hung up, Jacob glanced around to make sure no one noticed him, and then skulked down the street to his car, to go to Cooper's house. He could get there and do what he needed to do before anyone even realized he was gone. He would be back in the middle of things and nobody would ever know he left the party.

His plan was almost complete. His sister would soon know what justice was all about.

MONDAY

1:00 A.M.

In the middle of the night, Shep's cell phone rang. Ryan listened to his end of the phone call, hoping it was news on Henry Cooper. While a lot of evidence was found at Cooper's house, Cooper himself had never gone back home and had not yet been arrested. The evidence was all circumstantial, but convincing nevertheless, the most damning being copies of Ribson's police reports, including the report involving the shooting of Jude Lightell by the police. The child's name, Jacob, had been included in the report, although no additional identifying information had been given. It seemed as if Cooper had been the one responsible from the start, using Ryan's past as a red herring.

"You're kidding." From Shep's tone, Ryan knew the call wasn't good news. "I'll be there as soon as you send a patrolman here." He hung up and sighed.

"Did they find Cooper?"

"No. Shooting on Claiborne. I guess your dad was serious about me catching the new homicides."

"Be careful." She kissed him before turning back over and going back to sleep. She was just getting back into a deep sleep when she heard a noise from the kitchen.

At first, she thought Shep had come back for something. And then she saw the outline of a form in the room with her, and knew Shep hadn't returned. She tried to reach for her gun, which was inside the nightstand next to the bed.

"You won't be needing this, bitch," the figure said, yanking the phone from the top of the nightstand and throwing it across the room.

Ryan opened her mouth to scream, hoping whoever was in the patrol unit outside would hear her, but the form punched her in the jaw, stunning her for a few seconds. She was still unable to react a second later as he put duct tape across her mouth.

"Nobody will hear you now," he whispered, climbing on top of her. She was wearing one of Shep's SID shirts, with nothing underneath. The man brought his face close to hers. She tried to claw him, but he was wearing a rubber Halloween mask. "I've been waiting under your house for a while. These floors are so thin." Ryan could see a glint through the eye holes of the mask. "I could hear you screwing your boyfriend. What were you doing to him to make him moan like that?" He grabbed at her breasts through the T-shirt. "Maybe I'll take the tape off your mouth and let you do that to me."

Ryan knew what he was after. She had also had a suspicion who he was, although she couldn't be entirely certain. The blow had left her a little disoriented, and the voice was intentionally disguised.

He started to lift her shirt and her survival instinct took over. She pushed his hands off, clawing at them, drawing blood, hoping to have DNA under her nails in case he killed her. She couldn't imagine how he had gotten in, but she didn't have time to think about it now. Her goal was to get him off of her, and then go for her gun. It was the only way she could possibly hope to escape whatever he had planned for her.

He punched her in the face again, while she continued to struggle.

"Bitch, you can make this easy or you can make this hard. Come to think of it, you're already making it hard." He laughed at his own joke as he put his hands around her throat. "I've wanted to do this for so long, I can't believe I'm getting paid for it. I guess I'll finally get to find out if your snatch really does have teeth. Now, you just follow along and do what I say and I won't have to kill you." She knew without a doubt the identity of her attacker.

Ryan didn't believe him, and she wasn't about to get raped and killed without a fight. She searched her memory for the self-defense tricks her father tried to teach her. She had never taken him seriously. She had always been cocky, telling her father she would just shoot somebody if she had to. She thought back. Eyes and throat. The captain always said to punch the throat and jab the eyes. It would buy her time, if she could incapacitate the man for just a few seconds.

She punched the man's throat. He flinched. In that second, she lifted both hands and jabbed him in the eyes with them. The man reached for his eyes and when he did, Ryan moved quickly, knocking him off her. Without his hands to catch him, he fell to the floor, hard and loud. Unfortunately, he landed directly in front of the nightstand, blocking her access to the gun.

She had to make a new plan. She pulled the tape off of her mouth as he was standing up, and started screaming as loud as she could, hoping to get the attention of the patrolman outside. Then she ran toward the kitchen, thinking she could either escape out of the back door and run to the patrol unit, or she could pick up a knife and stab the attacker.

Ryan felt like she was in a horror movie as the man in the mask chased after her. She couldn't escape through the kitchen door because the key was lost. She thought she had been so clever keeping that information from her father, and now realized how stupid she had been.

She grabbed the kitchen phone and hit 911 just as the intruder snatched it from her hands.

Trying to hang up the phone before the call went through occupied him for a moment. Ryan wrapped a dishrag around her hand and punched out the window, screaming as loud as she could. Hopefully, the patrolman outside heard.

The attacker grew angrier. He threw the phone across the room and then lunged for her. Ryan leapt across the floor and grabbed a knife from the butcher block. Her father's words echoed in her mind. A woman should never attempt to use a knife against a man. A man was stronger, and would take the knife away. Unfortunately, she had no other reasonable alternative at the moment. She could pick up the knife, or she could let him rape and kill her.

The man came at her again, and she slashed with the knife, cutting his forearm. It wasn't a serious cut. He grabbed her wrist with one hand and punched her in the face with his other. Blood poured from her mouth. She gasped as he twisted her hand, the tendons in her wrist stretching like rubber bands about to pop. The pain was too much, and the knife thudded as it landed on the linoleum floor. He bent down and reached for the knife. Ryan jerked her foot up, making contact with his chin, and bolted to the bedroom.

He chased after her and tackled her before she made it to the nightstand. Ryan crossed her arms in front of her face and chest, and tucked her head down. The knife sliced the flesh on her forearms, and a searing pain flashed in her forehead.

A noise from the front of the house made them both freeze. The man slashed at her one last time before jumping up and running back toward the kitchen, bringing the knife with him.

Ryan jumped up, ignoring the burning sensation in her chest, and finally reached the gun inside the nightstand. She ran into the kitchen. The man was unlocking the double bolt on the kitchen door with the key when Ryan started shooting. She hit him once in the back, near his shoulder, before he ran out the door. She fired the remaining rounds at him, watching as he fled from the back porch and into the backyard.

The gunshots were so loud she hadn't heard the front door being kicked in. Dubuc let out a string of curse words and called for EMS on his handheld radio. Ryan sank to her knees, feeling like she was about to pass out, wondering if she was hurt badly enough to die.

3:30 A.M.

When Shep reached the hospital, the Murphy family was waiting anxiously for news on Ryan.

"Where the hell were you?" the captain asked the second Shep walked in.

"Homicide call on Claiborne," Shep answered curtly.

The captain turned his attention to Dubuc. "How did he get in the house?"

"Ryan said he had the key to her kitchen door," Dubuc answered, a note of defensiveness in his voice. "She didn't know how he got it, but she said it's been missing for a while."

"Did she say who did this to her?" The captain's face was stark white.

The doctor came out at that moment.

"Captain Murphy." The doctor shook his hand. He was a younger ER doctor, well-known by many of the police officers.

"Doctor Mann, is my baby okay?"

The doctor nodded quickly. "She wasn't sexually assaulted, and she's very lucky her injuries are not serious."

The captain closed his eyes. "Thank you, God."

Dr. Mann continued. "She has a few superficial cuts on her arms, and a stab wound to the chest, but fortunately the knife just penetrated the breast tissue. She also some small facial lacerations that required a couple of stitches to her lip and forehead. We gave her a tetanus shot, and I'm getting X-rays to rule out any broken bones. I'd like to keep her overnight, though, just to be on the safe side."

"When can I see her?" the captain asked, his eyes filling with tears.

"As soon as she's back from X-ray."

An hour later, Sergeant Mitchell was the first one to see Ryan. He relayed the information she gave him to the captain. The attacker wore a mask and tried to disguise his voice, but Ryan was certain he was Henry Cooper.

A car had already been sitting on Cooper's apartment all night, but Shep had an idea that Monte would have better information about where to look for Cooper. He called Monte on his radio as he headed out the door.

6:30 A.M.

Ryan sat up in the bed of the hospital room and looked at herself in the handheld mirror the plastic surgeon had left in the room. One eye was swollen shut. The other had a small cut above it. Her lip and forehead were stitched, giving her the look of Frankenstein's monster. Not to mention the stitches in her left breast. She threw the mirror across the room just as the door opened. The mirror hit the wall and shattered, barely missing Shep as he ducked through the doorway.

"Can I come in?" He held his hands up, remaining by the door.

She nodded, and turned her head so he wouldn't see the tears starting to form. A nurse walked in.

"Everything okay in here?" The nurse smiled too cheerfully.

Ryan pointed to the pieces of mirror on the floor. The nurse's smile disappeared and she gave Ryan a look, but only called down the hall for maintenance to clean the mess.

Shep walked over and put a paper bag down on her tray. "I brought you the gun you asked for. Thirty-eight revolver, just like yours."

She nodded. "Can you put it in my purse in the bathroom? Mama thought I was crazy wanting my purse, but I don't want to be stuck here without protection."

Shep went into the bathroom. A second later he came out and sat in the chair next to her bed. "Well, this should make you feel better — Cooper's dead."

Ryan adjusted the bed to sit up straight. "Did you kill him?"

Shep shook his head. "No. I did find him, though."

"Right. But you didn't kill him."

"I swear. Ask Sean and Monte. They were with me when I found him."

"Oh." For once, Ryan didn't have an answer. She would have believed any one of the men might have taken out Cooper alone, but she knew without a doubt they would never have killed him together. Not that it would have bothered her if they had. She just hoped however Cooper had died, it had been painful.

Shep continued. "Monte had information on Cooper's girlfriend, one of Big Who's girls. We watched her house for an hour before she showed up. She hadn't seen Cooper since that morning, when he took her car. Then she saw the car parked down the street and pointed it out to us. Cooper was dead in her black Taurus the whole time we were out there waiting for her. Everyone at the station is getting a big kick out of our detective skills."

"Did my bullet kill him?" she asked hopefully.

"Nah, I'm guessing the gunshot to his head did the trick. But then maybe the shot to the dick killed him. My hope is that the dick shot was first, and after he suffered immense pain for a really long period of time, he was shot in the head." He frowned. "I just can't believe I was wrong, and that Cooper was behind it all."

"So who do you think killed Cooper, then?" Ryan asked, knowing what Shep was thinking already. "If he was the one after me, why is he dead?"

"I think you just answered your own question. How about your dad? Or one of your brothers?"

She shook her head and said softly, "Cooper said somebody paid him to attack me. I think whoever Jacob is, he paid Cooper to come after me so he could set Cooper up to make it look like he was behind the whole thing. You're the only one I've told."

Shep's eyes opened wide in surprise. "Why?"

"Everyone else still thinks Cooper was the one after me the whole time. Everyone except for the real killer. And he won't know that Cooper told me otherwise. He'll assume that I think it's over, and that I won't be ready for him. Shouldn't that give us an advantage?"

They were interrupted by a knock at the door.

Daubert stuck his head in. "Ryan, I told him to go away, but he said he wouldn't until he talked to you."

Battaglia pushed Daubert out of the way and entered the room. Battaglia nodded at Shep. "Detective Chapetti, if you wouldn't mind, I would like to speak to Ms. Murphy in private, if possible."

Shep started to protest but Ryan grabbed his arm again. "It's cool."

Shep looked as if he wasn't going to leave, but finally stepped into the hall.

"I just wanted to return this." Battaglia handed her a plain brown envelope. Ryan knew without looking that the videotape was inside. "Everything you said checked out. And Mr. Lejeune still refuses to name his attacker, so I guess there's nothing I can do in any event."

"I told you so."

"Ryan, I don't approve of your tactics. And I sure as hell don't understand why you didn't have Lejeune prosecuted."

"You wouldn't. So what are you going to do now? Are you going to go to my boss with this? Or the Bar Association?"

Battaglia shook his head. "As long as you don't beak the law, what you do is none of my business. So that's the end. I just can't see why you didn't tell somebody —"

"Thanks for giving me the tape back," she interrupted him. She wasn't sure he would, and a part of her had hoped he wouldn't.

"Before I go, I do have a few questions to ask you about the murder of Henry Cooper," Battaglia said. "I'm sure you heard that he was found shot to death early this morning."

"Cry me a river on your way out. The cop who tried to rape and kill me was found dead. Why are you here again?"

"You have the best motive for murder."

"And the best alibi." She pointed to the room around her. "Battaglia, I can't change my own tampon, and you think I snuck out of here and shot a man's penis off?"

Battaglia looked embarrassed now, more likely from her use of the word tampon than from his own stupidity.

"I don't guess your father or one of your brothers or maybe your boyfriend mentioned anything to you about Henry Cooper?"

Ryan frowned, the wound in her forehead throbbing as it creased. "I don't recall. I think the trauma of being brutally attacked combined with my standing order for morphine has my memory a tad fuzzy. But, by all means, leave me your card. If I remember anybody confessing, I'll be sure to call you first thing."

Battaglia smiled, and said over his shoulder as he walked to the door, "I'm going to find something on your father one day, Ryan. He got lucky this time, but one day I will catch him."

"I'll hold my breath." She watched as Battaglia walked out and Shep walked back in.

"What did that prick want?"

"He wanted me to tell him which one of you confessed to killing Cooper." She handed the envelope to Shep. "And to return the videotape."

"Why did Battaglia have this?"

"I gave it to him," she said, holding her hand up to silence whatever he was going to say next. "It's a long story."

"Don't you think it's about time you trusted me?"

"Do you remember Cedric King?" She didn't feel like going into the story here, but at this point she figured Shep had a right to know.

"That home invasion guy?"

She nodded. "He would hit rich people's houses, beat and rape the women, sometimes the men and the kids. None of his victims could identify him because he covered his face with a stocking. And he always used a condom so there was never any DNA.

"He made a mistake and hit the house of a couple of drug dealers who had a security system with a silent alarm. King spent too much time assaulting them and was caught in the act. But he wasn't the only one caught. The victims had fifty bricks of coke on the kitchen table.

"I got both cases. I reduced the dealers' charges to simple possession so they would testify against King. But once they bonded out, I never heard from them again. They're both still at large."

Shep's eyebrows went up. "So King got a sweet deal because the vics took off. Big deal. What does any of this have to do with Chad Lejeune?"

Ryan blew out a breath. "That's not exactly the end of the story. Without the testimony of the victims, I didn't have enough to pursue anything. I was going to have to dismiss the charges, and you know how much I hate that. But I had an incentive to offer Cedric King that convinced him to plead to simple burglary with probation, even without any kind of evidence against him."

Shep waited for her to continue, an impatient look on his face.

She sipped through the straw of the plastic hospital mug, wincing as the cold water hit her split lip. "King was motivated by the challenge of breaking into people's houses, and getting away with the crimes. He didn't care about the stuff he was taking or even the pain he inflicted.

"I knew my case was in the toilet, so I asked for a conference with King. Janet was his public defender. She didn't even stay in the room when I met with him. I told him I would probably be dismissing his charges, but that it wouldn't matter, because he was bound to get caught again. Everybody knew who he was and how he operated now, and he was going to have trouble finding unsuspecting victims.

"I told him how I even heard an attorney say he wished King would show up at his house, so he could shove a broomstick up King's ass. King was intrigued, and asked what I was offering. I told him simple burglary with one year probation. Right before he signed on the dotted line he asked me if I knew the name of the attorney who was waiting for him with the broomstick. I gave him Chad's name. That was it. I guess King found out where Chad lived, because Chad was attacked in his apartment the night King was released, exactly one week after he took that video of me."

Shep rubbed his chin. "So you did this because of what's on that videotape?"

She nodded. "Killed two birds with one felon, in my view. I got my conviction, and I got back at Chad. Win-win situation for all involved." She paused. "Except for

Chad, of course. But then, he probably enjoyed what King did to him."

"You told all this to Battaglia?"

"Every word. I wanted him to know why I gave Chad's name to King. And I didn't break the law. I didn't conspire with Cedric King to hurt Chad. I guess King might possibly have thought I would only give him Chad's name if he took the deal, but I never told him that — as a matter of fact, I would have given him Chad's name regardless. Getting King to plead to the deal was just gravy.

"And I didn't know for sure King was going to do anything. I hoped he would, but wishing for something and conspiring to make it happen are two different things. I mean, they might have found something to charge me with on *Law and Order*, but in Louisiana there's no statute against wishing somebody would get the crap beat out of them. Not yet, anyway."

Shep was silent for several seconds, a frown on his face.

"What?" Ryan finally asked.

"Isn't that still an ethical violation?"

She looked at him in disbelief. "Are you going to report me?"

He shook his head. "Of course not. But Battaglia could."

"If I get spanked by the Bar Association then I'll deal with it," she answered. "I had to clear daddy."

"So does this mean you're going to finally let me watch the tape?" he asked.

She nodded again. "I still don't think Chad is some kind of mastermind. But maybe my judgment's cloudy. Maybe he is really Jacob. Or maybe he found out about Patti kidnapping me and used the information to set up Cooper. I just don't know any more." She tapped the envelope in Shep's hand. "You watch the tape. If you think Chad's responsible, you do what you want."

JACOB

Jacob went to his father's house. The man was still home, waiting for his dope.

His father didn't bother to take his eyes off of CNN. "About time. I've been waiting for you since last night." His tone had an edge.

Well, wasn't that nice. Here he was, thirty-two years old and still his father's errand boy. Enjoy your heroin, daddy. Jacob handed the vial to the man.

His father picked up a rubber tube from the coffee table. Without a word, he tied the tube around his arm, filled a needle with the brown liquid from the vial and injected it into a vein. A second later, the man fell to the ground in spasms.

Jacob walked into the study and grabbed a key from inside his father's desk. He used the key to open the safe inside the closet in the bedroom. The safe contained cash, which Jacob took, but the brass ring was a book that contained a series of numbers for bank accounts, complete with passwords and access codes. Jacob would be able to transfer the money from his father's accounts online. He took the book and the money and stepped over his father's body on the way out, turning to him one last time.

"Oh, I forgot to tell you. That's not the regular heroin I've been getting. It's ninety-eight percent pure. Hope it wasn't too strong for you, dad. You fucking junkie asshole." He knew the man was likely already dead, but he wanted to tell him anyway. His only regret was that his father didn't know in advance Jacob was going to kill him.

Jacob rushed back to his own house and logged on to his father's accounts. He emptied most of the money from his father's bank accounts into a joint account he had opened without his father's knowledge. By the time the police found his father's body, Jacob would have transferred the money several more times, and then withdrawn it, in cash. It was a total of eight million dollars — eight million dollars nobody knew about. His father hadn't gotten as far as he had by being stupid.

Jacob had one more stop to make. He hummed to himself on the way, double checking that he had his disk and that the digital camera had a memory card in it. It was going to be a beautiful day.

7:00 A.M.

Shep rushed back to the station to watch the tape, knowing he didn't have the luxury of time. He put the tape in the combination TV/VCR in the SID office. Fortunately, no one else was around.

The video opened with Chad Lejeune, standing outside the door of an apartment.

"I'm outside of Ryan's," Chad said into the camera. He was obviously holding the recorder himself. "She just caught me banging Laurie and broke up with me. And now for your viewing pleasure."

He knocked on the door. Ryan opened the door with the chain on.

"Let me in, Ryan," Chad said. "We're not finished yet."

Ryan tried to shut the door, fear on her face. Chad kicked the door before she could close it. The chain pulled. He kicked the door a second time and the frame pulled away, the door opening with a loud bang.

Ryan jumped back and ran down the hallway. Chad caught up to her and grabbed her by the hair, smashing her head into the wall. She fell, and remained down as Chad set the camera on the mantle of the fireplace in the living room. He aimed the camera down. "I hope this will get the shot," he said, looking toward the door of the apartment, out of the camera's view.

He then dragged Ryan, who was either stunned or unconscious, to the living room floor. He prodded her with his foot.

"Wake up, bitch. Time for fun."

She reached for her head with a moan, and Chad climbed on top of her.

He looked back toward the door again, and appeared to smile at someone standing there. He turned back to Ryan and tapped her face several times. "Wake up, bitch. We really need to talk. You're just pretending you're still out, aren't you? God, you are so smart. Smart and beautiful. Too bad you were such a lame fuck I had to slip a couple of roofies in your wine to have any fun with you." He started pulling her top up. She reached up and punched him in the face, surprising him. She tried to flip him off of her, but he pinned her down by putting his hand over her throat and pressing her into the floor. "So you were awake. I knew it. Maybe I should give you a few roofies now, to make this worth my while." He reached into his pocket and pulled out a foil pack. He popped a pill out of the back of it and tried to stick the pill in her mouth. Ryan bit his finger, earning a slap in the face in return.

"Worthless cunt." He turned toward the door again, and said, "Never mind the roofies. I don't want her unconscious for this. I want her to always remember it." He started lifting her shirt again, biting her neck and breasts. She fought back, screaming and clawing at his face. He laughed and slapped her again.

"Does it hurt yet, bitch?" He pulled her shorts halfway down. He jammed his hand between her legs. "Well, does it? Answer me, bitch." She clawed at his hands, and reached again for his face. He ignored her and pulled her underwear to her knees. "If you just admit it hurts, whore, I'll stop."

"I'm on my period," she said, struggling against him.

He laughed. "You think blood bothers me? By the time I'm finished, you won't even know where you're bleeding from."

He put both hands around her throat, squeezing until she went limp and her eyes closed. He let go then and started laughing.

"You'll be awake in a few seconds," he said, and pulled his own pants down. "See, baby, I can only get it up around you when you're unconscious. You're just not woman enough." He pulled a condom out of his pocket and quickly put it on before he penetrated her. "Wouldn't want to leave any evidence, Ms. D.A. No DNA in the ADA." He laughed as he pumped several times, apparently ejaculating quickly. "Oh, that was so good. But I'm not finished yet."

Ryan started to stir again. He flipped her over and bit the back of her thigh. "Does it hurt yet?"

"Yes," she screamed, barely lifting her face from the carpet. "It hurts. Please stop, Chad. Please?"

He smiled towards the doorway again. "I like it when they beg." He looked back down at Ryan. "Don't tell me you don't like it rough, bitch." He pulled his pants back up and took his belt off. He repeatedly struck her back, first with the belt and then with his fists. He continued to beat her, asking her over and over if it hurt yet. He then flipped her over with his foot, and used the belt to strike the front of her body. She whimpered as he hit her, shielding her face with her arms the entire time. Eventually, she lost consciousness again.

Chad finally stood up then and spoke to the unknown person in the doorway again. "That good?" He put his belt back on, kicked her crumpled form several times, finally walking up to the camera, putting his face close to the lens.

"I never even liked her," he said, smiling into the camera. "Going out with her was really just a big joke." Chad reached and turned the camera off.

Shep hit the rewind button and rubbed his chin. He tried to think of some way to calm himself down. Nothing came to him. When the tape stopped rewinding, he put it back in the envelope and stuck the envelope in his desk drawer and locked it. He clasped his hands together behind his head, trying to think. Remain calm.

Lejeune was talking to somebody off-camera in the video. The off-camera person appeared to be the one Lejeune was performing for. Was it the other girlfriend, or someone else?

Shep needed to meet with Chad Lejeune. Right now. He went outside to the Vette and opened the glove box. Inside was a .9 millimeter, not police issue, the clip loaded with hollow-point bullets. He concealed the Nine at his waist, and drove off to find Chad Lejeune.

Fifteen minutes later he was near Chad's apartment. It was almost 8:00 a.m. He hoped Chad hadn't left for work yet. Shep would be too limited in his options in a public place such as Chad's office.

He parked around the corner. No sense in being seen if something happened, which at this point was more than likely. Not that he had a plan in mind. He wanted information. If Chad was willing to tell him what he wanted to know, Chad might just get lucky enough to live for another day.

Shep knocked on the door and got no response. He knocked again, and this time heard a muffled cry from somewhere in the apartment.

Exigent circumstances, he decided, and tried the door. It was unlocked. The sight that greeted him when he stepped inside was more than a surprise. It was an ungodly shock.

Chad Lejeune was naked, hanging by a rope in the center of the living room, his toes barely touching a book that was resting on top of a chair. He was standing precariously on the book, as if he could fall off and hang himself at any second. The petite brunette had her head down on the table.

Chad's words were slurred. "Chapetti, cut me down."

"Answer some questions first." Shep walked to the sofa and sat down, putting his feet up on the coffee table.

"Man, just get me down first, please?" Desperation reverberated in Chad's voice.

"What are you doing up there, anyway?" Shep looked at the chair, and then at the rope, trying to figure out the mechanics.

"It's a game we play." Chad didn't even have the decency to be embarrassed. "Would you just help me already?"

"That's one hell of a game, although I can't say it looks like much fun to me." Shep studied the set up, noticing a thicker book underneath the chair. "So you set up two books on top of each other on the chair, hang a rope around your neck, and then jump off the books, hanging while you choke your chicken. When you start to pass out, or shoot your load, or whatever comes first, I guess, you reach your feet back to the books. Is that right?"

"That's the game, Chapetti. Now cut me down."

"So what happened to this book?" Shep picked up the larger book from the floor.

"If you just put it on top of the other book, underneath my feet, I can cut myself down."

"Is that a fact? So you get off on choking yourself and you get off on choking women. The term is paraphilia. But enough about your deviations. I have a few questions for you, if you don't mind." Shep dropped the book back on the floor. "Why not use just one book that's thick enough for your feet to reach?"

"Because if it falls off, then you're dead. This way, if one falls, you still have a chance." His breath came out in spurts. "Please cut me down."

"I like it when they beg," Shep said, narrowing his eyes at Chad. "Does that sound familiar? It's what you said in the video, while you were beating and raping my girlfriend. So tell me Chad, does it hurt yet?"

"Fuck," Chad moaned.

"Yeah, fuck about sums it up. So did you just go out with Ryan to terrorize her?"

"I didn't even want to go out with her," Chad said, a wild look in his eyes. "It wasn't even my idea."

"Who then, Lejeune? Who is after her?"

Chad's breathing came faster. "If I tell you, you'll leave. And if I die, she dies."

"Lejeune, be smart. I'm a cop. I'll let the law deal with you."

"Cut me down."

"Who?" Shep asked, standing directly next to the chair, staring up at Chad. "Tell me his goddamn name."

Chad told Shep the man's name. "Now will you help me? Please?"

"You're kidding me," Shep said, shaking his head in disbelief.

"Look in the camcorder," Chad said, his voice on the verge of hysteria. "The tape ran out by now, but the camera was recording while he was here. He didn't know. He gave Laurie some bad coke. I think she's dead. And then he pushed the book out from under me before he left. He'll be on the tape."

Shep found the camcorder partially concealed on a bookshelf. He took the tape out of the recorder and then checked the VCR, just to make sure the surveillance system hadn't caught him entering the apartment. The VCR was empty. Shep headed for the door.

"Please!" Chad yelled. "My toes are almost asleep. I can hardly feel them. If you don't cut me down soon, I'm going to hang myself."

"Isn't that the whole point behind autoerotic asphyxiation?" Shep asked, walking back and standing in front of Chad.

Chad's words came in butchered rasps. "I don't have the time to debate its finer points. Please, cut me down. Or just put the other book back so I can get myself down."

Shep headed for the door again.

"Chapetti," Chad yelled after him. "I'm going to die. You said you would help me if I gave you the name."

Shep snapped his fingers. "Damn, that's right, I did say that." He walked back one last time, his only regret that he didn't have more time to play with Chad right now. He looked at Chad for a second and picked up the book from the floor.

"Man, please hurry and put the book under my feet. I can't stay like this much longer. Let the law deal with me like you said. Please, I'm begging you."

Shep smiled. "Just like Ryan begged. That's kind of ironic, isn't it? But you know what you forgot, Lejeune?" He dropped the book on the floor, the smile fading from his face. "I am the law." He headed out of the apartment, catching a glimpse of Chad's legs flailing in the air as he slammed the door shut behind him.

The doctor who checked on Ryan was a middle-aged, potato-shaped balding man, with thick clumps of wiry gray hair growing out of his ears. Ryan guessed he was asked to show his credentials more than once in his career.

"If your temperature is normal, you can go home." He furrowed his eyebrows as he checked her stitches. "Everything looks fine." He handed her a prescription before he left.

A second later, Ryan's family took his place.

"You getting paroled?" Patrick asked.

"If I don't have fever," she answered.

"I saw Big Mike in the waiting room," Sean said. "Looks like Shep has some competition."

Nurse Tammy, a tall thin blond Ryan instantly hated interrupted the conversation to take Ryan's temperature.

"Did you get your card?" the nurse asked, knowing Ryan couldn't answer with the thermometer under her tongue. "Sheryl said a nice-looking young man left it at the nurse's station earlier." She pointed to an envelope on the hospital tray. "You want me to get that for you?" The nurse reached over and grabbed the envelope and handed it to Ryan. The short beeps of the thermometer stopped. Tammy looked at the numbers and smiled, as if she was personally responsible for Ryan's temperature. "Your temp is 98.6, perfect."

Ryan stopped listening as she pulled out the contents of the envelope. She heard a sound like an animal in pain, and then realized the sound was coming from her own mouth. She was trying to say no, but it was coming out as a low pitch wail.

She shook her head, finally closing her eyes to get the images out of her mind. Inside the envelope was a set of three pictures, all of Edie. In the first, Edie was naked, spread-eagle on the bed in a room, her hands and feet tied to the bed posts, a look of terror on her face. In the second, she was in the same position, with a plastic bag over her head, tied at her neck. The third was a close-up of her torso, bloody words carved into her chest. *Does it hurt yet?*

Ryan buried her face in her hands, unable to control the explosion of sobs. In all her life she had never experienced a feeling like this, grief so strong she almost couldn't breathe.

Edie had been brutally tortured, just to prove some kind of sick point to Ryan. He knew how to get to her. He hadn't succeeded killing her, so he did the next best thing.

Ryan didn't realize she was still howling until she felt the pinch of a needle in her arm. The sting shocked her into silence. She put her face down into her pillow and waited, hoping whatever the nurse just shot her with would make her sleep forever, or at least until her pain went away.

And suddenly, she needed to tell them that Chad had to be the one behind all of the murders. He was taunting her, thinking she wouldn't break her silence and explain what that phrase meant to her, how those words proved the person who hurt Edie was Chad. She couldn't believe she had been fooled all of this time, thinking it had to be somebody else.

She barely lifted her head and grabbed Sean's hand. "Chad Lejeune did this," she told him through her tears, barely controlling her sobs enough to get the words out.

"How do you know?" Sean asked, leaning in close, squeezing her hand.

"The question." She almost couldn't bring herself to say the words. "That's what he kept asking the day I broke up with him. He wouldn't stop hurting me until I told him yes. I've heard him ask me that a hundred times in my nightmares. I've never told anyone. No one else knows."

Almost like magic, the room cleared and the pictures disappeared. Ryan was relieved. She never wanted to see Edie like that again. She put her face back down in the pillow, drowsy, but unable to sleep despite the medicine the nurse had injected.

Something still didn't seem right. Her hell had ended. Chad was responsible. The pictures proved it. The police would get Chad and it would really be over.

But something was still out of place. A montage of images ran through her head. Edie, tied spread eagle to the bed. Chad, standing over her in her apartment, hitting her and talking to somebody she couldn't bring herself to look at. Durrell Wilson getting out of a black Mercedes.

And then she remembered the cologne worn by the kidnapper. Fleur De Lis. Who wore Fleur De Lis? Not Chad. And who was off-camera in the videotape, watching as Chad tormented her? Was it the girlfriend, as she suspected? Or was it someone else?

She could feel the medicine kicking in. Her thoughts were becoming muddled, too many ideas springing from her brain, too many images in her head to rationally focus. And then the phone rang. She thought about not answering, but was afraid to miss news about Chad.

"Did you like the pictures?" the voice with the distortion device asked. "I captured the true Edie, don't you think?"

"They're coming after you," Ryan said. "They know who you are. They're going to catch you and they're going to kill you."

Chad wasn't the killer. He would never have set himself up like this. She wondered if her brothers would kill Chad when they got there, and if Chad would even realize why. Not that Chad didn't deserve whatever he got.

The distorted voice let out a hollow, evil laugh. "Oh, you are so wrong. And nobody is going to catch me. As a matter of fact, you're going to come to me, right now."

"You're out of your mind." Ryan's voice was thick, the pain medication dulling her senses. Her throat felt like it was closing. "I'm not going anywhere."

"I have something here that might persuade you."

A second later, Edie's throaty voice was on the phone. "Ryan, he's crazy. He's going to kill me. Call—"

Ryan didn't find out whom Edie wanted her to call. The conversation was interrupted with a noise that sounded like Edie getting slapped, and then a whimpering in the background. Ryan sat up straight in bed, listening carefully.

"Wouldn't it be a shame for your friend's life to end over a whore like you?" the voice was back. "Her only crime was being stupid enough to be your friend."

"That's a tape recording. I saw the pictures. Edie's already dead."

"Poor Edie. She had to endure all that torture just to get your family out of the way. But I haven't killed her yet. Here, ask her a question."

"Who is it?" Ryan asked. "Who has you?"

"He said he'll shoot me if I tell you who he is." It was definitely Edie, and she was definitely still alive. Ryan was scared, but she couldn't let Edie die. She would figure something out.

The distorted voice was back. "I'm going to give you an address. I want you to go there, and wait inside for me. And don't bring any of your police buddies. If I see a cop, Edie will experience a slow, painful death. I'll be watching, from a safe place with your friend. When I see you're alone, I'll let her go."

"How do I know you're telling the truth?"

"You don't. But will you be able to live with yourself if you don't take that chance?"

"Where do I meet you?" She wrote the address down on the lunch menu.

"And I wouldn't advise bringing your little gun or anything stupid like that. I would just use it against you."

"The police took my gun when I shot Cooper. And how am I supposed to get there? I don't have a car here."

"That's your problem." He hung up.

Ryan thought hard. She had to figure out who he was. And how she would get to him.

Focus. Edie was in the hands of a monster. Edie might be killed, just to punish Ryan. Ryan began to get more angry than scared.

He's waiting for me, and he's got the upper hand because I won't know who he is until he wants me to.

Concentrate. The cologne. She had smelled it at the office before, but it was such a subtle scent it had never stood out in her mind. She now recalled smelling it at the Hole, the night Patti was killed. And at the D.A.'s fund-raiser. Who was wearing Fleur De Lis cologne? And then, like the sun breaking through the clouds, she knew. Even in her muddled state, she knew who he was, and she knew what she had to do. She would go to him, and she would trap him.

She couldn't take a chance and call the captain, or even Shep. If he saw them, he would kill Edie.

She could handle him. She was smarter than him. She had the benefit of knowing his identity. She also had the benefit of him not realizing she knew. She slowly started to get out of the bed, trying to think of how she would get to where he told her to meet him. She had to save Edie's life.

A second later, Bo Lambert stood in the doorway, his usual bland expression set in place. "Hey, is this a bad time? I can come back later if you want me to." He pointed to the hallway. "I saw Big Mike outside and thought you could have visitors."

She shook her head impatiently and stood up. She was a little dizzy from the medicine, but at least she didn't feel the pain.

"I need a ride," she told him.

"You don't look so good, Ryan. Why don't I get a nurse for you?" He started to walk back out to the hallway.

"No. Get back in here. I'm fine, but I need a ride. Will you give me a ride somewhere? Please?"

He looked confused for a second. "Did they say you could leave?" He pushed his glasses up and looked back to the hallway, as if looking for someone in authority.

"Yes, they discharged me," Ryan said impatiently. "I need to get out of here."

Bo looked even more confused. "Ryan, what's going on? Daubert's right outside, if you're in some kind of trouble."

"I'm not," she lied. "I just need a ride to this address, okay? Please?"

"I guess," he answered reluctantly, looking nervously around the room.

"Can you bring your car to the front entrance? I need to get dressed and I can't walk too far. And don't tell Daubert. I don't want anyone knowing I'm leaving."

"If you're positive I'm not going to get in trouble over this. I can bring my car around to the service entrance if you want. It'll save you some steps. You really don't look so good."

"Thank you. I'll be out in a minute." She took a deep breath. I can do this.

As soon as Bo left, Ryan went into the bathroom and changed into the T-shirt and sweat pants her mother had brought her to wear home.

When she was dressed, she reached in her purse and removed the gun Shep had brought her. She was sure Shep never imagined she would actually need it.

She checked to make sure the gun was loaded. The revolver had six bullets. Six chances to survive.

She thought as clearly as she could. She still had her holster, but he might search her. He would likely search her waist. He probably wouldn't think to search her legs. She could conceal the gun under the sweat pants if she could attach the holster to her leg. She grabbed the bondage tape out of her purse. Edie's penchant for the unusual may end up saving her life. She taped the holster to her left ankle, slid the gun into it and then pulled the leg of her pants back over the holstered gun. If he searched her and found the gun, she would just have to reach it before he did.

She copied the address onto her hand, and wrote a note on her menu, explaining where she was going and why, trying to reassure herself that the calvary would eventually arrive if something went wrong. She left the room, telling Daubert that she was going to the snack machine around the corner. She followed Bo's instructions and found his white Mercedes waiting.

Bo drove her in silence, seeming deep in thought. She would know for certain in a few seconds. Ryan watched as they passed the street where Bo was supposed to turn. Now she knew for sure she was right.

"You missed the street," she said. The subtle scent of Fleur De Lis tickled her nostrils.

"God, it's a nice day." Bo's smile was tremendous. Thunder rolled in the sky, followed by a flash of lightening. "You know what's really funny? That you just begged me to give you a ride."

"What are you talking about?" Don't let on you knew already. If he knows you already knew, he might look for the gun.

"You still don't know, do you? I thought you were supposed to be so smart."

"What?"

"I'm the one," he said. "I was always the one."

"You were always the one what?"

"The one who was making your life a living hell. Me." He pulled a cell phone out of his pocket, and showed her the distortion device attached.

"Where's Edie?" She needed to get him talking.

He shrugged. "You should be more worried about where you're going."

"Are you doing this because I was beating you for Strike Force?" If she could get him talking, she could figure out his plan.

Bo laughed. "You are stupid, aren't you? You think I would waste that kind of money and time planning this because you beat me to a promotion? Everything is always about you and your pitiful, pathetic, tiny little world, isn't it?"

"Where are you taking me?" Once she knew his plan, she could determine the best time to go for her gun.

He smiled. "We're going back to your favorite place — the St. Thomas."

"Why?" He thought he had trapped her, so he should feel safe enough to speak freely.

"You really don't know who I am, do you?"

"I thought you were my friend."

His laugh was hollow. "Don't lie to me. We were never friends."

Ryan tried to remain calm. "Where's Edie?" she asked again.

"Trunk."

"Is she dead?"

"Not yet." He laughed again. "But it's going to be hot today. I bet it won't take long."

Ryan shuddered. "Why are you doing this?" The medicine was still working, something she hadn't taken into account when she devised the plan to go against him alone. Her eyes wanted to close, but she forced herself to keep them open. "What did I ever do to you?"

The road ahead was blocked for construction, and Bo detoured toward St. Charles.

"Let me tell you the way it's going to be. You're going to keep your mouth shut for the first time in your life. I don't need to hear your stupid, lying, mouth. You're just like our mother."

"Our mother?" A second later she felt a slap to the side of her head.

"I told you to shut up. I guess you might as well know why you're going to die today. You see, our mother was a whore. Good old Patti. Humping anybody she could for a foil of heroin." He stopped for a red light. He had killed several people, kidnapped Edie and done God knows what else to her. But he stopped for the freaking red light. "To her credit, she did try to keep me." The light changed to green.

Ryan moved her leg slightly. The feeling of the holster pressed against her gave her a surge of confidence. "What does any of this have to do with me?" He slapped her face this time. She tasted blood in her mouth as the stitch in her lip ripped.

"Patti made the mistake of taking you back. She was out of money and the demand for used up, skanky whore was low, so she was going to trade you for heroin. One big score was all she needed. Do you remember? I tried to help you. I killed a roach so you wouldn't be scared. You were a bitch even back then. Instead of being grateful, you cried, and got me in more trouble."

"It wasn't dead," she said without thinking. "You didn't kill it all the way." She felt the slap before she finished the sentence.

"It was a fucking roach. It couldn't even hurt you."

"They bite." Ryan licked the blood from her lip.

Her plan had not included getting the crap beat out of her on the way to wherever Bo was taking her to kill her. Certain thoughts were entering her head now. Such as, what if his plan was to pull a gun and shoot her in the car? And that the note she had left on the menu was useless. While it would let her would-be rescuers know who she was with, it would not tell them where he had taken her.

Bo stared straight ahead, his gaze glassy. He seemed unaware of his surroundings, although he continuously obeyed the traffic laws. Just as he always did. Too scared to speed but he could kill without a second thought.

He finally continued speaking. "You ruined everything. When Patti heard the police outside, she sent me away with Jude. I told you to tell the police about me, to make them come back for me. I told you I didn't want to go with him. You saw what he was like. You knew what he was going to do to me. And you didn't bother telling them." He turned to face her. His expression was chilling. Hatred, mixed with pure evil.

She tried to reason with him. "I was only four years old. I didn't know." She wasn't sure if she was slapped this time or not. She seemed to be fading in and out, trying to concentrate.

He ignored her and continued. "For an entire year I lived with Jude, doing things for him little boys shouldn't have to do. All because you didn't tell them I needed help."

"So this is about revenge? You want to get back at me because you were abused? And your life turned out okay in the end. I mean, you were adopted by a family that treated you so much better than Patti ever would have."

"Not revenge, Ryan. Justice." He closed his eyes for a second, and Ryan had a glimmer of hope that he would run into the car in front of them, and she would be able to run. She reached for the door handle, and then realized it had been removed. She couldn't escape.

He opened his eyes and hit the brake. The car screeched to a stop, just in time. The man in the car in front of them shot them the bird. Bo waved back apologetically.

"Getting adopted by the Lamberts was no accident," Bo continued, his eyes dark. "Beauregard Lambert was one of Patti's best customers. When I was finally discovered at Jude's, Social Services tracked Patti down in prison and tried to force her to give me up for adoption. Patti contacted my father and blackmailed him into adopting me. She threatened to expose his sordid urges and drug addiction to the world. And he was, after all, my biological father." He smiled at the surprise on Ryan's face. "Chad's father handled the paperwork. Beauregard thought it would be a good influence for me to hang out with Chad. He had no idea."

The cars began moving again.

"You know you can't get away with something like this," Ryan said. "My family will never let this go."

Bo shrugged. "That's where you're wrong. I can get away with anything."

She decided to try a different tactic. "I don't see why you're blaming me for your crappy life. I didn't leave you with Jude. Patti did. You should have been mad at her."

He nodded in agreement. "She was also responsible. That's part of the reason I killed her."

"You killed her?" She felt another slap to the side of her head. Her ears were ringing, but she wasn't in pain. At least if her plan failed and he killed her, death wouldn't hurt.

Bo's lips stretched into a demented, but amused, smile. "It's your fault she's dead, you know. I overheard you at the Hole, planning your little visit. With Patti's dementia, she probably wouldn't have even remembered my name, but I couldn't take that chance. So I killed her. Not that you should be upset. If she hadn't told me about you, I would have never been able to find you in the first place. She hated you as much as I do."

Ryan glanced out of the window. They were driving down St. Charles, nearing Jackson Avenue.

"So you killed those people to get back at me for something I had no control over?" She still couldn't believe it. She had thought the killer would be somebody dangerous. Not a wimp like Bo Lambert.

"The only person I killed was Henry Cooper. Oh, and some bum on Claiborne. I had to get Detective Asshole out of your apartment last night. But the rest of them, they killed each other."

"Why kill them at all?" She waited to see if she was going to get hit again, but Bo seemed preoccupied for a second. "Why did you want people to think somebody was killing my defendants for me?"

"To ruin your life before I killed you. My plan was ingenious. I looked through the old dismissal reports to find the defendants. Then I gave a list to Cooper, who arranged everything for me. Cooper simply paid them to kill each other."

"Why now?" It still didn't make sense to her. She had known him for four years, what was so special now?

"You are so inquisitive. I don't think you've spoken this much to me in the entire time I've known you. But I guess there's no harm in telling you. It's our anniversary. Exactly twenty-four years ago today you let Jude take me. But I've been planning this since Patti told me who you were. And I've given you ample opportunity to prove to me that you weren't what Patti said you were. I gave you the last four years to prove you didn't deserve to die. But you didn't even try to be nice to me. Patti was right all along. You are nothing but a selfish bitch."

He drove down St. Thomas Street into the development, past Felicity, and then over the sidewalk. Just beyond the empty units, he turned on a gravel road that led to the first inhabited building. He stopped the car behind the building. The car couldn't be seen from the street. Maybe the resident of the back apartment would look out and figure out something was wrong.

Bo pointed to the open window of the apartment and smiled. "Oh, I don't think Eulah Mae will be giving us any trouble right now. She's taking a nice long nap. Now get out. And don't try anything cute or I'll blow a hole in your head." He pointed a forty-five at her.

She wondered if she should try to run. Nobody would even know she was here to save her. Before she could make the decision, Bo opened the door and grabbed her roughly by the arm.

Shep needed to call in a warrant. But it might be difficult to explain how he arrived at a suspect without mentioning the fact that he had just spoken to Chad Lejeune, who was likely dead by now. Shep was nearing the station when he heard the dispatch ordering all available units to Lejeune's apartment, who was wanted in connection with the murder of Edie Guilliot.

Shep wondered if Chad had somehow killed Edie before Shep had found him. And then he had another thought. While everyone else's attention was on Chad, Ryan would be easy prey. If she thought Chad was the killer, she wouldn't be prepared to defend herself against anyone else.

Shep quickly dialed her room at the hospital, and felt a chill when she didn't answer. He called Angie next.

"Check on Ryan, right now." He was on his cell, driving around in his car. His only problem was he didn't know where to go. "I'm going to stay on hold. If she's not in her room, page her."

Angie didn't ask any questions. Shep assumed she had been a cop's wife long enough to know better. A few minutes later she was back. It felt like an hour to Shep, who had pulled over to wait for the information.

"Shep, Daubert said she went to the snack machine a while ago, and hasn't come back yet. He said she had a visitor right before she left."

"Did he know who it was?" He felt his heart pounding against his breastbone.

"Bo Lambert."

Son of a bitch. Chad had told him the truth. It was Bo Lambert all along.

"And Shep, there was a note from Ryan on her meal tray. It says that Bo Lambert has Edie, and Ryan went with him to help her. She left an address. Shep, what is going on?"

"Call the captain and tell him to send a unit to that address," Shep ordered. "I don't think he took Ryan there, but maybe he left Edie. I'm trying to figure out where he took her. Tell him Bo Lambert has been behind this from the start. He's Patti's son." He hung up.

He put out a call to send a car to Bo Lambert's apartment, as well as to Bo's father's house. Shep doubted Bo would take Ryan to either one of those places, but he didn't know where else to try. And then he thought about the St. Thomas. Of course. But exactly where in the St. Thomas? It was a massive development, and Shep didn't have time to go door to door looking for her.

He dialed Monte.

"Carlson."

"Monte, Bo Lambert has Ryan. He's taking her somewhere in the St. Thomas. Where?"

"You on drugs man? The SID is taking down Lejeune for being behind this."

"Chad Lejeune is already dead. And Bo took off with Ryan. So where is he taking her?"

"How would I know?"

"Monte, you know more about this than you're saying. And if Ryan dies because of you, I will kill you, I swear to God."

"I don't know where he took her," Monte said again. "He might have a hidey-hole in the St. Thomas somewhere. One of my regulars heard that a D.A. was walking around the abandoned buildings one night. Maybe he's got a place in there."

Shep turned around and drove in the direction of the St. Thomas.

"You didn't think the information about a D.A. might be relevant?"

"It wasn't my business. I got tips that the homicides were going down, and that a D.A. might be financing them. All these guys were cases Ryan lost. I figured maybe she was settling the score."

Shep bit back what he wanted to say. "Well, she wasn't, and now Bo Lambert is going to kill her if we don't find her first." Something was coming back to him, something he had pushed to the back of his mind as unimportant at the time. "Sean took a report from Eulah Mae Simpson about a new tenant in her building. He moved in around the time Ryan started doing crime scene duty."

"I know where Eulah Mae lives," Monte said, "and I'm right down the street. I'll meet you there. Park on St. Thomas and Felicity. The building is the second one from where Smith was found."

Shep immediately dialed the captain. "I think he's got her in the St. Thomas. Two buildings behind where we found Smith's body. I'm down the street now."

"Wait for backup," the captain ordered. "I've got units on the way now."

"She'll be dead by then." Shep hung up and pressed on the gas, using only his flashing lights. He didn't want the siren to give him away as he got closer to the complex.

Ryan looked around the St. Thomas apartment, amazed the room was tastefully furnished, as if a normal person lived there. Bo caught her staring.

"Nice place, huh? Kudos to the drug dealer that used to live here. He had a very refined sense of style." Bo shoved her to the sofa, still pointing the gun at her.

"You're going to be caught, you know," Ryan said, surprised that her voice didn't reveal the desperation she felt. She had to thank Nurse Tammy for that one.

"I've got eight million dollars. Nobody will ever catch me."

Maybe if she could keep him talking, somebody might figure out where they were. "So was Chad working for you?"

"Of course. Why do you think Chad went out with you in the first place?" Bo asked with a superior tone. "He never would have looked twice at a girl like you. I knew how much he could hurt you. And I knew you'd never tell on him."

"You don't know anything about me," Ryan answered.

Bo smirked. "I know you better than you know yourself. I studied you for a long time before I decided your fate. Way before I ever started working at the D.A.'s Office. But I think we've really talked this thing to death. If you're hoping somebody's going to find you if you yap long enough, you're wrong. Even Chad didn't know where I was taking you."

Ryan looked around the room, trying to figure out what Bo's plan might be. "Maybe there's some way we could work this out. There's got to be something you want."

He began pacing. "The only thing I want is to finish what I started. I've thought about this a lot. You've had all the chances you're going to get."

Ryan thought that this might be the time to react. She had to decide. She could try to make it to the door and hope to outrun him, or she could go for her gun and hope she got it before he shot her.

As if reading her mind, he grabbed her by the hair and jerked her from the sofa.

She instinctively brought her knee up between Bo's legs as hard as she could. He winced and released her hair, but didn't fall, and didn't drop the gun. It was a bad move.

He shook his head slowly. "That was so stupid. I was going to take my time with you, but now I think I'll just hurry up and get it over with."

He brought the gun to her temple.

Ryan braced herself for the explosion, realizing she should have been spending the last few seconds praying and asking God's forgiveness for her sins so she could still get into heaven.

Then Bo laughed. "I'm really enjoying this too much to end it so soon." He pulled the gun away from her head, and roughly shoved her down to the floor.

He began pacing again, and then walked across the room to the entertainment center, the gun still in his hand. He picked up a CD case off of the shelf and looked closely at it. "Do you want some crystal meth?"

Ryan didn't answer. She was trying to figure out a way to reach up under the loose pant leg without him seeing her. A second later, she felt a hard kick in the stomach.

"Don't you dare ignore me. I asked if you would you care for some crystal meth. I expect an answer."

"No, thank you," she whispered, trying to catch her breath.

He walked back to the entertainment center and put the CD case down with a sigh. "Too bad you don't want to party before you die. But since you don't, I'll just kill you now." He pointed the gun at her.

She curled her body in the fetal position, and turned her back to Bo. "I think I'm going to throw up," she lied.

Bo laughed. "Oh good, I get to watch you vomit before I kill you. What fun for me. Not that I haven't seen it before. Remember that night I gave you a ride home? You probably don't, since you were trashed beyond belief. I was so nice to you. I even helped you into your house, to your bathroom, so you wouldn't puke all over the place. It's how I got the key to your back door. You've made this whole thing almost too easy."

She made a gagging noise as she curled her knees to her chest, and slowly reached with her right hand under the elastic at the bottom of the left leg of her pants. A second later Ryan had the gun in her hand, hidden between her knees. Bo walked back and stopped, standing behind her, his gun still pointing at her.

"I hate to end this so soon. But eventually those buffoons at the police station might figure out where we are, and I would hate to get into a big dramatic car chase."

By the look in his eyes, he saw the gun just as she raised it. They fired at the same time.

A single explosion sounded, and a circle of blood appeared on the front of Bo's shoulder where the bullet entered, a red stain spreading outward from the center, across the pinstripes of his shirt.

Bo's gun only clicked. God was looking out for her. Bo's gun had misfired.

"You shot me?" He looked at her incredulously, and then touched his own blood with his hand and looked at it, perplexed. "You bitch. You had a gun hidden on you the whole time? I never would have thought you could be that clever."

She stood up, her hand trembling violently, and took a step backwards, trying to put distance between them. She had just shot him, but he wasn't acting as if he was hurt.

Ryan kept the gun trained on him. "I figured out you were the murderer. I'm not only a better attorney than you, I'm also smarter. You didn't set this trap for me. I set it for you. Now put the gun down."

He pulled back the slide of the .45, making Ryan realize that Bo's gun hadn't misfired — he didn't have a bullet in the chamber. His eyes showed a glimmer of disbelief. And then his expression changed to one of awareness.

Ryan knew she wouldn't get lucky twice. She fired again, hitting him in the chest, watching as he fell to the ground on his back. The gun fell from his hand.

He clutched his chest, blood streaming through his fingers, as his eyes closed. "You fucking cunt-faced bitch." He was gasping for air, blood bubbling from his wounds. Despite his profuse bleeding, Ryan felt as if he might jump back up at any moment and try to kill her.

She could hold him until somebody came. She looked around for a phone, wishing she had thought to tape her cell phone to her other leg.

"I gave you every chance to be nice to me," he said, his words choppy. When he opened his eyes, Ryan saw no fear in them. She hoped he wasn't going to grab for his gun. He was just a foot away from it. He could still shoot her.

She took a step closer to him, determined to overcome her fear long enough to kick the gun away. She took a second step. He stared up at her, a deranged smile on his face. He wasn't dead. His chest was still rising and falling, a raspy, labored sound coming from his mouth.

"All women are cunts," he said, still smiling as his eyes darted to his gun, a foot away on the floor. His hand jerked. Ryan wasn't sure whether he was reaching for the gun or if the sudden movement was a spasm.

She didn't wait to find out. She pointed her gun and squeezed the trigger, firing three more rounds into Bo's chest.

"I just wanted what I deserved," Bo rasped, blood now trickling from his nose and mouth.

Ryan sank to her knees. "And that's exactly what you got." She crawled away from Bo's bleeding body, watching intently as his eyes finally closed, a demented grin frozen forever on his lips.

She sat on the floor, watching for any sign of life from Bo, praying that he was really dead, knowing she had one bullet left in the gun if he should open his eyes again. She wondered if she should sit there and wait for the Calvary, or if she should get the hell out of Dodge and find help on her own. Her question was answered when she saw Shep in the doorway.

Shep pulled up to the complex, right as Monte was getting out of his own car.

"Please God, let her still be alive," Shep said out loud.

Before either man had a chance to move, a series of gunshots filled the air. They both drew their weapons and rushed to building 23. The breezeway was eerily quiet.

Ryan sat on the floor, Shep's revolver in her hand. The room smelled of burned gun powder. "Shep?"

Bo Lambert's body was lying near the center of the room. Shep ran to Ryan, and felt her for injuries. Monte went to Bo's body, checked for a pulse and shook his head at Shep. He then picked up the gun with the edge of his shirt, smelled it, and frowned.

Shep took the gun from Ryan's hand. "Everything's okay, baby." Ryan seemed to be in shock. He hoped nothing had happened to her. "It's all over."

"Lambert sure won't be hurting anybody else," Monte said, but he was still frowning.

Ryan shook her head and her eyes filled with tears. "He was going to kill me. He killed all those people. And he was responsible for everything Chad did to me."

Shep helped her stand up. "I know he was, baby. And you don't have to worry about Chad Lejeune ever again either."

Monte looked over at him but didn't say anything. Shep knew Monte would never mention what Shep told him about Lejeune to anyone.

The sound of sirens grew closer.

Shep pulled Ryan close to him. "Did he hurt you?" He noticed blood on her shirt. "You need to go back to the hospital."

"I'm okay. Can you check on Edie? He said she was in the trunk of his car. And Eulah Mae."

"We'll check on both of them." Shep didn't want to tell her that Edie and Eulah were likely both already dead.

A minute later, the captain rushed in, followed by what seemed to be the entire Sixth District police force. The captain grabbed Ryan in his arms.

Doug was already there to transport the body to the coroner's office. He stared down at Bo's lifeless form and said, "Most of the women I know only carry pepper spray."

Ryan pulled away from the captain. "Bo tried to kill me." She was shaking uncontrollably. "He wouldn't stop. Even after he was shot. He kept moving. Like a cockroach."

"Well, he won't be coming back to life now," Doug said. "I promise."

"I had to shoot him," she said. "I didn't have a choice. He was going to kill me."

"You didn't do anything wrong, baby," the captain said. "Everybody knows that Lambert was a killer. Nobody's going to blame you for defending yourself." The captain glanced around the room at everyone, as if daring them to disagree.

"I killed him," Ryan said, seeming barely able to comprehend what she was saying. "Bo Lambert was my brother. And I killed him."

"I just can't believe one of our own was that screwed up and nobody knew it," Doug said grimly.

Shep followed the captain and Ryan out of the St. Thomas apartment.

JUNE

Ryan walked up the steps of the Sixth District Station, careful not to trip in the new Monolo Blahnik spiked-heel mules. They had replaced the Ferragamo's lost to the St. Thomas. That project had taken enough from her.

She waved at the officers in roll call, drawing a disapproving look from the sergeant when one of the men whistled. She smiled, glad she had decided to wear the low cut Ralph Lauren dress.

Shep was waiting for her in the SID office. "You look good enough to eat," he whispered in her ear. "In fact, I think I will."

She smiled up at him. "Good. I have something special planned." She opened her purse, knowing when Shep looked inside, he would see some black lace, a can of whipped cream and the John Mayer CD. "I need some serious stress release. I've had the most tedious day."

"I would have thought your first day back would have been exciting," Shep said with a worried look. "Especially your first day in Strike Force."

"I guess some things aren't as important as I thought," she answered.

"What about getting Gendusa back from Kellie?" he asked. "That had to feel good."

She shrugged. "It wasn't as big a thrill as you'd think." Then she sighed. "I wish I knew about Edie. Work doesn't seem right without her. Every time the phone rings I expect to hear her voice on the other end. I keep thinking that since Bo didn't kill Eulah Mae, maybe he didn't really kill Edie. Maybe she's alive somewhere, still waiting to be saved."

Shep put his arms around her, squeezing her in a quick hug before letting her go. "They might never find her, Ryan. I know that's not what you want to hear, but I have to be honest with you. You can't keep waiting for her to show back up, as if this was some kind of joke. You'll only drive yourself crazy."

"I know." She paused. "Do you think if I would have been nicer to Bo, none of this would have happened, and Edie would still be alive?"

"Absolutely not," he insisted. "You can't blame yourself for whatever the hell went through Lambert's psychotic mind. No matter how nice you would have been to him, it wouldn't have been nice enough."

"If I had just told somebody back then that he needed help —"

"You were only four years old. You didn't understand what was going on."

"Even after everything he did to me, I can't help thinking that he was still a victim," she answered. "The things that he went through —"

"Ryan, do not make excuses for him," Shep interrupted, his tone suddenly harsh. "He tried to kill you."

"Did he really?" Ryan asked. "Why wasn't his clip loaded then? It just doesn't make sense."

Shep shrugged. "Maybe he was just trying to scare you with the gun, and he planned to kill you with his bare hands. I doubt we'll ever know what he was thinking. The only thing I can tell you for certain is that he's a killer, plain and simple. Nothing you could have done would have changed that."

She clasped her hands together tightly in front of her. "Daddy said more or less the same thing, in between his rants that I should move back in with him and mama."

"I've already told you my place is plenty big enough for both of us. Or we could start looking for a new place."

She shook her head vehemently. "I'm not being chased from another apartment. And I don't know what everyone's so worried about. If nothing else I've at least proven that I can take care of myself."

Shep smiled. "Just don't break into a chorus of *I Will Survive* right now, okay?"

Ryan narrowed her eyes at him. "I think I saw Monte when I came in. I bet he won't make fun of me."

Shep grabbed her hips and pulled her body against his. "I never doubted for a second you could take care of yourself. Hell, you could probably take care of both of us. But I don't feel like talking about Carlson right now. At this particular second, I'm more interested in your sleeping arrangements for the night." His look made her blush. He nibbled her ear and whispered, "Why don't we get out of here."

Her stomach fluttered from his breath in her ear. "Only if I can sing *I Will Survive* in the car," she answered.

"You can do anything you want," he said, his tone suddenly serious. "I mean it,

Ryan. Just tell me what you want, and I'll do my best to make you happy."

She put her head on his chest for a second, and then grabbed his hand and pulled him toward the door. "Good. Because I've got some very specific things in mind for you tonight."

Down the hall, they ran into Monte.

He looked Ryan up and down and winked. "Looking hot, babe. Can you spare a smoke?"

"I quit smoking again," she told him. "Cold turkey."

He looked surprised. "Good for you. How'd you manage that?"

Shep looked annoyed at the conversation, but Ryan gave Monte an evil grin. "You just have to find a better focus for that oral fixation."

Monte grabbed his chest. "All that wasted on a fag like Chapetti."

Shep relaxed and smiled, holding up Ryan's hand for Monte to see. "And she also quit biting her nails."

"Damn," Monte said. "Chapetti must be the luckiest man in the free world."

"Absolutely," Shep agreed, as he and Ryan walked out of the station.

At the top step, Shep stopped and finally gave her a long, hot kiss.

Her day was definitely improving.

RUTH

Her mother had named her Ruth. She had been called so many different things in the last twenty years she was surprised she even remembered her given name. Names didn't matter to Ruth anyway. for the past three years she had been Edie Guilliot, and no one had found out. Well, Jacob had known, but the whole thing had been his idea to begin with.

Jacob had a whole lot of ideas, although being dead wasn't one of them. Ruth had always known that if someone else didn't kill Jacob, she would eventually have to do the honors herself. It was the only way to get Jacob's money, and, for Ruth, it had never been about anything other than getting the money.

Jacob had been right about one thing, though. Past inequities had to be resolved. Why should Jacob have so much, when Ruth had so little? They were, after all, blood. And she had suffered every bit as much as he had.

She watched from a block away, through a pair of Jacob's high-power binoculars, as Ryan and Shep left the police station, Shep's arm around Ryan's shoulder. Ryan smiled, and then they kissed. Ruth sighed happily and smiled with them.

Ruth wanted to find some way to thank Ryan, for getting rid of Jacob for her, and for being her best friend, even if Ryan had never figured out that they were sisters.

More than that, Ruth wanted to tell Ryan what she did for her. If Ruth hadn't switched the clip in Jacob's gun when he had gone into the hospital, Ryan wouldn't be here at all. And Jacob wouldn't be dead, in all likelihood. What chance would Ryan have had if Jacob's gun had actually been loaded? Yes, sisters should always stick together.

Ruth would have given anything to see the look on Jacob's face when he realized that he was defenseless. Especially when he must have realized that Ruth had betrayed him. She smiled again. She couldn't save the others, but she had saved Ryan.

Ruth and Ryan, they helped each other out. And justice really had been served. Maybe one day, when Ruth was far enough away from New Orleans, she would drop Ryan a note to let her know.

About the Author

Holli Castillo is a criminal appellate public defender and a former New Orleans prosecutor. She was born and raised in New Orleans, and lives in the metropolitan area with her husband and two children.

Her screenplay, *Angel Trap*, was a finalist in the Spring 2009 Wild Sound Feature Screenplay Contest. Gumbo Justice is her first novel.

To learn more about the author, log on to www.gumbojustice.net or www.hollicastillo.com.